MENTORED IN FIRE

Also by K.F. Breene

DEMON DAYS VAMPIRE NIGHTS WORLD

Born in Fire
Raised in Fire
Fused in Fire
Natural Witch
Natural Mage
Natural Dual-Mage
Warrior Fae Trapped
Warrior Fae Princess
Revealed in Fire
Mentored in Fire
Battle with Fire (coming soon)

DEMIGODS OF SAN FRANCISCO

Sin & Chocolate
Sin & Magic
Sin & Salvation
Sin & Spirit
Sin & Lightning
Sin & Surrender

LEVELING UP

Magical Midlife Madness
Magical Midlife Dating
Magical Midlife Invasion
Magical Midlife Love
Magical Midlife Meeting

FINDING PARADISE SERIES

Fate of Perfection
Fate of Devotion

MENTORED IN FIRE

By K.F. Breene

Contact info:
www.kfbreene.com
books@kfbreene.com

CHAPTER 1

OUT OF BREATH, bone-weary, and above all things determined, Penny staggered up to the lone door in an unassuming mound of earth, the entrance to the vampire lair. Darius had better be in its depths. Reagan was being held by the elves. The shifters and warrior fae who'd vowed to protect her had been forced to retreat from the elf castle to regroup, and Darius was their only hope for getting her back.

Penny just hoped Reagan would be alive long enough to rescue.

"This is it?" she asked, chest heaving, trying to catch her breath.

Emery stopped beside her and wobbled a little, bracing his hands on his hips. "Yeah," he panted, only still going because Penny had pushed him. She was the better runner, able for longer distances. He was hardier, though, experienced in pushing past his limits and ignoring pain. He was the absolute best guy to have in a pinch, something he'd proven again and again as he led them at a breakneck pace through the Realm, taking the absolute fastest route to the lair.

Penny brushed her sweat-soaked hair from her face and nodded, pushing forward. “Okay then.”

Not great at kicking in doors, she used her magic instead, fashioning a sort of explosion. It ignited and then concussed, bursting through the doorway and billowing into the space beyond. The door ripped off its hinges and clattered to the ground with the burst.

This wasn’t a time for skulking, and magic wouldn’t hide them from the older vampires. They’d sense someone in their midst even if they couldn’t see or hear her and Emery sneaking around. No, it was time to embody Reagan’s swagger. For Penny to show her power and make vampires think twice before attacking the strangers in their midst. At least until they found Darius.

He had better be in there!

“Grab those sticks, Emery,” she said, straightening to her full height as she pushed her shoulders back and strutted forward like Reagan would.

“Torches,” Emery murmured, pulling his backpack around.

“Right, torches, yeah.” Emery had grabbed them off some goblins who had tried to ambush them and steal their stuff. They’d gotten their bodies sliced in half for their efforts. It was Emery who’d insisted on rifling through their things and taking anything of value.

There were no heroes in the dangerous parts of the Realm.

A sucking darkness enveloped them as they entered the vampire lair, the narrow hallway opening up into a huge sort of hall. A path ran between a series of large stone pillars, the darkness shrouding what lay at the end.

Light flared from behind her, and Emery handed forth a torch, the flame licking the chilled air. Rough-hewn stone tried to catch her toes as she made downward progress into the lair's depths.

"They will be all around us in moments, if they aren't already," Emery said softly.

He needn't have bothered to explain. Penny could feel the vampires' predatory magic curling around her, flirting with hers. She could sense the bleating *warning* of a breached territory crowding the air. She could sense the presences drifting closer, hostile, hungry, and *playful.* These types weren't interested in a quick meal.

Penny didn't say a word as she continued along, mostly because Emery didn't. He was right behind her, the glow of their fire sticks—torches—creating a halo around them.

A woman's sultry voice slithered out of the darkness. "What, no magic from our illustrious natural mages?"

"I'm not here to fight, but I will," Penny said in a

strong, sure voice that she did not have to work at. Apparently, blind fear for her friend had brought out some heretofore hidden well of inner strength. Reagan wasn't the only one she was embodying on this journey—she'd been acting a lot like her mother, who took nonsense from nobody, and she wasn't even sorry for it. "We're looking for Darius."

"They know why we're here," Emery murmured, and Penny could feel the placating spell being woven behind her. He didn't intend to kill any of these critters if he could help it.

She had no such reservations.

"If they know, why aren't they leading us to him?" Penny said through clenched teeth.

A body appeared up the way. The vampire was in what Reagan referred to as its monster form—swampy green with lank black hair framing a long, drawn, and, well, monstrous face. Long white fangs dropped down from black gums, and its claws clicked together as it wiggled its fingers.

It hissed, and stringy drool dripped from its mouth.

"Rumpelstiltskin's foreskin, what is it trying to do, scare us?" Penny wove elements together at a blinding speed.

"No, no, wait—"

Emery's hand on her shoulder was too late. She let her magic slam into the swampy monster. The spell burrowed between its ribs, making it jerk back, before igniting. Guts and grime flew everywhere, slapping off Emery's hastily erected shield, something Penny had forgotten about. Getting slimed with that stuff would've been gross.

The remainder of the body dropped to the floor. Other vampires in monster form pushed away from the path, and a couple of creatures, unseen in the deep darkness, hissed.

"That might…cause a problem," Emery murmured. "We should try to remain peaceful."

Penny marched on, uncaring, the image of Reagan fighting a crowd of enemies, *alone*, seared into her mind. She'd done that so Penny and Emery and the others could get away. She'd sacrificed herself to a terrible fate so they could run like cowards.

"Fuck 'em," Penny said with lead in her stomach. This situation was worth that real swear. She'd never get that image out of her head. Never. And if something happened to Reagan before Penny could get there—if Reagan was killed—Penny would never, ever forgive herself. They needed to hurry, and no swampy monster trying to intimidate them would get in her way.

A female form appeared on the path down the way, hips swinging exaggeratedly, legs ending in long, spiked heels. A bustier hiked up her ample bosom and a leather duster billowed around her. Her plump lips pulled up into a sarcastic sort of smile before she came to a stop.

"Hello," she said in a velvety voice, her gaze skimming Penny and then lingering over her shoulder, clearly on Emery. "You are trespassing."

"You are in the way." Penny kept her pace even though she recognized the vampire as Vlad's right-hand woman. His assistant, if vampires could be said to have them. His protégée, maybe. They'd met in Ireland, at the meeting that had been held prior to the storming of the Mages' Guild.

"She's right..."

This time Penny did slow as a second female form appeared beside the first. Shorter, dressed in a *chic* white dress that draped around her shapely calves, Marie was no less beautiful. Her smile was equally condescending, but it was not directed at Penny.

"My oh my," Marie said, taking a step past the first vampire. "You are sure making a habit of choosing the wrong side." Marie held out her hand for Penny, the large ruby on her middle finger glittering in the firelight. "Come, Penny. Darius is waiting for you."

Penny heaved a sigh of relief and let her guard slip a little. Unfortunately, that also prompted her magic, which had been on high alert since the scene at the castle, to let loose.

"No, no, wait—"

Vlad's assistant's face never changed, haughty and

arrogant. But suddenly she was airborne, caught up in a blast of wind and magic, turned end over end as she was propelled backward. She landed out of sight, the repeated *thuds* echoing around the vast space. Penny didn't even know where she'd picked up that spell, but she was pretty sure the vampire would tumbleweed for a while before she could break free. She'd come out bloody, but she wouldn't die.

Marie laughed in delight. "And that was just a mere fraction of what she is capable of. Imagine."

Penny was well aware that Marie was pandering to the crowd. She and Darius needed to get vampires on their side—and away from Vlad—in preparation for the war that was surely coming.

That was all well and good, but first they needed to save Reagan. She was the only one who could help them win said war.

"Okay…" Penny made a *hurry up* gesture. "Let's get to Darius. I have news."

"Yes, of course." Marie led them past a host of gawking younger vampires, their inexperience indicated by the green hue of their monster forms, but the vampires recovered quickly, and the path was soon clear again.

"What has Darius—"

"No, no." Marie *tsk*ed at Penny. "Let's discuss our private business in private."

"Right. Fine. Good. Hurry up."

"You are so tired you are nearly falling down." Marie hooked an arm that might've been lined with steel around Penny's back, holding her up.

"I'm good."

"You certainly smell good."

"Gross."

At the end of the path, in the bowels of the earth, a cavernous room awaited them, with three thrones sitting side by side.

"Really?" Penny said, rolling her eyes.

Chests of gold and gems were arranged around the thrones, the treasure glittering in the warm glow of candles and larger sticks—torches—in metal rings along the walls. A table stood off to the side, laden with food, and Penny's stomach growled.

"Come." Marie led them down a hallway to the right, then another passageway, both lined with large paintings that were probably worth something. Pausing at a large door with a cross on it, she pushed it open and stepped aside. "Here you are."

Penny stepped through with magic at the ready. Marie had always been on Darius's side, who was on Reagan's side, who was on Penny's side, but that didn't mean one of those sides hadn't flip-flopped since. One could never trust a vampire.

Darius looked up from a round table in the center

of the room, beneath a large crystal chandelier. A massive four-poster bed rose behind him, crisply made. At the side of the expansive chambers, beside a marble fireplace, sat a desk strewn with papers. Candles glowed from many surfaces, and a fire warmed the hearth.

Where does the smoke go? Penny couldn't help but wonder. Sometimes, it still felt like she was new to this magic thing.

Emery closed the door behind them and then sealed it with a spell to lock Marie out. "Darius," he said, strutting over to the table.

"Yes, Mr. Westbrook, welcome." Darius stood from his chair, looking fresh as a daisy. His hair was perfectly styled, and he had on a three-piece suit. The guy could do suave in his sleep. "Miss Bristol."

"Oh my God." Tears welled in Penny's eyes. "Darius, you have to help. Reagan has been taken! The elves—"

"Yes, I know. Please." He gestured to one of the chairs. "Have a seat. Would you like something to eat? I had a meal prepared. I can send someone to get you something. It's probably not wise for you to leave these chambers just now. Not with your…theatrics a moment ago. I'll need to smooth a few things over before you are free to roam."

Penny wiped at a tear that got away. "You know that Reagan has been taken?"

"Yes." He glanced at Emery before resuming his seat, clearly not planning on pressing them to sit with him. "I received word a couple days ago. She was being tortured for information."

Penny sagged under the knowledge. She'd known that would be the case, but it was still hard to hear, and his blasé tone stuck something sharp in her middle. "Do you even care?"

Emery was there in a moment, trying to guide her to a seat. She waved him away.

"Do you even care?" she repeated, louder. "Did you actually even love her, or was that just a vampire trick?"

Darius scribbled something on a parchment before laying down the pen and leaning back, his focus narrowing on Penny. "I have spies in and around the elf castle. Word was sent to me that she was taken by the elves. From then, I've received regular updates. Of her torture, of her rescue, of her current situation…"

Penny held Darius's gaze as she stilled the magic gathering above her head. "Her rescue?"

"Yes." Darius braided his fingers together in his lap. "Lucifer got word of her entrapment before I could get her out. He stormed the castle, as it were, and took her with him back to the Underworld. She is now in his inner kingdom, heavily guarded but looked after. Safe, for the time being. News of her has not spread through the Underworld. Not yet. I am not sure what that means in relation to our situation."

This time Penny let Emery help her to a seat. A few tears escaped her eyes, the stress and anxiety of these last few days giving way to a different form of stress and anxiety. "Safe?"

"Yes. For the time being. He does not plan to kill her."

"But does he plan to let her go?" Emery asked.

Darius's eyes narrowed slightly. "That is the question, is it not? I would guess the answer is no, but she has only been in his care for a day. It's hard to say how things will progress."

"Okay, well..." Penny looked at the papers and parchment spread across the circular table and nearby desk, maps and notes and drawings with labels she couldn't read. "Okay." She took a deep breath and wiped the tear streaks from her face. "Now what? How do we get her out?"

Darius studied her for a long moment. "First, you rest. We can do nothing with you at this level of fatigue. You need to eat, sleep, and restore yourself to optimal levels."

"But—"

"She is safe right now, Penny." Darius's gaze took on a keen edge. "She is treasured, and she is not alone. A druid was seen leaving the elves' castle within Lucifer's fold."

"Cahal?" Emery asked, pulling a chair from the table and sliding it nearer the wall, putting distance between himself and the vampire.

"I would guess so, though I cannot be certain. He is the only druid I can think of that is capable of entering the Underworld."

"Not to mention he has a vested interest in Reagan," Emery added.

"Just so. He will guard Reagan, as best as he is able," Darius said. "He will steer her, guide her. He is her best chance at keeping her head."

"Keeping her head?" Penny sat forward. "Why? What's down there?"

"She has been through trauma, and now she will be a treasured pet to the man who is the master of lies. She will discover how much Lucifer cherished her mother. Listened to her mother. Left when her mother asked him to. That will be alluring to Reagan. It'll make her think she has some control in this situation—that his fondness for her mother will translate to a similar fondness for her. She is only stubborn to a point. Her mother is a weakness. Lucifer will exploit that weakness to gain her trust. I am hoping Cahal, when the situation arises, can shine a light in a dark place."

"And if he can't?" Emery asked.

Darius tapped his pointer fingers together, the only indication of his agitation. "Then it will be incredibly dangerous for us."

"So you have a plan?" Emery asked.

"Of course," Darius replied, and Penny let a breath whoosh out of her. "I have been planning for this moment since we first entered the Underworld. I feared it might come to this, eventually. This or something similar. I have made extensive networks and some allies. Unfortunately, I haven't been able to properly infiltrate the inner kingdom. They are incredibly loyal to their master. Still, we should be able to sneak in. I have a couple of routes plotted out."

Penny stared at him with her mouth hanging open. He hadn't mentioned to Reagan that he was preparing for something like this, that he was worming his way into the Underworld *just in case.* If he had, she would've told Penny. Reagan wasn't good at secrets.

All this time, the vampire had been playing the long game, strategizing how to get Reagan back before her father even knew she existed. Any doubt that Penny had possessed about his intentions toward Reagan dried up completely.

"Wow." Penny glanced at the large bed behind Darius. "Okay. Food. Rest. Then we storm the Underworld."

"More like slink through it, but yes," Darius replied. "You will need all your wits. This will be unlike anything you have ever experienced, and if we lose, we lose everything."

No pressure.

CHAPTER 2

I OPENED MY eyes slowly, and then closed them slowly. My wince didn't do the pain justice. It vibrated through my entire person, pounding in some places, aching in others, hot in my joints and thudding behind my eyes.

I took a deep breath, and it felt like fire through my esophagus. Oh, right. Unlike the rest of the Underworld, there was no air in the inner kingdom. That was probably for the best—it hurt to breathe anyway.

I gave the eye-opening thing another try, and it took a while to get used to my surroundings, mostly because there was so. Much. *Gold.* Golden-hued bedding laced with cream and a matching canopy billowing overhead, tied with golden tassels to cream and gold bedposts. A hideous gold and cream pattern lined the walls, which Darius would scoff at, and to one side of me there sat a mirrored desk (gold-trimmed, of course) and a gold-upholstered chair. Not all real gold, of course, but enough that I would be running out of here a lot richer. If I could run, obviously. Or move without setting off an earthquake of agony.

Cahal sat in a cream chair beside me, a book in his lap and his ankle rested on his knee. He stared at me silently. I stared back, just as silently. Usually I was the one who spoke in our relationship. I didn't much feel like speaking now.

My fingers were all straight, so that was good. I could bend them, too, though it hurt to do so. Bruises adorned my arms, and I didn't much care to lift the sheet and inspect the rest of me.

Someone had dressed me in what looked like a super-luxe hospital gown.

"How do you feel?" Cahal asked, and his voice had an echoey quality to it. Magic carried words here, since there was no air. Though I did remember him saying he could breathe down here because his godly magic negated the airless spell. Regardless, his words had that strange, tinny quality to it. Just another little stop on the mind-fuckery train.

"Like I got beat up, actually." I thought about sitting up. Then thought better of it. Then did it anyway to see how far away I was from healing.

Cahal pushed to standing and helped, fluffing my pillows and getting me situated. Usually I wouldn't accept that kind of help, but usually I didn't feel like sausage on the other side of the meat grinder, wrapped in too-tight casing.

"How long have I been in this godawful room?" I asked, taking a break from moving and closing my eyes against the onslaught of gold.

"You've been out for three days." He pulled a sack from the floor and extracted a wriggling magical snake. He quirked an eyebrow, silently asking if I wanted to use it.

"I know they heal wounds, but can they really heal broken bones and things?" I asked.

He glanced between me and the snake. "I don't know. I've never used one. I was told to offer this when you came to."

I *had* used one before, so I knew it would make me feel less like I'd been hit by a truck that had then backed up and hit me again, but I hadn't had internal injuries last time. And while I'd seen one of these buggers crawl out from a demon's insides, I wasn't sure I wanted one taking a jaunt through my body.

"Maybe not," I said.

He stowed the snake and straightened up, not moving back to his seat.

"What?" I asked.

He looked like he wanted to say something, but instead he stepped back and resumed his seat. I hurt too bad to be curious.

I looked around the glittering gold room before remembering there wasn't any human technology in this place. No cameras to watch and hear what was being said. "I'm in the castle, then?"

"Yes. You are in a transitional suite. You will get to choose your living quarters when you are able."

"So…the first thing he wanted me to see was a gaudy room from yesteryear?"

Cahal's eyes twinkled. "I assume he wanted to impress you."

"Ah." I flexed and unflexed my fingers again. As it was, I couldn't hold a sword. "Go, go gadget healing!"

"What?" Cahal asked, confusion stealing across his expression.

"Nothing. It's an old cartoon. So what's the plan here, do you think? Obviously I need to heal. I assume dear old Dad will let me do that?"

"That's a certainty, yes. You will not be harmed while you're here. You can heal in peace."

"Groovy. And after that?"

"He'll take up your training."

"Awesome. After that?"

Cahal's expression turned grim.

I nodded. I'd figured as much. There was a big question mark as to Father Dearest's end game. But now that he'd found me, I had a feeling I wasn't going to get sent home with a pat on the back.

As if on cue, the door opened up, and my father strutted into the room in his human form, his shoulders swinging as his slow steps ate up the dark wood floor. A grin pulled at his wide mouth and excitement and mirth sparkled in his brown eyes. It was like he'd sucked all the confidence from everywhere else in the worlds and donned it like a superhero's leotard.

"Good evening," he said in a medium-range voice before stopping halfway down the bed, on the side of Cahal. "Reagan Somerset, isn't it?"

"Yep. You knocked up my mother."

His grin pulled wider. "And you are the result."

"Two for two. And you are…" I quirked an eyebrow at him. "A rescuer? A kidnapper? A jailer?"

"Yes." He laughed, a rich, hearty sound. "Welcome. May I?" He glanced at the edge of the bed.

"Knock yourself out."

"Fantastic." He sat, giving off the vibe that he was incredibly comfortable with this situation, which made me uncharacteristically uncomfortable with it. The shoe being on the other foot would take some getting used to. "I've brought you a plaything."

"That sounds gross." I paused, and then the light clicked on. He meant Cahal. "I assumed you would be training me."

"And so I shall, but you need someone to practice on."

"I'm sure you have minions for that. Cahal is more of a drinking buddy. He's too chatty for anything else."

Lucifer's smile was bright and broad. "Is that the case? Hmm. Well, then, he can be your confidant, how is that? Or your tour guide to this new place. When you tire of him, however, you will get rid of him. He is only welcome here until you say he's not."

"And I assume I can choose how to get rid of him?"

"That all depends on what he knows when he is no longer needed."

I curled my lips under while nodding. "Gotcha. Tire of the druid, then slip a pair of cement shoes on his feet and send him down with the fishes."

A small crease formed on Lucifer's brow. "I am not sure I quite remember what fish are. I will have to look it up. Or, better yet, you can create them yourself when you require the watery grave."

I laughed despite myself. "How did I end up in this fucked-up situation?"

"You are my heir, Reagan." The smile dripped off his face. "You were always going to end up here. This is your birthright. It is where you belong. You'll see that, in time. For now, what can I get you? Do you need to eat, like your druid? Or just heal? Use that snake. It'll cut down the healing time considerably."

My stomach rumbled, but I knew it was just because it was accustomed to getting food, not because it needed it. I'd realized I didn't need food to live when I was bonding Darius. "I don't *need* to eat, no. And for now, I don't think I will. It'll probably hurt. But eventually, yes. I enjoy it."

He stood. "Fantastic. I will make sure food is prepared for you when you require it. I'll leave you to your…"

"Babysitter," I supplied.

He laughed again, and I could tell it wasn't forced. He was a man who liked to find humor in odd things. Another trait I'd gotten from him. This whole situation was probably going to blow my mind before it was through.

He stopped by the door before pointing at his head. "Remember, some of us can hear thoughts. You know how to keep your thoughts to yourself, don't you?"

"If not, then you must think I am incredibly simple, since I doubt you've heard any thoughts since you entered."

And you can hear them, too? he thought, obviously testing me.

Correct, I responded.

He smiled again and knocked on the doorjamb. "When you need something, broadcast the thought. I will have an attendant outside this door at all times. When you are able, leave this room at will. You are not a prisoner of this castle."

"Just this world?"

His smile was sly. In answer, he winked before leaving the room and shutting the door behind him.

"You and he are now playing a game," Cahal said after giving Lucifer a few moments to *adios*. "He means to manipulate you into wanting to stay. Forever. You will need to fight for your freedom before the siren call of your heritage changes your life forever."

"Jesus, man, are you always so dramatic? First you were talking about me owning my heritage, and now you want me to be wary of it?" I rubbed my eyes, but the pain in my fingers made me wince, so I eventually just dropped my hand. "Give me the snake. I need to get better, and then I need to get out of here."

"You need to train. The only way you'll ever be free is if you fully realize your power and no one can keep you a prisoner."

I closed my eyes, suddenly exhausted. "Fine. That still requires getting better. Get that snake."

CHAPTER 3

"WHAT DO YOU want to eat?" I asked Cahal. Two days had gone by, and I was feeling much better. Those snakes really did work wonders. They didn't even try to get into any orifices, which was probably the greatest news. I'd been a little nervous I'd end up with a reptile enema.

"It doesn't matter. The food here isn't great."

He turned a page in his book. I might be allowed to wander the castle, something I wasn't in any shape to do yet, but he wasn't. It certainly seemed like there was bad blood between him and Lucifer, but he got evasive every time I asked about it. The good news was that Lucifer seemed to have an incredible supply of books. Whatever either of us asked for, we got, hand-delivered by a creepy little demon that didn't seem to like either of us very much.

Hamburger. I blasted the thought for Cahal's order, like yelling through the walls. *With lots of French fries.*

"That's just because you got used to Darius's cooking when we were on the island," I replied, swinging my feet over the edge of the bed. The white hospital gown I'd been wearing to recover rode up my legs and split open along the back.

And my clothes, please. Bring my clothes. I'm ready to check this place out.

"Very likely. He is exceptional." Cahal turned a page.

"Has this place changed much since you were here last?" I asked, rotating my ankles. Only a small twinge of pain vibrated up my calves.

"Some things. Not others."

I stared at him for a moment, knowing he wouldn't offer any more information, and contemplated whether I felt like dragging it out of him. But really, what help would it be? It was all new to me regardless, except for the outskirts I'd already seen.

The door started to open but stalled halfway through. The hunched little creature I'd grown accustomed to peered around the wood, its bald and leathery head coming to about thigh height. Its large yellow eyes sighted in on me, and I could just see the edge of the tray it carried.

"Come in," I said, rolling my shoulders and then my head. "What about my sword?" I asked Cahal, ignoring the demon. If you showed it too much attention, it wigged out and curled up into a ball until your focus went away. I was pretty sure its function was to be neither seen nor heard as it carried out its duty.

"What about it?" Cahal replied.

"Is it still with the elves? Did someone grab it?"

"Yes."

I waited for a moment. When nothing else came, I scowled at him. "You're torturing me because I cannot physically beat your ass, is that it?"

"You could magically beat my ass, if you were so inclined." He licked his finger and then turned a page.

"Gross, you're getting your spit all over someone else's book." I lifted a leg so I could bend and straighten it, working my knee. The demon froze, its long fingers wrapped around the edges of the silver tray, halfway to the desk at the side of the room where I'd given it a mental push to leave the food.

"No one is noticing you," I told it.

Its head turned very slowly until its chin was even with its shoulder, looking straight at me. When it saw me looking back, it slowly swiveled its head away and then crouched down a little lower and froze.

I rolled my eyes and looked back at Cahal, working my other knee. Only a small ache.

"Yes, it is still with the elves, or yes, someone grabbed it?" I pressed.

"Both. You don't need it. There is no point in lugging it around."

"Says the guy with the enormous curved blade."

"I don't have the same magic as you. I need my sword."

"You can kill a man with your thumb. Why do you need a sword?"

"A sword is faster."

"Speaking of..." Out of the corner of my eye, I noticed the demon was on the move again, creeping across the floor. The food would be cold by the time it got out of the room. "Where is your blade?"

"In Lucifer's private quarters, I imagine. He doesn't want me to have it."

"Why is that? Surely he doesn't think you can take on a kingdom of demons..."

"No. But I know the demons that he values most, and I could kill those if I felt so inclined. It seems he'd rather not chance it."

I stuck out my lips while nodding. "Good call. Right, okay." I clapped once and turned back toward the demon, now setting the tray on the desk. "What about my clothes?"

The tray of items clattered to the table, the porcelain jiggling. The demon set it down and scampered away as though burned, the long nails on its feet clicking across the wood floor. The door closed with a thud and silence reigned in the room.

"Does that mean no clothes? What the hell is the deal with that thing, anyway?"

"The service staff, as we will call them, are the invisible workers." Cahal closed his book and stood, crossing to the desk. "They are low in power and have zero status. It's best if you don't speak to them, and they would never dare to speak directly to you. Don't notice them. To do so…stresses them out. The last heir would curse them for any misdeeds right before killing them."

"He sounds like a real peach."

"That's the way it was." He bent over the food. "Mystery meat. Great."

I chuckled at his sarcastic tone and pushed up to standing, turning so Cahal didn't get an eyeful of my derrière. I stretched to one side and then the other, working out the ache. Padding across the room, adding a little fire below my bare feet to combat the chill, I snagged a French fry and popped it into my mouth.

I crossed to the grand closet, which was completely bare.

I need my clothes, I thought, and then decided, since I was finally up, I might as well just take a peek out the door.

A demon fashioned after a human woman stood to one side of the frame, half my height but with jutting boobs far too big for its petite body. Red leather covered it from neck to ankles, one big jumpsuit without zippers, hinting that it never had to take the thing off to use the restroom. Hooves took the place of feet, and the hair on its knuckles curled up in soft puffs.

Standing with its back to the wall near my door, the demon stared at the lovely garden mural painted on the opposite side of the wide corridor. The ceiling soared above us, more than ten feet high, and a white carpet ran down the center of an otherwise dark wood floor. No gold adorned this area, which had a somewhat modern look and was painted and accented with deep earth tones.

I glanced back into the sea of gold from which I'd come.

"If it looks like this out here, why is my room so hideous?" I asked.

The demon turned to me, and I honestly wondered how it didn't topple forward with the size of those breasts.

Its yellow eyes took me in for a moment, and I could feel its intense power thrumming around us. *Glaciem* magic—ice magic, as I thought of it—and a lot of it.

"Good evening, your highness." Its voice was scratchy and deep like a drum, the perfect accompaniment to the bushy mustache on its upper lip.

"Don't call me *your highness*. I don't intend to take the post."

"Unfortunately, I must address you by a title."

"Your *heinous* will do just fine."

"As you wish, your heinous. In answer to your question, your room is a hideous sort of gold because the Great Master wanted to see if you'd get the joke."

"I didn't."

"Fabulous. I will let him know. You may choose your quarters whenever you would like. Clothes are currently being collected for you, and then I will show you the way."

"I thought I could roam freely?"

"And so you shall, but the palace has undergone many changes since your insufferable druid companion was here last. You will get lost inside of a human minute."

"I have an excellent memory."

"Which will greatly help you in places that do not habitually change."

I wasn't sure what that meant, but I didn't plan to explore far today anyway. My body was getting better, and movement wasn't too painful anymore, but I didn't think I had a lot of stamina. Not yet. I needed that snake to work its magic for a little longer. The thing was currently slithering around my torso.

I retreated and waited for my clothes, and after the creepy demon placed them on the desk, removed the empty plates and tray, and scampered away, I changed into a new set of leather pants and a tank top. It felt strange not to have any weapons to strap to my person.

"Looks like I'm going to have to go commando. And braless. They didn't bring underwear." I palmed my boobs. "This is more comfortable now, but if I have to run, things might get dicey."

"Yes, you'll give yourself a black eye."

I couldn't tell if he was joking or not.

Cahal picked up his book and faced me. "I'm free-balling it, too. They didn't bring back underwear after they took my clothes, and I didn't feel like explaining. My dick and balls won't affect my running."

I scanned his dark pants and black shirt, loose over his muscular frame. I hadn't noticed they were clean clothes. Then again, I hadn't exactly been lucid when he found me in the elves' cell.

Something occurred to me.

"Where have you been sleeping?"

He glanced back at the chair.

I lifted my eyebrows, checking his chiseled face for signs of fatigue. No dark shadows pooled under his glacial blue eyes. The planes and angles of his bone structure, almost severe with a slightly hooked nose, fit with his aura of lethal confidence. They did not, however, broadcast any wariness or exhaustion. He stood tall, well over my height, with his shoulders squared and back straight, his bearing loose and agile.

"You slept in the chair?"

"I've slept in many places all over the worlds. Some

more comfortable than others. I've grown accustomed to getting the rest I need in any given place."

"Huh. What a terrible life you lead."

The corners of his lips pulled upward. Many would think it was the beginnings of a snarl, but I knew it was his self-deprecating humor, only expressed once he got to know someone. The guy was like a block of ice. It took a while to thaw him enough to get to his personality.

"Right. Let's go pick a new place to stay." I headed toward the door. "This room is some sort of joke, it seems."

"I figured as much."

"My old man has a sense of humor, then?"

"That's what he could call it, yes."

"And what would you call it?"

"Usually? Dangerous."

Tits McGee led us slowly down the hallway, pausing halfway down as the walls around us shifted. A door disappeared, a wall appeared in front of us, and another hallway opened to our right. The demon turned that way, and I glanced back at a dead end that no longer reached as far as the room I'd just left.

"And that's why you grabbed your book," I murmured, watching a table appear beside me and feeling the magic thrumming from it. It wasn't real, that wood. That flower in the vase on top of it. It was an illusion made of magic, like the majority of the Realm, like the scenarios I could create myself. Well, kinda. On my best day, I couldn't create something so detailed. Not yet, anyway.

Cahal was right: I needed to hang around until I learned how to properly wield this magic. If the war did eventually come, and I was the one in charge of stopping Lucifer from destroying the Realm, I had better figure out how to make that possible.

The demon stopped again, and this time I reached out around me as the landscape shifted, feeling the various fibers of magic, picking them apart to see how they were constructed. Much of the hall was real—real wood, real paintings, real wallpaper or paint—but magic added the occasional door or glowing light fixture. Sometimes false walls masked whole rooms, blocking them from passersby. Or was it just blocking me?

As we turned toward the left, I unraveled it all. Plucking illusions apart was easy for me—putting them back together less so. Making them solid was a total no-go, but it was clearly possible. The illusion fell away, revealing a high-arched ceiling with chandeliers hanging down, much more fashionable than the setup in the elves' castle. Stately furniture was arranged on a large deep crimson rug, and each wall was completely covered in row after high row of books.

"Wow," I said, angling my head up to see the top row, where the bookcases met the edge of the ceiling. Not a single ladder to help people reach the volumes at the top, so I figured anyone working in this area had *Glaciem* magic. They'd need to levitate to reach.

The demon waited until I'd had my fill of looking, saying nothing about my pulling down the illusion. When I turned, it began walking again.

"Emery would do just fine in this place. His jokes would be commonplace," I mused, revealing a hidden pocket in the hallway and the creepy little demon that hid inside—not the one that had waited on me but of the same variety. It caught sight of me looking at it and took off running. When I found the next little pocket, I ran my hand through it first, making sure it wasn't solid. They weren't trapping the little critters in, they were just creating places for them to retain their invisible status.

I ripped it down and then grinned when another creature took off running.

"You think that is funny, but you didn't get the gold room joke?" Cahal asked, not even glancing at my antics.

"How is sticking me in a hideous gold room a joke? The rest of this place is gorgeous—why even have a gold room? Is it a throwback to the elves' gaudy decorating?"

"Probably, in a way." Cahal studied a mural of a battle as we passed, a robust demon ripping a wing off an angelic creature. Blood spurted from the creature's back. Fire crawled along the edges of the painting, near the frame. Bodies littered the ground.

"Salt-of-the-earth people around here, huh? Sugar and spice and everything nice," I said, leaving the next little alcove alone. I didn't want to stress them out too badly on my first day out of my room. I would give them a chance to get used to me.

"Is only Lucifer—" I stopped when Tits McGee hissed.

"When speaking to his underlings, you are to use his title," Cahal instructed me. "Either the Great Master, his highness, or Father."

"Is *your* Great Master the only one who can create these illusions?"

"No," it answered in a disapproving tone. "Those in the top echelons of power can construct the designs laid out by the Great Master."

We traveled up a wide, curving staircase, and then another, nearing the top of the castle now.

"Where is Father Dearest's room?" I asked, marveling at the great decorating and elegantly appointed halls and rooms, dotted here and there with some lovely paintings, some sexy ones, and some incredibly gruesome battle depictions.

"The Great Master occupies the Northern Tower," it

said.

"That is a change since I was here last," Cahal said, his eyes snagging on a painting of a type of flower I'd never seen before.

"A lot has changed since you were here last, druid." The demon nearly spat the term.

"I don't think they like you very much," I murmured as we crested the last set of stairs and paused.

"They blame me for things that I did not cause," he replied.

The demon hissed softly but did not comment. "This level has access to three sets of lodgings that would befit someone of your station."

"Three? Luc—Father Dearest was hoping for a brood of kids, huh?"

"Once upon a time, elf royalty or other members of the royal court in high standing used to visit," Cahal explained. "After the last war, though, the castle is only host to the *lesser.*"

"The lesser, and then below that…you, it would seem," the demon said.

"*Oooohh, burn.* Don't worry, I won't be moving you down to the dungeon, bud." I winked at Cahal.

"We shall see," the demon muttered, turning toward a section with columns on the outside of a balcony-style hallway. Beyond and down a corridor sat rooms. "Would you like me to show you to the various collection of rooms, or would you prefer to explore for yourself? Everything in this area is as it seems. The pathways stay constant."

"The pathways everywhere stay constant if you tear down the magic," I replied.

The demon didn't comment.

"I'll find my way, thanks." I turned left and started walking, then stopped when the demon trailed behind me. I quirked an eyebrow at it.

"I will be on hand should you need anything," it said.

"Can you make yourself scarce?" I asked.

"Of course." It took one step to the side and then looked away. I had a suspicion it still intended to follow me, just at a distance. That would take some getting used to. And it would likely chase me out of here quicker.

"Have you ever been up here?" I asked Cahal, intending to walk only as long as it took me to find a door. I'd stake a claim on the first set of rooms.

"No. The last heir took up a collection of rooms in the south section of the castle."

"Huh." At the end of an open hall flanked by columns and large windows looking down at the kingdom below, I found a large hearth with two double doors to either side. Chandeliers with tiny, flickering fairy lights swooped down between the doors, in front of the hearth. I hadn't seen their equal in the palace. I wondered how Lucifer had created them, because electricity didn't exist in this world.

We went through one set of doors, into a set of rooms cavernous enough to fit my whole house, both stories. Two rows of windows adorned the far wall, giving an impressive view of a kingdom riddled with gardens, lush little landscapes, and buildings with gothic spires. The blue sky above went on forever, even though I was almost positive a cave ceiling existed above us somewhere. When I managed to pull my gaze away, I saw the doors dotting the other side of the living space, various rooms for me and my guests. There was enough space for all of my friends, including those from my neighborhood, to come and stay. There would be plenty of room, and surely plenty of creepy little helpers scurrying around.

Not plenty of air, though. And obviously, the non-magical wouldn't be allowed in anyway. To stay here forever would mean giving up a massive part of my life.

I stopped in front of one of the large windows and remembered the last time I'd been to the Underworld. I remembered having Darius by my side.

A pang hit my heart.

He must've heard I'd been taken from the elves, but he'd probably know that I was safe here. Safe from physical harm, at any rate. Even though I missed him, I didn't need him, so hopefully he would keep working on the vampires and not attempt to do something crazy, like try to rescue me. I was the one who'd gotten us through the Underworld the first time, for the most part, and even that had been close. I didn't want him to try to find me, get caught, and have Lucifer turn him into a hostage situation. That would just complicate everything.

Still, though, it would be cool to stand here with him and take in the view.

"I guess you get a bed now," I commented to Cahal, standing just inside the doorway.

"It seems so." He pointed at the door at the back of the room. "That is yours. I'll take the room next to it."

"How do you know?" I zigzagged though the furniture and opened the door into a well-lit room with more of the fantastic view. The colors in the room were deep and pleasing, dark and saturated. The enormous bed backed up to a paneled wall. A little writing desk faced one of the windows and couches took up the other side, so I could lounge without going into the common area.

I blew out a breath and braced my palms against my hips. The arrangement of the furniture, the view with the gothic spires, the height of the room—as though I lived on a cloud—and the decor made me feel comfortable in a way that unnerved me. All of it blended together into a pleasing sort of utopia.

This felt like my room. Like I'd been living here all my life.

"Why did you say this was my room?" I asked, raising my voice so Cahal could hear.

"Because—"

I startled and ripped my elbow away from the guy who had snuck up on me and now stood two feet away. I clearly hadn't been paying attention to my surroundings, something that didn't usually happen in foreign and dangerous places.

"Because," he started again, "it is the corner room and the largest in this wing. It belongs to the person with the highest status. You."

"It's breathtaking." I chuckled to myself and shook my head. "He used that gaudy room to heighten the pleasure of ending up here."

"You get the joke."

"It isn't a joke. It's a lure." I shook my head again. "And it's a good one."

CHAPTER 4

PENNY GRABBED EMERY'S arm as they slowed in front of the gate to the Underworld. Dead flowers and twisted vines lined either side of the path before it descended into a hazy black maw that threatened to suck travelers in if they got too close. Intense magic seeped into the air around them, pulsing with menace, violence, sex, and love, the mixture not as pleasing as Reagan's brew of magic, but darker and more sinister. Beyond that maw would be an incredibly dangerous place, Penny could feel it.

She did not want to willingly walk into that.

"You've been this way before?" she asked, gulping, resisting the urge to take a step back.

Darius unslung a pack from his back and pulled out a torch. "Yes. Many times. It's the safest entrance point I've found into the areas I usually traverse." He handed the torch, unlit, to Penny. His normal vampire swagger, the one she was as accustomed to seeing as his suits, had been replaced with the sort of ruthlessness he showed in battle. His magic swirled around him, heady and vicious. "You can magically light this, correct?"

"Yes." She took the torch. "How many times have you been down here?"

"Through this particular entrance—two dozen or so. There are others I've used, including the first area I visited with Reagan. I have business in the Edges, as they're called. Your magic has helped me make good connections. Connections we will need now." He glanced down at her fanny pack, one of Reagan's old ones. Scuffed up and beat to hell, it still did the trick, holding a small fortune in spells.

Emery had a similar pack, his being newer, a designer brand, and bright red. He'd made a case for using a satchel instead and lost the argument, and then lost another argument when he suggested wearing cargo pants and using the pockets for all the spells. He did not enjoy the fashion that had been pushed on him, and his sour expression, even here, proved it. In addition to the fanny packs, they had on leather pants and sweaters, all in dark colors, much like Darius.

"If you need to use those spells, do so," Darius went on, handing Emery a torch. They all had backpacks, but Emery's and Penny's were full of supplies humans needed, like food and water. Darius held all the essentials for the trip. Anything they couldn't bring, they planned on stealing. "Refraining is best."

Penny nodded and did everything in her power not

to back away from that black maw in front of them.

"Set?" Darius's stare was still beating into Penny.

"I'll be fine," she said, gripping her torch much too tightly.

"Remember, you will need to follow my lead," Darius said. "You will need to do as I say. Only strike out when I say so. Only strike out at *whom* I say to. It will take all of my effort to navigate this place. You need to take my commands and *follow my lead.*"

"Yes, yes, I know. I heard you the first eight hundred times," she grumbled, losing the battle of wills with herself and taking a step back.

"Hunch for all you are worth, stay behind me and in front of Emery," he continued. "Keep your hands down. Do not make magical clouds. Do not get startled and accidentally strike out. Use your magical concealment spell for sight, smell, and sound. Do not release it unless I say otherwise."

"I said *I know.*" She scowled at him.

His stare pummeled her for another beat before he nodded and turned around, facing that horrible maw. She swore she saw him take a deep breath before starting forward. Any place that made Darius nervous was nowhere she wanted to go. But heading to a noose wasn't appealing either, and she would've been pushed onto the platform if not for Reagan.

She reached back and clutched Emery's hand as she

stepped into the blackness, the two of them silently weaving a concealment spell that she then pulled around them. She squeezed her eyes shut and held her breath. An unnatural cold slithered over her skin and seeped into her blood, the feeling closer to fear than magic. Or was this magically induced fear? She couldn't be sure.

Blinking her eyes open did no good. The world beyond was pitch black. She bumped into Darius's muscled back and jostled against Emery's front.

Something splattered against her forehead.

"Flipping flapjacks!" She released a plume of magic she hadn't realized was ready to go. Or maybe it hadn't been. It zipped into the sky and bloomed in the darkness, a flower of blues and pinks and purples, light in a dark place. It showered down like a firework, raining sparkling light.

She felt Darius turn, his breath dusting down on her face. She could feel his anger thrumming between them.

"Sorry," she whispered. "Something hit my head."

"Drops of water," he replied, turning. "The ceiling drips. Do not do that again."

"Once was probably plenty to get noticed," Emery murmured.

Yeah, it probably was, especially since it was still streaking the ink-black sky.

"Light your torches." The heat from Darius's back

dissipated, cold taking its place. He'd stepped forward. "These are stairs. Take caution."

"Right, right. Stairs to go down," she said, conjuring up some fire to cover the tip of her torch.

Emery stepped beside her as the flame slowly grew, illuminating the tiny bubble around them. Together they descended, Darius a few steps ahead and not needing the spell—he'd been down here before. Emery flinched.

"What?" she whispered.

"One of those drops. It's disconcerting."

"I have a feeling this whole place is going to be disconcerting."

"You're probably right."

She stumbled at the bottom, expecting a step and not seeing one, having been looking ahead rather than down. As if someone had flicked a switch, low light flooded the area. The light skimmed the rough-hewn ground. Large walls made of sharp rock, twelve feet high or so, rose in sections, creating dry canals. Creatures crowded into the little pockets of darkness, their movement suggesting they were communicating in some way. This had to be the market.

Darius veered right, aiming for a large opening between one set of the walls. They passed three of the seller stalls, not unlike the ones that had populated the medieval village she'd worked at in Seattle. Only two were active, one with a crowd of hairy creatures and the other with a lone troll, watching them with a grumpy expression.

Darius slowed at the fourth stall, stepping to the side and out of oncoming traffic, which comprised of a few demon-looking creatures. They'd aimed to come at the low tide, as Darius called it, when the market was the slowest. Apparently he'd cataloged such things.

He bent to the stall owner, a goblin reminiscent of the Red Cap from which she'd *inherited* the boost of godly magic she now carried.

"I am seeking passage to the inner kingdom," Darius said softly, his words barely reaching Penny even though she waited right beside them. "For three."

"Can't get you there right now," the creature grated, its voice like a knife blade pulled across her bones. "They found the heir. She's up at the castle. The Great Master has locked the inner kingdom down tight. Everyone coming in and going out is monitored. Can't get you through."

"I don't need passage, I need a guide to get us there. We'll get through. Send word."

"Who is this *we*?" the goblin asked, his eyes narrowed.

"Someone the heir will want to see. She will repay you for your help."

"Yeah, sure. But the Great Master will skin me alive

if he finds out. That's not worth it."

"Everything has a price," Emery murmured as Darius pulled the backpack around and reached inside. He came back with four filled casings and laid them on the flimsy table.

Penny recognized their special markings. It was an incredibly ancient and potent spell Darius had found in a spell book and copied down by hand, not trusting the light of a copy machine against paper or parchment that old. At least, that was what he'd said. As they'd done the spell while in the vampire lair, Emery suspected Darius had taken it down from someone else's book. The spell was so robust that they'd needed four casings to hold it all.

She and Emery had taken two days to prepare a few of those spells. Days they could've been on the road to Reagan. But Darius had assured them that the time was worth it. Necessary, he'd said.

The goblin licked its lips. It clearly recognized the casings and coveted them. The spell would allow a creature to change into any form it desired and live in the human world undetected by anyone. Not even shifters or vampires would smell the magic on him. It was like witness protection for magical people. For a creature like this, who basically couldn't blend in in the human world, that was apparently an incredibly big deal. For people like Reagan, with demonic magic that

Lucifer could track if he had a close, personal object of hers (news to Penny), it might mean the difference between freedom and servitude.

There was only one person that seemed to have such a handle on ancient magic like that. Ja. Emery had mentioned to Penny that he wondered what Darius had had to trade to get it. It sure would've been nice if they'd had it before all this.

"For that"—the goblin pointed at the casings—"I can get you near it. Then you're on your own."

"I need someone on the other side," Darius pushed. "Someone who can get us in and out of Lucifer's castle. No deal until we are out of the Underworld."

"Are you crazy?" The goblin leaned forward. "Do you know what you're asking? Do you know what kind of heat me and my associates would be in if we were caught?"

Darius touched the spell on the table. "Once you take this, I will set you up for life. You can disappear forever. Live as a wealthy human. Visit the Realm whenever you like. With this spell and my resources, you can have the kind of life you've never dared to dream of. It would get you out of here."

The goblin shook its head, leaning back, not taking the bait.

Darius pulled a vial of blood out of the backpack. The goblin's head stopped shaking. Its eyes widened in recognition.

Unicorn blood, a secret the vampires had been keeping for generations. It was essential to their creation of new vampires, but it also imbued anyone who drank it with certain powers. The vampires kept it a closely guarded secret for obvious reasons, but they wouldn't need to anymore if they were allowed to return to the Underworld. Something about this place awakened their ability to procreate, a secret that Cahal had blabbed to everyone on Darius's island and now probably wouldn't be much of a secret anymore.

"One spell and vial for you," Darius said softly. "And one for whoever meets us on the other side. Plus disappearing into the human world forever. If you don't, you'll be on Lucifer's front line. I doubt you will last. Take this offer. It's the best you will ever receive."

The goblin stared at Darius for a long time. Seconds trickled by, then minutes. Darius did not shift or fidget. He just waited.

"He has him," Emery said softly, his voice concealed by the spell.

"Fine." The goblin reached forward to swipe the spell off the table.

Darius was there first, infinitely faster. "You will get half of this spell now. You will get the other half, and the vial, when we pass through the Edges on our way out. Your associate will get the same deal."

The goblin pulled back his hand, waited for Darius to deposit two of the casings, and then slipped them into his pocket. "Meet you beyond the river. Usual place. I assume you only want your most loyal allies knowing of this?"

"Yes. Don't dally." Darius packed his things away and turned, heading farther into the area.

"I knew he'd been setting up a magical trade down here," Emery whispered as they followed, still walking beside Penny and not behind, like Darius had said, "but I had no idea he carried so much favor with these people. They must really trust him to agree to something like this."

"Reagan is not going to be pleased he's been keeping secrets of this magnitude. If he's got this going on, what else is he hiding?"

"He's an elder vampire—my guess is a lot."

Darius didn't breeze through this place like he always breezed through the Brink. He didn't stroll or strut, confident and arrogant. He trudged along like a creature at the end of his rope and ready to snap. He walked like he might snap into violence at any provocation. Like he would kill if he did. Like the doomsday cloud he really was.

Shivers washed over Penny at the change. He was clearly a master at knowing what persona was needed in any given place, and she was seeing it carried out in the flesh. Thank God he was on their side. Or…Reagan's side, anyway, and Reagan was on hers.

If Reagan ever had to break up with him, she'd need to kill him. That was all there was to it. He was too dangerous to be an ex.

The feel of the ground changed beneath her feet. Squishy now, almost. She swore she'd stepped on a clump of something. Looking down, though, it was still the rough rock.

The walls started to taper down and then stopped, another invisible clump catching Penny's notice. And then the landscape changed entirely. One minute they were walking through a leaking sort of cave, and the next they were on a wide, desolate beach that went on forever.

"What kind of messed-up place is this?" Penny said softly, clutching Emery.

"Pull away the magic. I need to see you," Darius said, an edge in his voice.

Emery did so without hesitation.

Darius grabbed her other arm, pushing in close. "Stay together. If we separate here, the illusion will change. We'll lose each other."

She'd already had a hand on Emery, but he adjusted it so they were more tightly pressed together. The guys clearly thought she couldn't be trusted.

She flinched when a drop hit her forehead out of a

bland gray sky.

"I hate this place," she murmured.

"You will find that it gets worse. Try not to think about it, and it isn't so bad. Come on." Darius started forward, Emery reading his cues and moving quickly. Penny was dragged between them. "It's an illusion. Much of the Underworld is. Like what Reagan does, only more detailed and on a much larger scale. We will be going through a sect that is going to…broaden your voyeuristic horizons. I doubt you will be embarrassed by much after it, and I doubt you will be comfortable during it. It is the safest sect we can traverse, however. They are enamored by my kind."

"You better not have cheated on Reagan, or when this is all done, I'll not only tell her, I'll help her torch your body and bury your black sludge guts in the yard."

"I would never bed another," he replied, and he had better be telling the truth, or Penny absolutely would help Reagan do something awful. "I certainly would not bed a demon. But I am a predator of humans, gifted with traits this sect of demons covet. They can sense my magic. They delight in it. Merely being in their presence… Well, you'll see. I passed through a similar sect on my first journey through the Underworld, but this one holds much more power. Their power draws out my gifts. When we come back through, they will delight in seeing Reagan by my side, and she'll…probably give in to my enhanced predatory traits. You will get to see quite the show. I know how you delight in such things…"

Penny's face burned at the reminder that she'd walked in on him and Reagan, twice, and Emery chuckled, the jerk! "Seriously, this has got to stop! *I was not trying to catch you two!* It's not my thing, honest!"

"We shall see."

"Oh my God, I hate you." The squishy sensation beneath her feet turned into the hollow thunk of wood. It matched the look of the pier.

Emery looked around, his gaze coming to rest on the fog in front of them, near the end of the pier, if she had to guess. "And that's the fog you want us to take down?"

"Yes, but not yet." Darius stopped in front of it. "That would alert Lucifer to a breach."

"Obviously." Emery's eyes were still moving across it, then coming to a stop. His brow lowered. "This is incredible magic. The weave is intricate and tight. It would take a while to get through it. Maybe we should've left Reagan here for longer. Let her learn first."

"She'll have time to learn." Darius got himself situated, adjusting his jacket and then his backpack, as if he were gearing up for what came next. "Once we get into the sect, we won't be rushing. Can't rush. One wrong step, and we'll be hunted. We need to play this safe."

"We only have food rations for a week, though," Penny said. "That isn't a lot of time for her to learn."

"There is human food here, as well as various animals to hunt. They probably won't be appetizing to you, but if you're hungry enough, you'll eat them. I have a store of canned goods hidden away in various sects for just such an occasion. We are aiming for Reagan being in his care for another two weeks, making it three total. We can push to four, but any longer and I fear she won't want to leave. She is an incredibly fast learner—even Cahal mentioned his surprise. It'll be enough time for her to learn the basics. She can build her knowledge from there."

"She'll want to leave." Penny nodded as she studied the fog. Emery was right: that thing was a beast. It wouldn't take forever for them to rip it down, though. All it would take was the spell Penny had devised to cripple Reagan's magic.

"Ready?" Darius spared them a glance, and then he was easing into the fog, his body tensing up. That meant it hurt, probably pretty badly for him to show it.

"Do you think it will hurt us that badly?" she asked Emery, a quiver in her voice that she couldn't quite help.

"No." He didn't sound sure. "Ready?"

She took his hand and stepped up to the fog. It

licked her front, stinging, questing, hunting for the key that would allow them through.

They kept pushing forward. Magical needles pierced her, and she gasped. It felt like it was probing, trying to get at her blood. Wanting a sample of what granted her admission.

Emery tugged on her, forcing her farther into the fog. The pain increased, digging into her now, ever searching.

She knew what it was doing—it was seeking out the godly power she'd accidentally stolen from that horrible little goblin. She offered up what it was seeking to help it along.

The fog sizzled, peeling away from her tiny string of magic and then her body, deadening the pain as it let her pass.

It slithered around Emery's body next, now popping and hissing, before letting him pass too.

She frowned as they stepped into the area beyond, where Darius waited with a watchful gaze and loose posture. A single boat waited at the end of the pier, occupied by a solitary figure at the bow.

Despite Darius's posture, the tightness around his eyes suggested that he'd wondered if Penny and Emery would make it.

The hissing and popping continued after they passed, the thick white fog turning black. The magic peeling away. Evaporating. The change in fog racing into the sky…but not stopping there.

"What's happening?" Darius asked, alarm in his voice.

"I…don't know." Penny watched as the magic continued to sizzle and pop and eventually burn away, exposing other piers with boats waiting at the ends. "I just offered up the magic it was searching for…"

"It looks like it's unraveling the whole spell," Emery said, still holding Penny's hand, looking back at the beach, and then the sky. "Did you use the spell that deadens Reagan's magic?"

"No! That's a complex one—you've seen it. This was literally just me allowing it to find the magic I got from that Red Cap. The godly magic. That's it, I swear!"

"Reagan is of the Underworld," Darius said softly, and the sudden hard lines of his body made Penny jolt with adrenaline. It advertised his alarm. "But she had a mage's magic through her mother. She has a godly touch. The two halves must exist in her in a unique way. Godly magic doesn't unravel her Underworld magic this way. Come. Quickly. This will be noticed and reported immediately. We must go. *Hurry!*"

Penny jolted backward as a drop splattered across her forehead. "How did he come up with all that so fast…" she said as Emery tugged her on, rushing to the boat at the end of the pier.

The people in the boats down the way were looking upward. Some had turned in their direction.

"Donkey balls dipped in milk," Penny swore, allowing Darius to grab her other arm and help Emery lower her into the boat. This was not a great time to be clumsy. She did not want to fall into the stagnant yet murky river water. Lord knew what was in it.

"I've been thinking about her unique magic for a while," Darius answered. "It has never seemed to fit with any other magic I have read about. The balance of the two magics within her is a logical conclusion. It fits a few of the pieces together."

"Logical to whom?" she asked as Emery climbed in beside her. Darius took the middle.

Now nothing stood between them and the beach that seemed to go on forever. The boat rocked and pitched, as though actually on a quickly moving river. The man at the bow stared straight ahead, and Penny belatedly realized that he wasn't a person at all but some sort of creature in a dark gray robe with a hood over its head. Grayish skin covered its kind-of-human face, but the eye sockets remained empty, bone divots more than actual holes.

"Ugh," she said accidentally, clasping her hands in her lap.

"Plan B," Darius said as the creature in the boat animated.

It looked at Darius. "Hello, Walrus."

CHAPTER 5

PENNY'S EYEBROWS SANK low. "What… What?"

The creature's face turned a little, and adrenaline beat a drum in Penny's veins. People were gathering on the beach now, looking their way. The magic just kept on unraveling, the sand turning into hard rock and then some sort of green-gray plant matter. The water that had once been concealed by fog rocked and swayed, a decided contrast to the smooth river beneath the boats. Far, far above, the sky was starting to peel away and lose its light. Her simple action was somehow undoing the whole magical façade.

"Who are you?" the creature said as Penny tapped the side of the boat.

"We need to go," Penny said. The other creatures were all turning to look at their boat now. "We need to go now."

"Black Sheep," Emery said beside her.

"Black Sheep," the creature repeated, as though saying hello. Its sightless gaze came to rest on Penny. "Who are you?"

A creature came jogging out of the rocky path whence they'd come, heading straight for them across the rapidly unraveling sand.

"Sparkly thongs," she swore, tapping the boat harder now.

"Sparkly Thongs," the creature repeated. "Where do you go?"

"We have to immobilize those other boats," Emery said urgently as Darius rattled off some name across the river. "Otherwise they can just follow us."

A drop plunked down on the top of Penny's head. She absently wiped at it as she analyzed the magic she could feel. *Transport. Safety. Steady.*

"The boats are designed to get people to and from the area safely," she said softly, looking over the side. The tranquil waters didn't stop the boat from rolling and rocking, but there was magic attached, which seemed to lessen the impact. "I can't generate rapids or anything. I'm not an elemental."

"You've gotten mighty good with magical explosives, though," Darius mused, as though there wasn't some guy pointing at them as he loaded into a boat. As though the rest of the people or creatures in the area weren't watching them in surprise. There went their freaking cover. There went sneaking in!

"I did this, and I didn't even mean to," she murmured, magic crowding around them, Emery forcing it to take shape. "It wasn't even a spell that I did." A thread of doubt wormed through her. Or had it been? Maybe she'd accidentally used a sort of spell to give the fog what it had been seeking.

"It doesn't matter, Turdswallop," Emery said, his face closed down in concentration, his fingers moving. "This isn't the only thing that will go wrong. We need to rebound."

"Yes, exactly. Something was always going to go wrong. Now it has. Adjust," Darius said.

"How can you be so calm?" she ground out, taking stock of Emery's spell. Looking back the way they'd come, she felt her chest tighten. Two boats had taken to the water now, drifting after them. They might not be following, but they definitely knew who'd caused all the mayhem.

"My dearest always said that you are the most effective when you are running for your life," Darius replied, and had the gall to entwine his fingers over his knee. Penny had the presence of mind to notice he didn't say Reagan's name. She needed to remember that. "And now you are. Make miracles."

"Yeah. Sure. Fine." Penny threaded fire power, magic borrowed from the creature in the boat, through Emery's concoction. Letting Emery handle the rest, she turned to the creature. It would need to be magically gagged. It would be asked who'd eroded the fog, and she couldn't chance it spilling its guts.

A swell of power left Emery's hands, but Penny didn't look up to see. The bank on the right drifted closer, the creature magically aiming for whatever place Darius had requested.

She pulled ingredients from the magical cloud that constantly traveled above her, weaving the most potent of the gag spells she knew. It might kill the thing but…well, this was life or death. It was time to get serious.

A distant peal of thunder made the boat rock and roll, just barely stopping before it took in water on the right side.

"Do that spell again," Penny said, letting the gag order dissipate and now working on the spells attached to the river. They kept the boats safe, kept them going to certain locations, kept them from capsizing. The magic was all connected, grounded, like Reagan had described the magic in the Realm.

She peered over the side. Her stomach rolled with what she was about to do.

"Horse dongs and singalongs, hold on." Another peal of thunder reverberated off walls and a ceiling she couldn't see. A ceiling that kept dripping. She ignored it and formulated the spell that deadened Reagan's magic. She elbowed Emery, and he helped out, making it bigger. More expansive. More potent.

The riverbank drifted ever closer. The boat rocked and rolled some more. The thunder died away, and she glanced around. One boat was sinking fast, two bodies floating away from it. The other was in pieces amid some sludge that probably used to be demon parts. Emery's spell had taken them out in short order.

"Right, okay, good work." She breathed deeply, and he worked quietly, accustomed to being around mayhem and carnage, and also causing it. You'd think she would be too by now.

She released the spell and then immediately faced front again and restarted the spell for the gag order. Emery jumped in quickly as Darius waited patiently, watching the bank, the point at which they needed to have all the spells done.

"Wait..." Penny stilled as her and Emery's spell ate through the Underworld magic like it was nothing. Breaking it apart. Sizzling it. Eroding. The illusion in the river dissolved, and now the torrid current jibed with the rocking of the boat. "We don't have oars."

"We do." Emery continued to work on the gag spell.

Penny glanced downward as the boat caught a current that pulled them back to the center of the river. Darius bent to his feet.

"No, Walrus. That is not your job," the creature said, still mostly placid.

Penny stilled for the second time as the magic wafting toward her changed. This wasn't the magic creating the illusion, but that of the creature in the boat. *Restrain. Capture. Question.*

"Hold on there, Darius," she said softly, feeling Emery tense. He must've caught the tone in her voice. The *something is about to go very wrong here* tone. "Just take it easy."

"I'll handle it," Darius said, and he all but launched forward, the speed and ferocity of his movements making Penny jerk back and cover her chest. If she had a string of pearls, she'd be clutching them so hard her knuckles would turn white. Even Emery jerked back.

In a display of unbridled violence, Darius reached the boat man and slashed his throat with his lengthening claws, raking them down the gray flesh of the creature's chest. He punctured the sternum and then wrenched off its head, tossing it aside. The quickly decaying body followed.

With wide eyes, frozen stiff, Penny watched as Darius pulled down a sweater sleeve, adjusted a strand of hair that had gotten out of place, and then bent for oars that had been tucked along the floorboard.

"Now you won't need to rely on a gag spell," the vampire said, holding an oar out to Emery.

Emery shook away his reaction and took the proffered instrument. Penny continued to stare.

There was one thing she would never, ever say: Darius wasn't vicious enough to date a girl like Reagan.

There was one thing she would never, ever do: pick a fight with him.

She'd seen him in battle, but they'd never exactly fought side by side. She'd never watched as he…handled things. It was jarring, to say the least. Reagan had found her match.

Penny licked her lips as the guys put their oars into the water and started paddling quickly. "How did you know he—it—was about to…cause a problem?"

"You advertise your reactions, and Mr. Westbrook…has certain tells when he feels danger coming," Darius responded. "My solution was easier and quicker, though we need to put some muscle behind these oars or we're going to miss our point of entry. The sect beyond isn't as…savory as the one I'm aiming for."

"Very eloquent speech after that display…" Penny murmured.

"I didn't *see* our lives in danger," Emery said, speaking of his special magical ability to get a mental picture of his demise right before it happened. It allowed him to change things up and avoid death, something that had saved them both a million times, it seemed like. He pulled harder on his oar.

"No, the Boatmen do not resort to extreme violence very quickly or very often," Darius said. "They are not programmed for offense or even defense. Lucifer could've changed their roles to keep people like me out, if he'd wanted, but instead he created the fog. It did its part but left ample room for error. I have not figured out why this decision was made. Possibly one day I'll be able to ask him about it."

"After you steal back his daughter and work to thwart him in battle?" Penny huffed. "Fat chance."

"Yes, there will be that issue lying between us. Can't be helped, I'm afraid."

"No, it cannot," Penny mumbled, leaning to get a look around Darius. The river buckled in places and rolled in others. Rocks marred the way, forming eddies. No plants grew. Nothing floated along the surface, not even the ruins of the other boats or the bodies of the passengers and Boatmen, as though something had sucked them under.

Penny looked down into the murky depths, not able to see very far, wondering if something lurked in these waters. "Don't tip us over," she whispered.

"How did you know about the design of the Boatmen?" Emery asked, and Penny knew he was trying to figure out this world, similar to Darius. He'd want to understand the rules, the better to survive. It was a skill Penny needed to learn in case she was separated from them. She'd been helpless under her mother's care. And although Reagan had a habit of pushing her into dangerous situations to make her shine, she never attempted to take control when traveling with Emery or Reagan, always happy to go along with the stronger personalities. Well, time for that to change. She'd be damned if she'd lose another person she cared about like she'd lost Reagan.

"I've tested them. I have never killed one before, but I did have to thwart an attack. No punishment was doled out for my misbehavior. I am not sure if actually killing one will change matters."

"Three, and their passengers," Penny corrected him, seeing the guys strive harder, trees on the bank whipping by. They were going faster now, the river picking up speed. Darius's movements increased pace and fervency to match, but Emery wasn't able to keep up. Darius looked back at him with obvious irritation.

"I'm not a vampire. I don't have the same abilities," Emery responded.

"So it would seem." Darius turned and looked farther down the bank. "We're going to miss it. Pull for all you're worth, Mr. Westbrook. The next sect over isn't ideal, but we can make it work. The one after…"

Penny hated when Darius was formal like this. It meant bad things. Dangerous things. A vampire holding on to his fleeting control, tooth and nail.

"What happens if we land there?" Penny asked in a small voice, trying to think of a spell that might help. She just didn't want to rock the boat too much. She didn't want to misjudge the amount of magic that was needed and send them flying into the water. Something told her a dangerous sect, whatever it was, was better than what possibly waited in these waters.

"Then we must use all our speed and stealth, and hope that you do indeed work best when your enemy is closing in."

CHAPTER 6

"I SEE YOU are up and going today."

I paused with my hands in the air, having just taken down a fake wall. My intention was to change it into some sort of mind-fuck, but I was having trouble narrowing in on a good one. These people had a patent on mind-fuckery—I had to come up with something vicious.

"Say, listen." I dropped my hands and turned to find Father Dearest, wearing the same clothes as the last time I'd seen him. Then again, I'd gotten another set of clean clothes that morning, as had Cahal, and they were exactly the same as the day before. Still no underwear. This time I'd described what I needed, though. Commando with leather had the ability to chafe. I wanted to nip that problem in the bud. "What's a gal gotta do to get a little whiskey around here?"

Lucifer pushed away from the wall, uncrossing his arms. I didn't mention that I hadn't heard him approach. Or that I had no idea how long he'd been standing there. Cahal and I would have to have a little talk about what things to mention, and what things to omit. No, I didn't need to know when I looked tired, but yes, it would be nice to get a heads-up when my kidnapper-rescuer was watching me unravel the handiwork of his minions…

"Whiskey…" He looked skyward in that way people did when they were thinking. "Remind me. I'm not placing that one."

"Yeah, my mom wasn't really into the hard liquor. She was a wine and beer kinda gal."

"Your mother, yes. I wanted to speak to you about her. I have something to show you." Butterflies filled my stomach and longing grabbed hold of me, like it always did when I thought about her. I still missed her. I would always miss her. I wanted to talk to her, just once more. I wanted to tell her about Darius and Penny. To let her know that I'd connected with Callie and Dizzy. I wanted her.

She was beyond my reach, but I could maybe learn a little more about her while I was here.

"First, whiskey." He wandered closer, an easy sort of stroll that held all the swagger of a prized pony. Not that I knew what one of those really looked like. "Remind me. I'm sure I know of it."

I filled him in as I stepped away from the wall I'd torn down, wondering if I'd be chastised. It had been a good one, intricately made and pumped full of power, completely solid. I'd marveled at it before I labored to rip it away, knowing in my gut that it had been created by the Great Master himself.

"Hmm, yes. It has a burning sensation." He smiled. "I remember it. We have something similar here. I'll show you. It's more potent, though. You'd best watch yourself."

"That sounds like a challenge."

He laughed. "Indeed, it is."

His eyes twinkled as they beheld me, velvety soft but brimming with power. Brimming with an ego he had earned. He was the master of his domain, and he knew it. I felt the call of it, stirring in my blood. The power welling up in me. The excitement for what was to come.

I squished it down. That wasn't the right frame of mind to fall into down here. I couldn't let the siren call of my magic change me. I was perfectly content being nothing more than what I was—a girl who liked her bad neighborhood, full of people who would take a bat to someone's head on her behalf. Some might accuse me of thinking small, but I didn't want to think big. If I wanted servants, I could get them from Darius. If I wanted to rule people, I could just hire a staff…

With Darius's money.

Lucifer tilted his head to the side. He'd heard that thought—I'd let it slip. He probably also read the annoyance in my posture.

I gritted my teeth and focused on appearing neutral to him. I needed to be better about watching myself around him, about not letting him realize how good it felt when I fully gave in to my power. That was something he could exploit.

Without commenting on my slip, or whatever he saw in front of him, Lucifer shifted his attention to the illusion I'd torn down. "I am incredibly impressed."

I lifted my eyebrows, following his gaze. Cahal, his eyes on my face, took this opportunity to step into my line of view. His focus was fixed on me. He thought I'd just messed up something, I could tell. I'd probably get a lecture later. A very dramatic lecture.

Hopefully Pops came through with the whiskey beforehand.

"With…what, exactly?" I asked Lucifer.

He furrowed his brow at me then indicated the large space in front of us. "I put up this wall myself."

"Yeah, I gathered. It was really well done."

"It was at the height of the power scale."

"Also that, yeah."

"How long did it take you to rip it down?"

"Oh…" I formed a duckbill with my mouth and glanced at Cahal. "Fifteen minutes? Twenty? It was a doozy."

"Seventeen," Cahal replied.

I took a moment to try to read Cahal's face, because

that had been very specific. All those planes and angles were very attractive in a hostile, severe sort of way, and very hard to get a read on. One would think I'd be better at it by now. Then again, he was incredibly closed down when Lucifer came around, and with him, that was saying something.

"Okay, then," I said, pulling my gaze back to the large area that used to hold a solid wall made entirely of magic. "Seventeen minutes, says the guy without a watch."

Lucifer laughed. "What our brooding druid is not telling you is that he is constantly comparing you with your predecessor."

"Your other kid?"

"Yes, exactly. It took him months to learn which walls were magical and which were real, and months more to work out how to tear one down. But you can do it in"—his eyes darkened as they flicked Cahal's way—"seventeen minutes. Did our illustrious druid teach you that?"

"No. Demolition was always one of my strong suits. He basically taught me how to take a punch." I grinned, then frowned when neither of them reacted to my joke. I let it go. "But I can't make anything solid. I can't build as easily as I can take down."

"Curse breaker," Cahal said, clasping his hands in front of him. "The very magic that allows you to stay down here will make it harder for you to create down here. That is the magic that has allowed you to gain admittance to carefully constructed worlds and then, well, ruin them. You are the true demolisher, for not even the land of angels would hold up to the Underworld magic you wield."

Curse breaker.

I didn't know if that thought came from myself, Lucifer, Cahal, or a memory. Callie had said it. She'd told me I was one. She hadn't elaborated, though, and certainly Cahal had never mentioned anything about it. But now, as I watched Lucifer's eyes spark with a cunning gleam, I wondered what exactly Cahal was playing at. Clearly that was something he should not have advertised.

"This other magic…" Lucifer let the sentence trail away.

"The godly power, on her mother's side," Cahal replied, and I was getting closer to knifing him so he'd shut up.

To my surprise, though, Lucifer snorted. "*Godly* power? Is that a joke, druid? Those meddling fools are no more gods than those fool elves. Than *you*. They are cowards, truth be told. But fine, your point is made."

I wanted to think at Cahal, to ask him what he was getting at, but I couldn't without Daddy Dearest hearing it. I wondered if I could section off my thoughts.

I wondered if Lucifer would allow me to learn.

"Well," I said, trying to steer this conversation like a train that had jumped the rails and was hurtling toward a sleepy village. "Be that as it may, I *can* build, to a degree. If I work a little harder at it, I'm sure I can create something passable."

"Of course you can. Come." Lucifer turned and jerked his head. "Let us have a tour. I'll give you your first lesson." I stepped forward to follow, Cahal quickly falling in behind me. "No, no." Lucifer flicked his hand and an intricate sort of wall curled into existence, stitching into the air, starting at chest height and barring Cahal's way. "Not this time, Master Shadow. You are best taken in small doses, and I have had my fill."

I slowed, glancing back, considering whether to tear down that forming wall and push the issue. But Cahal stepped back and tilted his head to me.

Go, he thought. *I will be fine.*

"Of course he will." Lucifer hadn't slowed. "What am I, a barbarian? I would never harm my heir's treasured pet."

"Cahal as a pet..." With stinging doubt, I turned and hurried to catch up to Lucifer. I needed his instruction, and it wouldn't hurt to have more knowledge of his kingdom. If Cahal wasn't put out, he'd be fine. "I suppose it does make sense that I would have the surliest pet I've ever met."

I just wondered if I would be fine. Lucifer was tricky. Trickier than anyone I'd ever dealt with. Layers upon layers of secrets and lies simmered just beneath the caring surface he showed me. It was different with Darius. Although vampires were notorious for being manipulative, and he could manipulate people into pretzels, he genuinely cared about me. He'd gone so long without feeling that his emotions discomfited him. Which was what made it so easy to tell the difference when he was feigning emotions to manipulate me. I usually caught on pretty quickly and zeroed in on his motive. I took peace in knowing that.

But with Lucifer, I could feel his affection. I could see his excitement to have me around. I could even sense his pride in me, wrapped up in the strange push and pull he had with Cahal. He laughed, played jokes, messed with me, but made sure I had everything I wanted. It felt genuine—*he* felt genuine. He couldn't be, though. Not with the way he kept this place running. He was a lot more balanced than the elves, but he clearly had a ruthless underbelly. I just hadn't seen it yet.

I had a feeling most people didn't until it was too late.

I needed to stay vigilant.

"You did this place up better than even the vampires could," I said, marveling at the sweep of heavy velvet curtains that should've looked really dated and ridiculous but somehow paired nicely with the textured wallpaper and modern sconces lit with his special brand of lighting. "And how do you make those glow?"

I could just see his cheek lift in a smile as he stepped off the first stair on the grand staircase leading all the way down to the castle doors, and hovered above them at an angle. His glance back said he would like me to follow his lead.

"Simon says…" I did the same, not as smooth, maybe not as polished, but perfectly capable of the slow hover.

"Very good. You are much farther along than any heir I have met thus far."

"Why do you call them—us—heirs instead of children?" I increased my pace to keep up as he floated down. It felt weird that there was no air. It would have been much cooler if my hair were blowing out behind me.

"Because it hurts too much to remember lost children." He settled onto the ground gracefully. I bumped down next to him. He looked me in the eye and put his fist to his heart. "My hope is that you can survive, even with the magic of those suffering fools."

"The gods?"

His eyes narrowed. "They are not divine. They are merely angels. They have a world, like this one. They are immortal, but so am I. And the elves and many other creatures. Their magic is powerful, sure, but not unstoppable. Not for me."

"Right. Old grudges, picked scabs, a small bit of jealousy—I got you. Mum's the word."

He jerked back just a little, his face going blank except for a small crease between his brows. Something moved behind his eyes, something feral and wild. Something vicious and violent. I'd hit his weak spot. I prepared for a violent response.

He erupted in laughter.

It was my turn to jerk back, this reaction wholly unexpected.

His guffaws filled the huge room, big and full and delighted. "My gracious." He wiped his eyes and then laughed again, shaking with it. "Very good." This time it was pride that filled his gaze. "*Very* good. Very few people push my buttons, Reagan. Very few. You did it in such a way that it was every bit as infuriating as it was distracting. Tell me…" He put out his elbow, and I took his arm without thinking. Darius had trained me, it seemed. "Where did you learn a trait so valuable? Or, more accurately, how did you hone it? Because that trait cannot be taught."

"I've done a lot of surviving. It's a tool unlike any other."

"Hmm…" He pushed out a hand, and the grand

double doors opened before us. The sun shone down, utterly fake, I was certain, but warm and soft all the same. "You asked about the light…"

He turned us to the right, along a little path flanked with flowers. Service critters shuffled out of our way, dashing into the underbrush or dive-bombing into what looked like rosebushes, some with twisting black flowers and some with white lilies instead of roses. They clearly thought being in the Great Master's way was worse than any injuries they might sustain from getting out of the way.

"It is a very complex illusion, no different than the elves have in the Realm. Their sun isn't real."

"Yes, I realized that when I tore down one of their illusions."

"Very good, yes."

"But they use fairy lights more often."

"That is because they have a lot of fairies who have no choice but to work for nothing. We do not have fairies, and so I must expend the effort to light the dark places. Of course, most of my subjects see in the dark, so I don't have to light all of them…"

"Right, of course."

"That will be one of the last things you learn, I think. First, let's start simple." He put out his hand, palm up, and a little flower curled into existence very slowly, so that I could see each fiber as it stitched together, almost like sewing a design into fabric.

The resulting daisy was a little off color, dirty cream instead of white, and not totally detailed. It didn't look natural.

I mimicked him and copied it anyway. I knew from Cahal not to get ahead of myself. The battles I'd thought I was going to win always hurt the worst to lose.

The petals of my daisy showed up crisp white, the vibrant center dotted with various shades of yellows and oranges, to show the pollen. His pale green stem was more shamrock on mine, and I tried to color in some slight shadows on the petals that would work with the positioning of the sun. The added detail took a little longer, but he didn't urge me to move faster, or call me out for doing more than he had. Instead, he waited patiently, slowing his pace as I worked on the shadowing and then picking it up to a leisurely stroll once I was finished.

"Fantastic." He beamed, and his flower drifted toward mine. He lowered his palm, and I did mine, letting the two flowers hover beside us as we walked. "You improved upon my design, and you did a remarkable job. You put in touches that would fool the wandering eye. Now…" He held up a finger, and in a moment his design perfectly matched mine, except his shadows were relative to the faux-sun. His leaves were veined and his stem shimmered a little. "You do not need to paint on the environmental effects. If you do, it'll only be correct when the plant and sun are in that exact position."

"Right..." I lowered my brow, concentrating, and he halted his steps.

"Did you have a comment or question?" he asked.

"No. Just...learning."

His smile was soft and his nod slight. "Here, let's sit, and I'll show you how to create that effect."

I paid close attention to what he did so I didn't miss anything, but I needn't have tried so hard. He slowed down when I faltered, and explained more thoroughly when I had trouble grasping something. He was as patient of a teacher as anyone I'd ever met. Although my training in the past had usually involved some sort of violence, from my mother working with me on up, and I would have thought I'd be bored without it, I was too focused to notice. I was too enraptured with what I could create to want any other sort of training.

"Great Master!"

The urgent voice knocked me out of my concentration, midway through building a purple elephant that I planned to surprise Cahal with (he wouldn't be amused, which would amuse me more). A lady-demon with incredibly long legs—too long; it was weird—and a short torso glided to a stop at the edges of the garden in which we sat. If it had been anywhere else, she would've been panting. As it was, her carefully composed face and too-far-apart eyes conveyed perfectly well that she considered it an emergency.

"You guys need some pictures of what humanoid creatures actually look like," I murmured.

"Great Master," she said with more decorum, clearly because she hadn't expected me to be sitting with him.

"Yes, Victoria, what is it?" he asked curtly.

"There is an issue that...needs your attention," she said, a little too fast. "Greatly."

He studied her for a moment, her frame tense and shoulders tight. It didn't take a genius to know something had gone gravely wrong in his domain.

"Of course." His gaze slid my way. "Forgive me. How about dinner tonight—"

"No, Great Master, I do not think that would be possible," Victoria cut in.

"Is it because you will be sewing, since no one sells pants to fit those gams?" I murmured.

A smile drifted across Lucifer's lips. Victoria's eyes cut my way.

"Now is not the time," he told me.

The chastisement was slight, but it felt as though the teacher had slapped my hand with a ruler.

I furrowed my brow, surprised by the uncomfortable pang in my middle. I wasn't sure when I'd started to value his good opinion enough to affect me, but I needed to tone that down right quick. I was technically a captive. Stockholm syndrome had to be a thing between teacher and pupil. Or else he was just really good at manipulating emotions in a very short period of time.

"The issue is…rather…large in scope," Victoria said, back on track, eyes narrowed. She hadn't liked that comment very much.

Lucifer nodded stiffly, and I could tell he was confused and not used to hiding that fact. "Of course," he said, a little drawn out this time. Standing, he put out a hand to keep me put. "Please, enjoy this lovely garden. Practice. Be at ease. I'll have the whiskey—our likeness, anyway—sent to your rooms. Tomorrow we will see the garden I fashioned after your mother."

My heart gave a mighty leap and my stomach swirled, but I was careful not to show any of that on my face or in my body. Hopefully.

"Sure, sounds good," I replied, blasé, settling back. I wanted to see how much I retained of his teaching. Then I needed to go find Cahal so we could figure out a way to get a message to Penny and the others, telling them to turn back. To stay safe. That I would get out of here somehow, without their help, and didn't want them making this situation worse.

Because if there was anyone in all the worlds who could create an issue that needed the Great Master's direct attention, a situation that was "very large in scope," it was her. And while I didn't have proof directly, I could read the room.

She'd be in incredible danger—they all would.

CHAPTER 7

WHAT...

Lucifer's mind stuttered to a stop when he flew into the vicinity of the river. The water boiled below him, this area home to some dangerous rapids that would overturn boats twice as big as those carrying his *navita.* Rough-hewn rock loomed above them, exposed. What should be the beach on the other side was melting away into the rocks and weeds and ugliness of the natural landscape.

Who... What...

He couldn't form a coherent thought. He'd never seen this before. Never, in all his years, had something dissolved his illusions to this magnitude. The elves had tried. The angels had tweaked and manhandled. But nothing had acted like a disease, like acid, and burned it all away.

What sort of being had this kind of power? This kind of magic? While the vampires who'd infiltrated his kingdom peddled magic, it wasn't to this magnitude.

Gathering himself, he flew forward over the river in

his demon form, Tatsu flying alongside. Victoria, also in demon form, rode her dragon, a shimmering green spectacle that usually caught the light.

Not so, now. There was no light. The sun had dissipated with the rest of the illusion. It would take days to fix, as it had been one of the biggest illusions, servicing a vast area.

Anger boiled within him.

Was this retaliation for what he'd done to the elves' castle? Could they be so stupid?

He could lay waste to their illusions. He could shelter the vampires in the Underworld. They'd come fleeing from the real sun, which would be exposed if the Realm's network of magic came crashing down…and they'd stay so they could reproduce.

In fact, he might just do that anyway. War was imminent, and the vampire Vlad was having some trouble wrangling all of his recruits. Lucifer might be the guiding shove they needed. They would join him out of necessity and help him tear down the elves, once and for all.

He landed on the far bank, in the heart of the destruction. The fog had been completely torn down in this area, not even a trace of it left behind. All the docks were visible, many of the boats physically tied up and bobbing against the ends. Six boats were gone.

"What happened here?" he boomed, in his humanoid form now, looking around at the gathered mass of creatures. They stood with wide eyes, blinking, stupid.

"Sire." A sniveling half-powered demon, no more than one of the creatures living in the Edges, hobbled up with a bowed back, its head low. "A vampire passed this way before…the disturbance."

Lucifer huffed humorlessly. *Disturbance* was putting it mildly.

"A vampire? Do all this?" Lucifer scoffed. "Preposterous. What of the boats? Six are gone—where did they land?"

"I have that list here, Great Master." Victoria, back in humanoid form, her dragon off to the side, unrolled a scroll and held it out to him. "Two boats are completely unaccounted for. The Boatmen can't be found."

Lucifer tapped one of the sect names, where the record indicated that three boats had landed and dropped off living cargo. "Vlad the vampire deals heavily with this sect, does he not? They visit him in the Edges."

"Yes, sire." The sniveling half-powered demon wrung its hands. "Six vampires crossed the river behind the group that created this commotion. There was a clear leader, though we aren't sure…" Its voice trailed away within Lucifer's severe gaze. "There was a clear leader. Vlad, certainly."

It wasn't convinced, clearly, but that was no matter. Who else could it be?

Lucifer lowered the scroll a little, staring down at the cowering demon without seeing him. “He snuck into my kingdom when it was vulnerable?”

“Yes, sire. So it would seem, sire.”

“Here are the Boatmen.” Victoria held out her hand to indicate them, walking in single file, led by a wrangler. Their backs were bowed and knees awkwardly bent, not used to time on land. They rarely left their boats. There was magic stopping them from doing just that.

“And you said two boats are unaccounted for?” Lucifer asked Victoria as the Boatmen drew near.

“Yes. Their living cargo and the Boatmen with them. Another landed…” Leaning over the scroll, she tapped on the sect name. A warlike sect, low in status. “The boat was found downstream, however. Empty.”

“The boat was intact?” He handed back the scroll.

“Yes, Great Master. The Boatman was gone, however. Lost.”

“Killed, you mean. That sect has no outside affiliations that I know of. They are not inclined to deal with outsiders.” He speared Victoria with a glare. “What have they said?”

“A lone vampire, Great Master,” she said. “I have someone asking questions. There was chaos, last I heard. The *conspector* was killed, his dragon released.”

“A vampire.” Lucifer put his hands on his hips. “A

vampire did *all* this…" He swept his hand out, a trail of fire in its wake. "A *vampire* took the safeguards off the water, killed a Boatman, and killed a *conspector* out from under a dragon? A *vampire*."

Victoria lowered her gaze. "Despite the illogic of it, those are the reports we have so far."

A blast of frigid air thundered out from him, sending the lesser demons flying, landing where they may. Fire was quick to follow, coating his body.

"Boatman. Come here." He pointed in front of him.

The wrangler ushered one of them forward.

"Hello, Great Master," it said. "What can I tell you?"

They were a species of wraith, altered for his purposes. They had been magically connected, and what one knew, they all knew. It was the safest way to monitor the comings and goings of his kingdom. Given that those leaving and entering knew that, they would know there was no point in killing a Boatman.

A stranger was in their midst.

"Who tore down the fog?"

"I am sorry, I do not know."

The perpetrator hadn't done it from a boat, then. The Boatmen were only active when they were needed. It prolonged their shelf-life, as it were. They were gruesome to make; Lucifer hated doing it.

"Of the last six boats to leave, who was in the one that landed in the Warsol sect?"

“Walrus piloted that ship. He landed at the Warsol sect with Black Sheep and Sparkly Thongs.”

Lucifer shook his head, his brow furrowing. “Repeat the names again.”

“Walrus, Black Sheep, and Sparkly Thongs.”

“I don’t…” He looked at Victoria.

“Walrus is the vampire Darius,” she said. “He must know we would have that name. Once you give your name to a Boatman, you can give no other.”

Lucifer half thought he was losing his mind. “The Boatman allowed him to cross the first time—any time—using *Walrus* as his name?”

“Yes, sire. He traveled with Eggman at first. We believe that is the heir.”

Lucifer let his breath out slower. Her magic—the strength of her mighty magic—would be enough to addle any Boatman. Once the name was accepted, it was set. “Black Sheep and…*Sparkly Thong*?”

“Sparkly Thong*zzz*, yes. Plural. It’s English from the Brink. Black sheep is a furry sort of animal. For the other, sparkly, you know. A thong is a small slip of undergarment you likely have encountered—”

“I know what it is!” His voice thundered across the way. Anyone who wasn’t expressly needed in the area ran. Everyone else withered where they stood. “Those aren’t names. They are not proper magical identifiers. What are their names? *Who are they?*”

"Ah. Well..." Victoria forced herself to straighten, and Lucifer could see the effort behind it. "I am honestly not sure why those names were accepted. The heir was accounted for, of course. So there really is no explanation."

Lucifer turned toward the river, scanning where the fog once was. "Whoever it was, they were powerful enough to get through my barrier and rip down my illusions. Check that sect. Get any information you can. I want to know what sort of being has infiltrated my territory. If it is the angels after that accursed druid..." He tightened his hand into a fist. "Just find out who they are and trap them. I will deal with them myself. Their deaths will be a public spectacle."

"But the heir enjoys that vampire, sire."

"It will be easy to sow mistrust. He's a vampire, after all. She is probably just addicted to his bite. We will cure her of that. I need to get that druid out of there, though, before he poisons her mind with thoughts of leaving. He will remind her of the life she had. Of her humanity. If that happens, she will go the same way as the last heir. I cannot have that."

"Yes, sire."

Victoria turned to leave.

"And Victoria?" He waited for her to turn back. "Find that vampire Vlad. Take him to the castle. I would like a word."

"How will we keep him here, sire? He is cunning. Able to get out of tight spots."

Lucifer's smile showed his teeth. "Call the most powerful *conspectors*. They will help me create a barrier not even an angel could tear down. The Underworld is closed until further notice—no one in or out. I want those trespassers—*all* of them."

CHAPTER 8

I SLOWED AS I reached the set of double doors that led to my collection of rooms. Brain watery and body weary, I didn't at first register the pulsing, icy magic covering the wood. I'd stayed in that garden for what felt like days. In reality, it had only been until the sun dimmed and finally went out, not sinking like in the Brink, but dimming in the manner of a ceiling light.

I could now make a perfect flower. Granted, the colors were probably still off, in Romulus's opinion anyway, but the details were spot-on. I understood how to achieve that precision now. Unfortunately, it still wasn't solid, and the whole thing had been incredibly taxing.

Now, ready for that Underworld whiskey, and maybe a bite to eat because I missed the act, I stopped in front of the ice blockage and wondered, *What the fuck?* Both sets of double doors had them.

"It is to keep the druid out," said my stalker demon with the ridiculous boobs.

"He has no interest in this place. Ask him to stay

where he is, and he'll stay." I rubbed my temples.

"If you didn't return when he thought you should, it was thought that he might seek you out."

I turned to meet the demon's eyes, and when it lowered its gaze, an unfamiliar spark lit in my middle. Dawning understanding curled through me.

I was its master. I was its supreme being.

With Darius, there were people waiting on me, helping me (often against my will), and doing things for me, but they weren't answering to me. I wasn't in charge.

Here, I *was* in charge. Only my father had more say than me.

I'd just called him my father.

"This place is fucking with me," I said to myself.

"Yes, your heinous." The demon bowed.

I was too tired to figure out if it was agreeing with me, which meant this place was fucking with me on purpose, or if it was acting like a yes-man so I wouldn't lose it and kill everything in sight.

I also didn't really care.

"Cahal—the druid—is acting in my best interest. If he wants to check on me, he can check on me."

"Yes, your heinous. Of course. Except when the Great Master forbids it. And then he will be locked in your rooms."

Annoyance flared through me. I continued to stare

because I didn't really know what I wanted to do with that information. Given what I'd seen of Father Dearest today, he would probably accede to my request to allow Cahal some freedom. He'd been incredibly patient and forgiving of my mistakes. Eager to make me happy. He seemed like he'd hear me out.

But he wasn't here now, and this creature couldn't do squat about the situation.

"Great. Well, then, there is only one thing to do." I stripped away the simplistic magic, leaving bare the closed and probably locked set of double doors in front of me. Even if they weren't locked, their fate was written.

I strode up and kicked out. The sole of my boot connected with the latch area—the sweet spot on heavy, well-made doors.

Crack.

Nothing to it. The doors swung open with such force that a hinge tore loose. They flew toward the wall, but hadn't been designed to go that far. Metal groaned and wood splintered as more hinges tore. The right slab of wood wobbled wildly, and the rest swung back.

I kicked it again, then took two fast steps and did it again, sinking into my anger. My fury at the elves, at being kidnapped by Lucifer, at Cahal's treatment, and at my own murky future. When it broke and clattered to the floor, I marched to the other double door, but this time from behind it. From the direction it would swing, had it been opened, just to make it harder.

More rage to spew, more uncertainty, more fear of what was in store for my friends, who were surely in the Underworld with me, those fools—I kicked harder. Again. Again and again, battering the thing even though it had nowhere to go. The lock broke, then the handles. It bounced against the frame and came back, only to be kicked again. Once more. My boot opened up a hole. The hinges loosened from being jammed so hard, released, and jammed again.

Finally, sweaty and depleted, I stepped back, my body burning because I was trying to suck in air.

"And another thing!" I looked upward, the ceiling in my way. Two thick jets of hellfire, thicker than I'd ever managed before, blasted from my hands and sliced through the wood. I made a sort of messy oval, like a kindergartener would draw with a crayon, before punching the wood out and away, taking the spire above with it. I launched it off the side of the building. Out of the corner of my eye, I saw it fall past the windows.

Then I started rooting around in the magic up there, looking for whatever spell was tied to airlessness. I was sick of this place being so different than the Brink. I was sick of not eating and breathing.

Or maybe I just wanted to remember how much I

liked those things. Because I was starting to like my magic an awful lot. I enjoyed working on it, perfecting it, feeling it sear or freeze within me, and especially the feeling when both types swirled together, boosting me to what felt like impossible heights. I liked when I was nearly out of control with it, nearly about to blast everything around me, but containing it just enough to etch out the perfect illusion.

I liked it here, too.

Even the garden I'd sat in earlier had been amazing. It wasn't like the Flush, which was lovely and pretty and sweet smelling. This one had plants with jagged, poisoned thorns that made you appreciate the flowers you stole from its vines. It had odd color pairings, and illogical lilies on the rosebush. I'd noticed a garden gnome when I was taking a break, nestled among the moss-covered, dense green rocks. On its face was a little sneer, and it held a painted dagger. I had half expected it to come to life and try to kill me. The fact that it didn't made me laugh.

Occasionally, a foul odor would waft through, like a farting dog. For funsies, I'd made the flowers wilt as the smell roamed through the garden. It was a detail that should've already been incorporated, and one that would surely make Daddy Dearest double over laughing.

It was interesting, the garden, a mixture of fair and

foul, with a hearty dose of the unexpected. I fit there. I fit in this collection of rooms. It felt like coming home.

But I fit in the Brink, too, in my house that Darius kept messing with. I fit with my off-kilter neighbors, looking out across the cemetery. I was two halves, just like my magic. I was growing to appreciate them both.

My magic was also swelling, even now. I felt it. I loved it.

Oh God, how I loved it. I felt *alive.* Its wildness, its power, its raging intensity—it cured my need to get drunk and chase shifters around. It was more dangerous than inciting Roger. It was more fun than lighting Cole the yeti on fire.

What did that mean for me? What did it mean for my future?

In my gut, I felt like this was a very precarious situation—a game of balance that could easily be lost as I struggled to own my heritage and hold on to my past. I needed time to figure things out.

I needed to talk to Cahal.

As my mind worked furiously, my magic found two possible sources for the airless spell. Because it *was* a spell, not an illusion. The difference was obvious, and I wondered if Lucifer had done this. It seemed more like a Penny situation than his magic. I dissolved them both; fuck it. The threads fell away, and I sucked in a thick, sweet breath.

Part of me wondered if I'd get in trouble, if I was poking the bear, trying to see just how patient and responsive Lucifer would be. I'd already proven I could spot his weaknesses, but maybe, just maybe, I wanted to see the ones that didn't make him laugh.

The stars disappeared from the sky.

Whoops.

Whatever else I'd done, I couldn't tell. Would I hear about it?

Cahal cleared his throat, drawing my attention to the easy chair he sat in by the window, a type of lantern magically glowing on the table near him so he could see. The other lights in the room, artful sconces on the walls, didn't emit enough light for someone to read this far into the room. For him, at least, given he couldn't see very well in the dark.

"All done?" he asked, closing his book around a torn piece of parchment and placing it on the table in front of him.

A glass canister filled with brown liquid sat at the edge of the table with two crystal glasses beside it. That had to be the demon whiskey. He picked up the canister and poured two glasses.

I fell into the overstuffed armchair near him, the seating set up around the table designed so people could converse. I unlaced and then slipped off my heavy boots before propping my feet onto the coffee table. He handed me a glass before sitting back down with his own drink, his gaze on me. His severe features were softened by the shadow, which made him incredibly striking. I said as much, projecting probably, just needing a compliment myself. Man, I was in a really weird place. I said that, too.

"Shadow visually softens all," he replied. "But it is only an illusion. The sun will re-emerge and show the sharp edges."

"Deep." I took a sip of the demon whiskey, crinkling my nose at the wisp of flowery taste within the punch in the mouth delivered by the alcohol. It was strong, sure, but the weird floral elements were just weird. Still, it would do the trick.

I leaned my head back and closed my eyes.

"Your watcher at the door can hear us," Cahal said.

Oh right, I'd kicked the doors in.

I flung up an ice barrier to block sound, something I'd picked up from Lucifer's spell earlier in the day. Very handy, that. Once I'd seen him do it, it seemed so obvious. Then I stitched a hasty, half-assed illusion over the gaping holes so I wouldn't have to see anything peering in at us.

Silence crept in around us, the air heavy with unsaid words. Cahal waited patiently, and I knew he'd wait all night. He'd wait for years, even, I felt. This wasn't like when he was trying to get me to out myself and claim my birthright. Now he was...guarding me, it seemed like, as I learned this new facet of myself.

"I'm in a really weird place," I repeated, and I felt like crying for the first time in...years. When was the last time I'd cried?

"You're exhausted."

"Yes. There is that."

"And you like it down here."

"I haven't seen enough of this place to know if I like it down here."

"Yes, you have. This isn't the first time you've been through."

"Right, well..." I thought back. "There are definitely parts I do not like. That crazy circus when I first came? Terrible. The worst. The weird desert with that big bird thing? Not awesome. The weird boats and that still river and the leaking ceiling—those are all mind-fucks, and I hate them."

"You are describing areas that are meant to be...less than ideal. Areas that Lucifer himself does not enjoy traversing, I imagine, though I don't remember ever hearing about a circus in my time here. This is a very large place, like the Realm. He must allow his citizens their exploits, even though he might not like them."

"Who could possibly like the water dripping from the ceiling?"

"It doesn't drip everywhere. Vlad occupies the nicer

areas of the Edges, I hear. He clearly doesn't like those traits any more than you do, and he's lived through some…unfortunate times."

I heaved out a sigh, and it felt good to breathe again. "I liked the garden today."

"Did you stay there the whole time?"

"Yeah, I was working on my magic." I paused. "And I like the view here. And the castle, except for the gold room, and yes, there were parts on the way here that were lovely. I did want to come back. I always have."

"And now that you're here?"

I rolled my head back and forth across the edge of the chair. I didn't want to admit it. Cahal didn't make me say it, though he probably knew.

"Why are you angry?" he asked, and this was probably the first time in all the time I'd known him that he'd tried fishing information out of me, like a psychiatrist.

It was the first time I'd needed it.

"I've hardly spent any time here," I said, and lo and behold, a bit of wetness slipped from the corner of my eye. Fatigue, it had to be fatigue. I downed the rest of the demon whiskey. "And the weird demons who wait on us annoy me, but…" I blew out a breath, then finally admitted it: "I do like it here, Cahal. I can't even totally describe why. Not really. I could create that garden in the Brink, but it wouldn't be the same. I could move to a place with gothic spires and greenery to get this view, but I wouldn't bother. It's not what I'm seeing, it's the feeling *plus* what I'm seeing. Something down here just...makes me feel like I belong somehow."

"You do belong."

I blinked my eyes open and lifted my head so I could look at him. "What's that now?"

"You *do* belong here. Of course you do. Your magic sings down here. Your display with the roof a moment ago will delight Lucifer to no end. Your power has increased tenfold in just one day of intense practice. You are overtired, but you are glowing in a way that makes you incredibly lovely in a way I haven't seen before, even with Durant. The part of you that came from the Underworld is singing now that you're here. You should embrace it."

"Right...but..." I narrowed my eyes. "I'm confused. Aren't you the guy who is supposed to keep me grounded? I need to be trying to get out of this place. Not..."

"Yes, you are confused. For now. And maybe that's a good thing. It is only the first day, and you are very tired, as I said. Give it more time."

"I may not have more time. Which brings me to the next issue. Penny's here."

He flinched, and I grinned, leaning my head back against the chair. He had history with Penny, having tried to guard her during our battle with the Mages'

Guild. Her unpredictable habits had put him off-kilter. Now he got antsy every time she might show up and ruin his controlled bubble, which was pretty much every time she used her magic around him.

"Here…where?" he asked.

"I'm not positive. But my training with Lucifer was interrupted by a very urgent issue that he had to see to immediately. Whatever the problem was, it was widespread. The…woman—demon didn't say we were under attack or anything, but it definitely seemed urgent."

Cahal didn't respond for a long time, probably mulling everything over, before he finally asked me to repeat what I'd heard, word for word. I was amazed it was all in there, like I'd been running a tape recorder. My vampire-boosted memory still astounded me. I loved it.

"If it was an attack, it doesn't seem like the elves," he said. "They could push back Lucifer's magic and, with adequate time, rip it apart in places, but it wouldn't result in something large in scope. Not unless it was a full-scale attack. Her message didn't make it sound like that at all."

"So…Penny, then."

"With the godly power—"

"That's a sensitive subject with Lucifer, by the way."

"I know. With that power, in addition to being a

natural dual-mage, in addition to her unprecedented unpredictability"—I chuckled—"I agree that it could certainly be her. It could also be…another entity."

I frowned. "What other entity?"

His face closed down, but his eyes sparked. I had no idea what that meant. "Maybe nothing. Get some sleep. We'll get up early to discuss everything. You will need your wits about you tomorrow. This show will not go unnoticed." He stood.

"You mean the door? The roof?"

"The flux of power. The last heir tried, when in an incredible rage. After he'd trained for some time. He didn't have the same effect. Not even close. You are not as you seem, Reagan Somerset. Not at all. Your mix of power is unique in a way I didn't properly realize until now. I knew in theory, sure, but I had no idea it would amount to…this. Tomorrow, Lucifer will realize what I have, and your hopes of escaping will dwindle. The battle for your soul will start tomorrow."

CHAPTER 9

A KNOCK SOUNDED outside my rooms the next morning, whoever it was needing to use the frame, since my pseudo-door—my magic—wasn't solid. I felt the strength of magic before I heard, *Knock, knock...*

With that magic, it could only be one person.

I squished the urge to grin. I snuffed out the excitement churning in my gut. But I couldn't help looking forward to what was to come, good or bad. My magic was a churning, boiling, aching thing inside of me, and I wanted to let it flourish. I wanted to cause havoc, to ruin things, to paint the sky in fire. And then I wanted to sit down and create something beautiful.

Who's there? I thought, lacing up my boots and standing.

Silence followed.

I stopped halfway to the door. He could tear down my simplistic block and come in at any time, so I wasn't sure what game he was playing. But then—

That accursed joke is the only one I remember from

the Brink. Madman?

The grin wouldn't stay suppressed. *Madman who? Madman feet...open the door. No, that's not right.*

I tore down the magic. Given the doors hadn't been fixed, there Lucifer stood, in the same white button-up and jeans as always, black hair slicked back and power brimming within his velvet-brown eyes.

"Fail," I said, laughing. "It's *Madam.* Knock, knock, who's there? Madam. Madam who? Ma-damn foot is caught in the door, open up!"

"Ah, yes." He laughed. "My mistake."

Cahal came to the doorway of his room and Lucifer's smile slipped, the sparkle in his eyes dimming. Something vicious and wild churned in them instead.

The moment passed in a blink, and he was back to looking at me, his lips pulling up at the corners. "So. You decided to renovate." He looked up and around, taking in the ruined doors. He tensed in a way I understood. "May I?" he asked, but I was already clearing out of the way.

He crossed the space to where he could view the gaping hole where the other doors had been, covered by my haphazard illusion.

"Not great work." He winked at me.

"No. I wasn't trying very hard."

"Hmm." He looked upward, at the gaping hole and indigo blue beyond. "The stars disappeared last night."

"Yeah. My bad. I wanted to breathe air, and the stars got in the way."

"Pesky things." If he was mad, or even annoyed, he didn't show it. His head stayed tilted, and his eyes roamed the harsh hole. Finally, he lowered his face to look at me. "Should we repair it? Or leave it?"

My eyebrows ticked up, and a glow warmed my middle. I was just about to ask, "You aren't mad?" like any kid would, ever. Like I'd asked my mother several times growing up, when she was doing her best to teach me and my train left the rails. It hadn't been like that with Darius, though, when he'd helped me with my ice magic. With him, I'd apologized, as an equal.

That thought made me hyperaware that everything in me recognized this guy in front of me as a parent figure, not just a mentor. It was…disconcerting. I never thought I'd think of him that way.

I certainly didn't want to give him the power of knowing that. Not until I had more power of my own.

Trust me to get into a screwed-up situation. It seemed to be my lot in life.

"Repair it, I think," I said, double-checking to make sure my thoughts remained mine alone.

He nodded, looking back up at it. "It's rough. The lines, I mean. The shape is…off."

"My goal was to get beyond it, not create a masterpiece out of it."

"Within destruction, there is always an opportunity for a masterpiece." He put up his hands, fingers together. A blast of hellfire streamed from each, through the center of the hole. He then moved his hands apart, the streams hitting the edges of the hole before traveling in a circle. Halfway through, he stopped. "I didn't even ask—did you want a circle or an oval? I can cut at an angle."

"Oval. Why go for the expected?"

He looked at me a beat too long, something I couldn't identify moving within his gaze. He went back to the ceiling. "Yes." He started again, and then paused. "Ye-es."

In a rush of movement, he ceased the hellfire, slapped his hands together, lowered them a little, and blasted out again, the fire now sweeping up the sides of the tower, just below the cut-off top.

"The unexpected," he shouted over the noise of grinding stone as he spread his hands apart wider and moved them through the air. He cut perfect waves into the ceiling, rolling berms, as though by a machine and not his steady hand. "The rush of power. The rage. Within it, the beauty. That is hellfire."

The small hairs stood up on my arms. Electricity lit my body.

"Catch it, or we'll be crushed," he said.

Dust rained down. Parts of the already-ruined ceiling broke off, hurtling right for his head.

I caught the debris without thinking.

"I could've just killed you," I shouted over the din as more of the building fell. I lifted my other hand, wanting the visual so I didn't mess up.

"No, *I* would've killed me. You would've just placidly watched my death."

He ceased the hellfire as the last of the cut was made. I shoved the detached area upward, now hovering in the sky. "Do you want me to drop it, or lower it, or…?"

He stepped back from the center of the room. "Lower it to where?"

"The ground? I don't know. Where else would I put it?"

"Can you lower it to the ground?"

This seemed like a trick question. "I'd probably have to follow it in a hover to see where it's going, but…yeah. Right? Why?"

"Well then. Shall we?" He swept his arm out, indicating I should go first.

"Just so we're clear." I hovered up toward the pile of building debris, which I kept in place until I was closer. "I do not have wings. I don't turn into anything else. So if you know something I don't, or are playing some sort of practical joke on me, and this ends badly… Well, it'll end *very* badly, get me?"

"You didn't let me die. I suppose I'll have to return the favor."

"Mighty magnanimous of you."

"Yes. I think so."

I huffed out a laugh as I followed the hunk of rock over the very smooth edge surrounding the badly removed spire. Lucifer followed me. Given I didn't hover very fast, I took in the sights as I lowered down, feeling the burden of hovering with a load but bearing it. I'd practiced hovering and fighting with large objects often, so I had great stamina. He hadn't chopped off much—I'd already pushed off most of the roof—so it was probably the equivalent of a few large rocks.

From this vantage point, I could see where I'd entered the inner kingdom with Darius, the road in, and the flower-lined fence of the sect we'd snuck into. A pang hit my heart, and I tried to feel through our bond again. It was all but blocked, whatever the elves had done to it still in effect. The memory of him was still there, though, unleashing an ache. I missed his face and his quips. His soft touch and the way he held me. I missed his boring lectures and the wicked ways he made them more fun, and most of all, I missed his grounding presence.

I took a deep breath and looked away, nearing the ground, finding Lucifer right beside me, peering at my face.

What? I thought, because it was easier than shouting.

You are not taxed.

No. I've had practice.

You've had practice lowering building tops to the ground?

I thought about that a moment. *I can't recall an actual building top, but it's possible.*

There was that smile again. *I had no idea you'd be so far along when I brought you here. I thought I would have so much more to teach you.*

A large divot dug into the dirty, scarred ground, and I figured this was where the spire had landed the night before. It had been cleaned away, as though waiting for this one. Or maybe they didn't just leave parts of buildings littering the grounds.

My feet bumped down after the debris, and I shook out my arms and body, which always tensed up when I hovered and moved things around at the same time. Lucifer lifted his hand, now on the ground as well, and I quirked a brow to ask what he was doing. A moment later, Cahal floated over the lip of the topless tower, his arms crossed over his chest, and though I couldn't see his face, I strongly suspected he was wearing a scowl.

"Oh wow, you can grab him from all the way down here?" I asked, shocked.

"You can't?" he responded.

I guess I had a new thing to practice. Cahal did not seem like he would be amused.

"I thought you might want your safety blanket today," Lucifer said, and I suddenly wondered if I'd let some of my thoughts slip yesterday. If I had, Mr. Boobs had a big mouth. Either way, it appeared Lucifer had a mind to be reasonable. "I heard you were out late in the garden yesterday."

"Oh yeah, how did that go, by the way?" I asked. "With the disturbance."

His eyes didn't so much as flicker. Nothing in his body tensed. And that was what gave him away, because if I had been asking about the dentist or something, he would've made some noncommittal movement. He wouldn't have been this carefully controlled.

I didn't read much body language, it was true, but I knew when someone was covering up something that affected me. Darius and a life of hard knocks had been excellent teachers.

Cahal touched down a few feet away, his arms still crossed. The scowl indeed in place.

"Thanks for joining us," I told him, making light of my loaded question to Lucifer. "Now you won't have to sulk all evening again."

Cahal's scowl hardened before his face went flat. He was playing along perfectly.

And now I knew what he'd meant about the battle

for my soul starting today. The guy was so melodramatic.

"The Edges have always been wild," Lucifer said, turning and gesturing for me along with him. "You remember. That's where you came through, correct?"

"Yes. And where I left, through flames from your dragon."

"*Yes.*" He drew the word out. "Right. She was upset that you escaped right out from under her. She expected to be punished."

I held out my hand, my guts turning cold. Then hot. Then exploding with excitement. "They can talk? I mean, communicate?"

Yes, he thought. *Like we can.*

"Right, right." I blew out a breath. Tried to play it cool. Failed. "Will I get to see one? Can I talk to one? Do they like being petted? The only ones I've seen were trying to kill me."

He laughed. "I should've known you'd be excited for a dragon. Yes, you will get to see one. And hopefully bond with one. They can only communicate with those they are bonded to. And each other, of course."

"How do they bond? Blood, or…"

He nodded at my hand. "We'll talk about all that when we go to see them. But first we must get you more up to speed with your magic. They are treacherous beasts. If they sense weakness, they'll kill you rather than bond you. Let's see what you learned from yesterday."

I called up the flower I'd perfected yesterday, and this time around it was so much easier, probably because I wasn't half as tired. The shadows fell just right, even as I walked, and the petals moved softly in the very slight breeze.

"Oh." I pointed at the sky with the other hand. "You added a breeze to the air."

"Yes. I did that early this morning. I noticed the change and thought I'd add a flourish. I didn't want to make it any stronger because we have leaves in some of the gardens, but no rakes."

Not mad, then.

"Makes sense."

"Yes, I thought so." He stopped and turned, bending to my palm. His eyes roamed before he called up his own flower. A small crease wormed between his brows. Straightening up, he held his next to mine and silently judged the differences.

"Hers is better," Cahal said, unasked. "More lifelike. You are out of touch with the human lands."

Lucifer's eyes lifted to mine in what I could only describe as a long-suffering, deadpan look. I giggled like a simpleton.

"Yes, Cahal, I see that. Thank you for ruining this fine moment." Lucifer's flower disappeared and he dropped his hand, his gaze softening. "Yours *is* better. After one day of intense practicing, you have outstripped the teacher."

"It's a flower. It's small in the grand scheme of things." I let it disappear as we started to walk again, feeling an outsized sense of accomplishment. It was…a good feeling, like I'd checked that box and could confidently move on.

"Cahal, would you mind filling her in?" Lucifer gestured to the right, where a cobblestone path diverged from the one we were on.

"I told her last night."

Lucifer turned to glance behind him. "You haven't gotten any more likable, druid, has anyone told you that?"

"Yes. Your daughter. The two of you are very similar, unfortunately. You both have a terrible sense of humor."

Lucifer sighed and then glanced upward. "Yes, that was a good change. I do like expressing actions through air. And breathing it. Sometimes it's just a tedious action, but it can give you something extra to do with your energy."

He stopped at a wooden archway made of actual wood, with ivy vines crawling along the top. The light caught the wavy leaves, and I touched them with my fingers, not sensing any magic. "These are real."

"Yes. I had soil from the Brink brought in." He stuck out his hand in invitation, and I ducked my head a little to enter, the ivy crowding the top and obscuring much of the view. Once inside, I lost my breath for a moment, because I instantly knew where he'd taken me.

I blinked, trying to keep the sting out of my eyes. Trying to keep the wetness merely coating the surface.

"Druid. Go with her," I heard. "I will follow at a distance."

The dainty wooden arch continued along the path for about ten feet. Rosebushes crawled up the outside, dotted with bright red roses peering in through the green-painted fencing along the sides. At the top, the green of the bush tapered off enough to let in the crystalline blue sky, an illusion on top of an illusion, since the sky was indigo outside the tunnel of roses.

"It's exactly like my mother's garden," I said, out of breath, a tear breaking free. I swiped it away with a knuckle. "She had a setup exactly like this leading into…" I let another breath loose when I reached the end, tears crowding my eyes now. Pressure lining my chest. A gazebo waited in the middle of a haphazard array of flowers, all different colors and varieties. More roses, daisies, bluebells, orchids. There was no rhyme or reason. No design. They just splashed the area in vibrant color and fragrance—

"No." I shook my head, following the little cobblestone pathway that led to the gazebo, the port in the sea of flowers. "That smell isn't right."

I slipped my hand around Cahal's arm and closed my eyes, salty wetness sliding down my cheeks. The memory bubbled up immediately, fuzzy and soft, years old. I wished I'd had my vampire memory back then so it would be crisper.

I let Cahal lead me slowly forward, and as he did, I dug into the magic of my surroundings and altered them to smell exactly the way I remembered, with a floral, sunbaked vibrance that seeped into my bones and lightened my mood.

Eyes open again, the image wavering through unshed tears, I adjusted some of the flowers. Only then did it occur to me that this was probably a rendition of a different garden—the one she'd had before she moved me into the forest, away from people.

I didn't care. I wanted it to match up with *my* memories, not his. I wanted her to live on as I remembered her, not as he'd met her. He likely wouldn't notice the difference anyway. He hadn't sat in that garden after she'd died, hours at a time, for weeks, sobbing until his voice was hoarse. Wishing she'd come back. Wishing she hadn't left me alone in a world I knew nothing of. Wishing I could go with her.

Crying harder, giving way to it, I felt Cahal pause and realized he was waiting for me to step up. I did, but my toe hit the edge and I stumbled. His strong arms wrapped around me and he hoisted me up, against his chest, walking me the last few feet into her sanctuary. The place where she used to retreat with her books, or her wine. Where she would invite me to sit with her and gaze at all of the beautiful flowers.

"I asked her often why she didn't make some sort of design out of them." I let Cahal sit me on the bench, taking the spot beside me. Then I took his hand and gripped it tightly, needing his touch to ground me. Needing him to keep me from falling into that dark chasm of despair that I remembered so vividly, vampire memories or no. "She said that nature wasn't organized. It was beautiful chaos. It was her favorite place."

"Well." Lucifer stood off to the side. "I will let you reminisce. I will ask you, however, to please not destroy it. I understand your pain, and you are welcome to destroy any other garden on these premises, but please not this one. It is special to me. It gives me fond memories, especially now that you are here."

He waited for my nod, offered me a bow, and then walked away. I watched him silently for a moment, then let my gaze roam the wild bushes that should really be cut down into manageable shrubbery. They were perfect.

"She hated pruning," I said, talking because I needed to. I needed someone to hear me. When I'd sat in this gazebo before—its likeness, at least—I'd been alone. I hadn't had anyone to share my grief with. I wished it was Darius with me now, but I was grateful for Cahal. "We never agreed on that. She didn't think it right to turn plants into precise shapes. Which, fine, don't shape them into elephants, but at least cut them back to a manageable size. They get wild." I leaned against Cahal's shoulder, and he let me. "She liked them wild."

"Maybe they reminded her of you."

My smile was slight. "Maybe they reminded her of Lucifer."

I expected him to try to turn the situation into a lesson of sorts, but he didn't. He let it drop, and I was grateful to him for that.

I let the tears fall, and a moment dragged a bagful of minutes behind it. Cahal never moved, never shifted in impatience or even because his butt fell asleep. He let me grieve all over again, offering me his solid presence and, if I asked for it, his protection. Not like I'd need it here. Not like I'd ask.

After a while, which would never be long enough, I took a deep breath and straightened up.

"I still have to look after the living," I murmured. "It's the only thing that dragged me out of the grief. It used to be just me." I lowered my voice so I couldn't be overheard. "Now it is Penny, and Darius, and Emery. Well...Darius isn't exactly living, but...still. You need to leave and find them. Send them home. I'll get the rest of my training, and I'll find a way to get out. You have my word."

"Your grief touches me. It gives me hope. It gives you protection. As long as you have this grief, you will remember where you came from and who you are. It will save your life in the end."

"Another deep one. But about the others…"

"It is not me you need to give your word to. It is the soul of your mother."

"Ah. Checkmate. Nice setup."

"As for your friends, I cannot help them. I cannot leave you, even if I wanted to. Lucifer and his watchers would notice my absence immediately, and they would hunt me down and capture me. My magic doesn't work as well with demons. They are used to the shadows. They would find me."

"You're speaking from experience, aren't you?"

"Yes."

"Why did Penny and them come in here?" I murmured to myself, my mind whirling.

"You know why."

"Yes, but…" I did, obviously.

"Durant is the most cunning vampire I've ever known, aside from Ja. He is highly intelligent. He will know you need to get training. He will know that, inevitably, you will also need to escape."

"And I doubt he knows what he's getting himself into."

"He has asked me many questions about Lucifer. I have told him all I know, which is extensive."

I pulled away so I could turn and look him in the eye. "He did?"

"Yes. He will not be going into this blindly."

I resumed sitting straight up, and my heart swelled. Of course he'd found out everything he could from Cahal. He'd probably done a crapload of research, too. Read everything he could get his hands on. He'd kept all of it from me, shouldering the worry by himself. That might have annoyed the old me.

"I miss him."

"Good. Then you will want to return to him."

"Bud, look, I'm not that last guy. I *will* leave this place. I'll get my training, and then it's adios. If Lucifer tries to hold me, I'll leave violently. Otherwise I'll say goodbye. But I *will* leave. I bet the other guy never said that."

"No, he did not. He didn't want to leave, even when this place was killing him. But it won't kill you. It'll call you."

"Home calls to me too. This place is just a nice vacation."

"I hope that remains true. For the sake of your future, I sincerely hope that remains true."

I rolled my eyes. "Did you take a course on melodrama? Because you really have a gift for it."

"Yes." He was quiet for a moment. And then, in a small voice, he said, "I never got to see the dragons with the last heir. He went off to see them, but we weren't friendly at that point. I've only seen them in the air, or from a distance."

"Yeah. Dragons." A surge of excitement cut through my grief. "It'll make this whole trip worth it, I bet."

"I hope so. I think we could use a bright spot at the moment."

I just hoped that bright spot didn't come with a heavy debt.

CHAPTER 10

PENNY CROUCHED BEHIND some sort of stone that felt like half-baked clay, her clothes grimy, her belly empty, and her energy nearly depleted. They'd been on the run for a week so far. The camp or sect or whatever the goat's tits it was called they'd first landed in had been filled with bloodthirsty creatures armed with huge teeth, large claws, and an appetite for human flesh. Sneaking around hadn't worked out so well—they'd only gotten a few hundred yards before a swarm of the creatures came out of nowhere and attacked. The three of them had left a trail of demon blood behind them. A trail that would be super easy to follow.

Darius had decided they couldn't then go straight to their destination. He was sure they'd be hunted, and he wanted to erase their scent, so to speak. They'd gone a roundabout way through a docile camp that had tents and flowers and a lovely smell to the air. No one had noticed them, too busy painting and making daisy chains and singing. It was not what she'd expected of the Underworld. She would've been just fine staying there!

But no, they'd only stopped for a moment in some sort of rest area, where there was apparently some rule barring communication, which worked out well for them. She'd eaten and slept for a while in a fluffy pink bush, too tired to be weirded out by the strange foliage, while Darius stared at the sky. He hadn't mentioned what he was looking for up there. Penny had been too afraid to ask. Bad news waited around every turn in this place.

Here they were now, though, in a part of the Underworld that was absolutely what she'd expected.

Fire covered the charred ground ahead of them, sweeping across it and curling upward into the sky. Within it, large cracks emitted blue flame, hotter than the garden-variety red and orange that swirled around the rest of the area.

On the other side of this field of awful sat their objective—a stone archway with metal gates. The gates stood open, the surface as blackened as the ground. No light shone from the sky, but it wasn't night. As they'd gotten closer to this field of despair, deep gray clouds obscured the glowing orb that passed as a sun. Unfortunately, the fire was bright enough for them to see the danger that lay ahead.

"The good news is, the metal on the gate isn't hot," Penny said, sandwiched between Emery and Darius.

One looked just as haggard and bedraggled as she did. The other was somehow still pristine, in his stupid designer sweater and styled hair. It was like he'd just turned up to take the next shift, rather than being the saving grace that had led the way and kept them alive through some extremely hairy situations. Sure, Penny and Emery had definitely pulled their weight, and Emery's gift of foresight had saved their butts a few times, but Darius was the mastermind who kept them moving in the right direction, who changed strategies at a moment's notice to keep them just on the right side of harm's way.

"How do you know?" Emery asked.

"It's steel, I think. Or iron. Those metals glow a reddish color when they are very hot. It is not very hot."

"Exactly," Darius whispered, his forearms on his knees, his gaze acute as he looked out over the burning fields. He'd reckoned it would take too long for them to go around, upping the odds they'd be discovered, and was hoping there was some way through. The sect they were going to was on the other side of Hell's Gate. A name she'd made up, which fit a little too well.

"So the flames are not hot," he continued.

"Well, wait..." Penny held out her hand, her nails chipped with dirt crusted beneath them. She lowered it again. "I didn't say that. Just that they weren't making the gate hot. So if we needed to close it...we could."

"I don't feel any heat," Emery said.

Penny's gaze roamed across Hell's Field. Blackened rocks in front of them led to the flat ground covered in flame. They were only about ten feet away from the open fire. If it was as hot as normal fire, they really should feel some of it.

"Don't you say it," she murmured.

"We can probably walk across," Emery said anyway.

"I have some ability to withstand the heat of fire because of my bond with Reagan." Darius adjusted his backpack, obviously getting ready to try what Emery was suggesting.

"I thought your bond was…muffled or broken or something." Penny licked her lips. She'd done a lot in this past week. A lot of running. A lot of spells. A *lot* of swearing. She didn't think she was ready for fire walking. Fighting was one thing, but fire walking? She had to draw the line somewhere.

They all did.

"Hey." Emery looked at her before slinging his arm around her shoulders. "We're almost there, okay? We're going to make it. Somehow, someway, we're going to make it. And if we get caught, we'll get to see Reagan rescue us again. Because she will, remember? She'll risk anything to rescue us."

A tear slid down Penny's cheek, and the memory of Reagan's last stand resurfaced. The feeling of walking away from her.

Penny choked back her fear and the desire to sob, hardening herself yet again. She fisted her hands and nodded. "Yes. Okay. Dogs dumping, okay. We can do this."

"Your swearing has certainly gotten much more…colorful after this past week," Darius said, standing slowly and looking behind them. "It will still annoy Reagan to no end. And no, the bond itself is not…subdued, just our awareness of each other. I retain her gifts, and she retains mine, I am certain of that."

"We've got the concealment spell going strong. No one should be able to see you," Emery told him.

"I think your spells will need to be tailored to the different demons we face. They aren't like humans." Darius checked over his sweater, of all things, like he was going to a meeting. "The suspicion has been growing since we passed through the first sect. I am not certain, of course. That is not my domain. But…think about it."

He stepped forward as what he'd said pulled at Penny's mind. Different spells for different demons?

Darius reached the edge of the fire, glancing behind him again. Seeing no one, he stepped out.

"Huh. That makes sense, since they don't all have the same magic. Some have ice, some have fire." And Reagan and Lucifer had both. The vampire tensed and lifted his hands away. "That means it hurts."

Her brain skittered off in another direction. She could make fire, even without Reagan present. She should be able to do the opposite…

She pulled down elements from her magical cloud, always hovering above her head, organized and ready for use. Darius stepped back onto the part of the ground that wasn't dancing with flames and bent to check his leather-clad legs. Emery saw what she was working on and leaned toward her somewhat, analyzing. In a moment, he jumped in, adding little fixes, plugging little holes. They worked so incredibly well together; it was miraculous. *He* was miraculous.

"If we get out of here—"

"When…" he interrupted.

"When we get out of here, I'm going to marry you. I don't care what my mother says."

"I'd like that." She heard the love in his voice. The hopefulness.

She wished she had hope. She was operating on determination alone. All of this was too much for her. She'd seen and done plenty since leaving her incredibly sheltered life, but this was beyond anything anyone could imagine. So far beyond that it was traumatizing. Who even had the imagination for all this crazy crap? What sort of twisted individual was behind it?

"I miss Reagan," Penny said, another tear falling.

She infused that emotion into the spell, her spells always stronger because she didn't just *use* magic—she poured herself into it. "She would take all of this in stride."

Darius crouched back down before them. "She didn't, actually. She thought a lot of it was a mind-fuck."

"She did?" Penny lifted her eyes to the vampire's. "Really?"

"Yes. She nearly broke on the boat ride. With the drops from the ceiling. Then we got to a circus sect and she about unraveled. You are showing your true grit, Penny Bristol. You have earned your place in Reagan's company. We all have."

Lead lined her stomach and more tears dripped down her cheeks as she continued to work on the spell. Creating something more than just a cooling spell. Creating a barrier of protection that would keep them safe *and* invisible. Fire and ice. She was using what she knew of Reagan, of her multifaceted magic, and infusing it into the spell.

"Thank you," she barely got out. "That helps."

He touched her knee briefly before standing and stepping to the side.

"This will work," Emery said to Darius, not looking away from the spell. "Penny has it. This will work for what we need, here and beyond." He chuckled. "You're a genius, baby."

"I am barely holding it together, actually." She tied off her portion of the spell and let Emery add the final touches.

"How hot is it?" Emery stood as the spell fluxed and boiled, condensing into a little ball.

"It is painful for me, but I could make it," Darius said. "You would…not."

Emery watched as the spell reduced, smaller and smaller, and then began to shimmer. Blue coated its surface, then white, before it began to balloon in size again, the color losing saturation as it became first cloudy and then wispy. Finally, it drifted to each of them and enshrouded them.

"This should withstand both types of magic, to a degree," Emery said, putting out his hands and watching the magic coat him. Darius, unable to see magic, just watched them. The spell had no feeling in it. No warmth or coolness. No impact. If Emery hadn't seemed so confident, she would've thought she'd created a dud.

"Let's go," Emery said.

She grabbed the back of his shirt and followed him toward the fire. If the ground weren't so rocky, she would've closed her eyes.

"We're almost there, Turdswallop," he said softly, stepping into the flame.

"Buttercrack fizzleshits," she said, following him.

"I'm telling your mother," he replied, laughing.

"I'm not sure what would be worse, her or this field," Darius said, stepping in beside Emery.

Taking a deep breath, Penny followed, her foot touching down on the crispy ground. The flame licked her ankle. Heat coated her calf. The bite of pain didn't chomp down.

"We're good?" she asked, following with the other foot. "We're okay?"

"You did it. Let's go." Darius was walking quickly before she could properly prepare herself.

"Okay, but…" She jogged to catch up with the other two. "What if it stops working?"

"That is why we are hurrying," Darius replied, and picked up the pace.

The flame rose as they hastened across the field, reaching past her waist now, up to her stomach. The heat pulsed, thick against her body. They passed through a short wall of blue flame, and pain slashed through her awareness.

"Holy flapjack crusty barnacles!" She hopped and danced, speeding up. "Screw this. Get me outta here!"

She ran past Emery and Darius and jumped over the next wall of blue. Her toes didn't quite make it over, and searing pain curled through her body. The heat intensified as they neared the gate, but it wasn't unbearable yet. She could withstand it. She could do this!

A waft of blue reached for her as she passed, like a pair of hands. It clutched her leg, blistering in its intensity. She cried out and wrenched away but refrained from using her godly magic to kill it at the root. She didn't want their passage through this field known. She didn't want Darius to force them through another week of torture.

The gate was just up ahead. Crackling orange flame reared up as she got closer, filling the entrance. The black gates still didn't glow with heat, but it was an illusion, obviously, because it *was* hot. She could feel its scorching heat, the flames at the onset nothing compared to these. Sweat drenched her brow. If it weren't for her spell, she'd have been roasted to a crisp. As it was, she bit her lip, pushing through the pain.

Trap. Scorch. Kill.

A trap. This field was set up as a kind of trap. Let creatures who thought they could handle it (like lesser powered demons) wander through, only for the heat to turn up at the end, like a stove dial cranked to high, and burn them alive. She wondered if someone had set it up for them. Or maybe this place was always this terrible—there was no way of knowing.

Regardless, they'd triggered the trap. Now, they had to get through before the heat bled through her magic.

"Hurry," she grunted out, putting on a burst of speed. "Hurry, Emery!"

Darius was beside her in an instant, looking at her face.

"Yeah, danger. Danger, danger!" she yelled. "Oh sure, *now* the metal starts glowing!"

The wall of flame waited. If Darius was to be believed, a safe haven waited for them at the other end of that field. She wanted that. Needed it. She could not handle another week of picking through back roads in this hellish landscape.

The fire raged ahead of her, heat blanketing her body and forcing out all of her air. Pain pounding, aching, throbbing. It overcame her thoughts. Blacked out rationale.

She increased her magic, feeding in a cooling effect. More of it. Trying to make ice and instead conjuring a chilled blast of air. It would have to do.

She flung it at the flame filling the archway right before she jumped through, the others behind her. Her hair crackled and lit on fire, the flame racing toward her head even as heat coated her face. Agony scratched along her skin and dug in, all the way to her bones. She hit the other side and turned, taking the pain, needing to make sure Emery would make it.

She needn't have bothered. He must've seen the elements she'd pulled and formed his own spell, one that worked a little better. The flames reduced within the blast of cold, and then he was by her side, grabbing her arm and ripping her along. Darius zoomed through a moment later, not needing the blast of chill air.

He shoved them from behind to get them moving again, and then they went rolling through the smoky agony.

It took a moment to realize that was a residual affect. The flames were gone. Her scorched cheek lay against green grass…

"Here. Quickly." A little vial was put to her mouth. Darius leaned over her. "Please, drink. Quickly!"

She opened her mouth and the most divine taste filled her senses, sparkling and fizzy and full of life and light and all things good. Energy filled her limbs. Her magic jumped and surged. The pain eased from her skin.

"Emery, here. Drink," Darius said, bent over him now, his sweater burned away. He still had his hair, though, the jerk. How'd he manage that?

"I'm naked, aren't I?" she asked as the invigorating elixir worked through her body, her cheek still pressed against the springy grass. It felt cool to the touch. But anything probably would've, given what she'd been through. "And I'm bald. I'm bald, aren't I? Do I have eyebrows?"

"No, you do not." Darius was back in front of her, his hands out. "Let's get up. The unicorn blood should start working any moment."

The air turned sparkly, and the colors around her started to change, a little too bright, like everything was oxidized. A rush of power pumped through her as she let Darius help her to sitting. Her nipples tightened, and her core ached with need.

"Oh my God, what did you give me?" She crossed her arms over her bare chest, blackened with soot, a couple pieces of fabric sticking to her flesh. Then she slapped her knees together, her legs scuffed and scraped but the leather holding up better against the flame. She could feel the burns healing, though.

"Unicorn blood has many effects, an aphrodisiac being one of them," Darius said, pulling open their backpacks and checking the contents. "This is in good shape. Here." He tossed a shirt at her. "This will make you feel better."

"That stuff is addictive, huh?" Emery said, running his tongue around his lips. Her core started to pound now, aching to be filled by him. To feel his touch. To invite in his tongue…

"Highly," Darius replied. "You must use it sparingly. You won't think much of the antidote."

"And that is?" Emery asked, pushing to standing. His bulge said he was feeling what she was, and his easy movements and calm demeanor said he wasn't nearly as stressed out about it.

"Vampire serum or a vampire bond. A vampire

touch can help, too."

"Not interested. We'll need to avoid the blood as much as possible."

"Which is why I haven't brought it out until now. Come. Let's go. We shouldn't be far now."

"How can you possibly be so chill right now?" she asked Emery as he helped her up, then yanked her hands away before she gave in to temptation and cupped that bulge and pushed down those pants. She squeezed her eyes shut, shrugging into the shirt Darius had tossed at her.

"I always feel this way around you, Turdswallop," he said, heat in his voice. "It's a constant ache. This is just a bit heightened. I'm used to ignoring it until you notice I'm in the room." He laughed. "It's just another part of surviving. I'd rather ignore this feeling than the pain a few moments ago."

"You won't have to ignore it for long," Darius said, and started off.

Penny hobbled after him, almost asking what he meant by that, and decided she really didn't want to know.

CHAPTER 11

PENNY EYED THE ground as they made their way to a sort of large cliff face with multiple holes dotting the sides. It almost looked like a rock honeycomb, but the ground seemed to be made up of a soft, springy material. It rolled in small hills and berms toward lavender fields that waved softly in a breeze she couldn't feel.

"It almost feels like a mattress," she said, bouncing a little as she half trudged along, feeling much better from the unicorn blood and healing faster than should be possible. "Like…" She bounced again. "I feel like I should take my shoes off."

Emery held her hand, walking beside her, as they quietly followed Darius. He hadn't made a peep, but he didn't seem tense. He was probably trying to take stock of whatever horrors lay ahead.

A shape moved down the path toward them, tall and slim and with slinky movements. Its hips swayed erotically, and its shoulders swung forward and back, like a model in front of a camera. Darius didn't slow as it neared, but the creature did, giving Penny ample time to check out its form.

Humanoid but obviously not human, it had short legs, slim thighs, and a long body. Its chest was flat, but it had rounded hips, and its face was the stuff of nightmares, with no nose, red eyes, and leathery skin.

"Oh great, yeah. Good." Penny shuffled a little closer to Emery. "I was hoping for more terrible things in this wretched place."

"Now you are starting to sound like my beloved," Darius said, passing the creature by.

It said something in a series of hisses and consonants that Penny didn't understand. Another language, probably.

Darius glanced back at Penny, and Penny realized she and Emery didn't have the concealing spell over them anymore.

"You will get a lot of opportunity to explore your…newfound tastes," Darius said.

"My newfound tastes—what does that mean?" Penny wondered.

"I think this is a lust sect," Emery murmured as they got closer. Two beings loitered by a large square hole in the rock, what probably passed for the entranceway. One was squat and round and wearing a tutu. The other was in full demon regalia, with a scabby body, insects crawling out of random holes in its hide, and limbs that could've used a little more fleshing out.

"Who could hold on to lust in a place like this?" she muttered. Then Darius's words finally registered. *Newfound tastes.* A new sexual appetite, he meant, for peeping. "He's making fun of me. Even here, he is making fun of me for *accidentally* seeing him with Rea—"

Darius spun so fast that Penny barely had time to squeak in surprise. His hand closed over her mouth before she could react.

In the next moment, he was magically bound and gagged and lying flat on his back, his eyes wide.

The beings near the door straightened up, now looking over. The short, round one smiled, its fleshy lips pulling much too wide, literally spanning ear to ear. She grimaced with the sight as it completed its turn, zeroing in on Darius lying prone.

"Hmm. The vampire is back. I *feel* it already. De-*light*ful," it said in crisp English, before bending at the waist. The one with the insects stepped closer, fastening its hands around the hips of the first, pulling back at the same time as it pushed forward. The resulting moan of the bent one explained what was happening.

"This better not be some elaborate joke," Penny said, looking away quickly.

Emery unraveled Penny's hasty spell around Darius and helped the vampire up. "She's got fast reactions."

"It seems so, yes." Darius dusted himself off. "Had I been trying to kill her, however…"

"Yeah, she's not quite fast enough, as…Bruiser would say." Emery took Penny's hand again, giving her a pointed look. "Remember not to say her name. We don't know who knows it."

She nodded, because yes, she knew that. She'd just lost her head for a moment.

"If I was waiting for danger, or didn't know you, I would've been quicker," she mumbled as they passed by the two thrusting creatures. "Well, let's be real, I wouldn't be this close—Oh God, there's more." She jerked her head away from the three creatures just inside the cavernous space, writhing and moving in a sort of dance she didn't want to see.

The springy material covered the floor of the cavernous space, dotted with the equivalent of beanbag chairs and pillows. The ceiling rose to about twenty feet, letting in light from holes in the cliff face but maintaining the overall dim lighting. Away right, a rock staircase spiraled upward, empty at the moment.

"Is it always this empty?" Emery asked as Darius moved toward the staircase.

"This area seems to be, yes, for the most part. I believe they have various festivals where neighboring sects come to…visit, and this large area hosts them. This sect is made up of a string of caves and caverns, though.

Certain areas are teeming with life at all times. This is the third lust sect I've been to, and its general makeup is very similar to the others. They like twisty halls and secluded rooms and hidden alcoves."

"Or just banging on the stoop," Penny groused. "So these…creatures just hang around and bang all day?"

She felt a little shiver. Then a little tingle, starting at the base of her stomach and sinking into her core. It pulsed there, aching, feeding on the unicorn blood and the thought of Emery so near. Meanwhile, her brain screamed at her to shut her eyes, uncomfortable because of her naivety, she knew, but uncomfortable all the same. She wanted to turn around and sprint out of here, much like her reaction when she had unfortunately burst in on Reagan and Darius. Twice.

"This might turn into the biggest mind-eff of them all," she murmured miserably. "They're like a bunch of bonobo monkeys."

"It'll do you good to…unwind a little," Darius whispered as they reached the next level. He didn't stop, leaving Penny to peer through the gloomy darkness. She didn't see any shapes moving in its depths, though.

At the fifth floor, when Penny's calves were burning, and she had to squint through the darkness to see anything, Darius finally stopped climbing.

"This is the leader's quarters," he said, stepping away from the stairway. "They call them *conspectors.*"

Those alcoves he'd talked about branched off to the sides, little cubbies with long, flat surfaces topped with piles of pillows. All of them were empty.

"They don't have any guards or anything?" Emery asked quietly. They approached a dimly lit doorway at the back of the space.

"No, not that I've ever seen," Darius replied. "They like the feel of my vampire magic, so I had no trouble gaining admittance and a meeting with the leader. From there, we worked to a place of understanding. I don't think they get a lot of visitors in this area. I was directed here by my contacts in the Edges."

Penny shook her head slowly. This vampire could clearly talk his way into anything he wanted. If Reagan ever thought she'd hear all of his secrets, she was sorely mistaken.

She chanced a glance behind them. Still empty.

They passed the empty alcoves, entering a dimly lit space with a couple of flickering lights on the walls—fairy lights, maybe?—mimicking the flickering candles lining the furniture along the sides. Couches crowded together, facing each other, no table in between. An assortment of beanbags and armchairs were arranged beyond them. Farther back, through another doorway, the ceiling dropped low until it felt like they were cocooned.

A being lounged near a bookshelf, an open book in

hand and its other hand between its plump thighs.

"Good gracious," Penny said, bumping off Emery's side.

"Hmm," the demon groaned before slowly closing the book and sitting up. It looked around, its eyes landing on Darius. "The vampire returns. Fan*tas*tic. Just in time for our weekly ritual. Your magic will be a pleasant boost to our usual efforts."

"Acacius," Darius said by way of greeting. "Let me introduce you to my associates." He slid his hand through the air. "Penny and Emery, a natural dual-mage pair."

"Ah." The demon rose to standing, up and up until it reached the height of nearly seven feet, Penny was sure of it. A sheet draped its chest, masking what might be lady boobs or man boobs, and slid down the lower half. Nothing tented it. "The origin of the spells you peddle in the Edges."

"Just so. Their craft is highly prized." Darius clasped his hands in front of him. "We've had a long journey. I wondered if we could rest here for a time. Get some food for them. Replenish. After that, we will continue on into the Underworld. We won't mention whence we've come."

The demon waved the sentiment away as though that didn't trouble it. Its smile was sly. "On one condition. They must attend the ritual."

"Oh no," Penny said immediately. "No, no, that's okay. We wouldn't want to impose."

The smile spread. "I insist. You are inexperienced, are you not? I can see it in you. I can see the yearning, the great passion…and the fear. I can see the confusion as you respond. We will release you, little *flenchlin*. We will let you fly."

Penny felt her eyebrows sink as her face twisted into a scowl. She stepped a little farther behind Emery, and the demon laughed.

"I will see that it is done," Darius said, and turned, his hands out, motioning for Penny and Emery to get going.

Outside of the room, with Darius apparently knowing where he was going, Emery asked, "What's the nature of the ritual? Penny won't go quietly to anything extreme, no matter how much she tries. You must know that."

"This won't be that sort of extreme," Darius said, and left it at that.

THEY ONLY HAD a scant couple of hours of idle time before Darius emerged from his little alcove in their joined room, nothing more than a rough rock cut out from the main drag on the third floor, outfitted with a few little sleeping cubbies encircling a firepit in the center of the space. A spit straddled the circle of rocks.

It had been slowly turning as they walked in, roasting a pig that must have been magically thawed when they first arrived at the compound. Darius was incredibly *extra* when it came to food, clearly. She'd been expecting to eat beans out of a can, cowboy style, and instead they would get fire-roasted pork. Now that she was finished healing, she could feel the hunger coming on.

The little alcoves didn't have doors. Just something similar to mattresses, plus lots of pillows. Penny had quickly fallen asleep.

"So…you don't have to participate in the ritual?" she asked Darius as she stepped out of her and Emery's little alcove. Darius had been annoyingly silent on what the ritual would entail, and Emery hadn't pressed for unknown reasons. She would've magically dragged it out of the vampire hours ago if she hadn't fallen head-first into a nap.

"No. They tried to make it a requirement of me at first, but I strictly refused. I told them I would engage in it when my beloved was with me. Not until then."

"But I have to participate?" Penny demanded. "How is that fair?"

"Because your beloved is with you. And because I *will* still participate; I just won't touch another."

"Well, I won't touch another," Penny said adamantly as they walked down the corridor. Other demons walked in the same direction, some hurrying and others dawdling. They represented all different forms, some resembling humans, others looking like creatures, and one a sort of man-goat. That one was really gross.

When they got close to Darius, many smiled, and some made lurid sounds.

"You'll touch me, I have a feeling," Emery said softly, and something in his voice lit a fire in her core, tightened her up in all the right ways while loosening her in others.

She struggled to breathe out of a suddenly tight chest, butterflies filling her stomach. She wasn't in the right headspace to comment on that.

"It's your seduction they like?" Emery asked Darius as they took to the stairs.

"Yes. Humans are easy prey when offered the fundamentals of their species' survival—food and sex. Our magic is seductive to lure them in, and this type of demon feeds on it. It heightens their…senses, I think. Or maybe just adds a little flavor, I'm not sure."

"So you hang around while they bang?" Penny asked in a harried tone. She knew she sounded like a prude. She knew she was theoretically clutching her pearls. But this was some sort of crazy. She'd only ever been with Emery, and she hadn't started with him all that long ago in the scheme of things. She wasn't ready for intense public displays of affection. Yes, okay, maybe she'd made love to him outside when they were becoming a dual-mage pair. But they'd been alone. And that had been a special circumstance…

"Yes." Darius led them off the stairs and down a wide stone corridor, the nicest area she'd seen in this strange, cavelike dwelling. "I read, typically, or think about other things."

"And it doesn't gross you out?" she pushed.

"No, quite the opposite. It makes me long for…my beloved."

"The leader didn't seem concerned about why you're here," Emery said, his fingers entwined with Penny's.

"No," Darius replied. "This sect mostly ignores politics. That is why I sought them out. They thrive around my magic and don't much care why I am here. It's a perfect setup for my goals. I'm not sure if…they will be suspected in harboring us or not. Likely not."

"And why is that?"

They turned a corner, the demons bumping and jostling now, the ground turning from stone into that mattress-like material. The room opened up into something similar to the cavern on the ground floor, although not nearly as big. The edges that seemed more like catacombs. There were little nooks and crannies everywhere, it seemed like, plenty of darkened corners for people to disappear from sight. And plenty of room for them to lie around, on full display, nestled in the pillows or along the soft ground.

A large cauldron stood in the center, raised on a stone dais. Creatures stood on the dais, dipping in golden cups and handing them to those waiting on the ground. Those that received the offering drank it down, handed the cup back, and moved on, choosing a spot in the open or grouping with others in the darkened areas.

"Do we need to drink that?" Emery asked in a low voice. He sounded unsure.

That made two of them.

Magic pumped and pulsed around them, pounding through her. It infused her blood and sank into her core. *Touch. Kiss. Please. Be pleased.*

"Yes, it is part of the ritual." Darius stopped behind a sticklike creature that only came up to Penny's chest. "I will be drinking it as well. It is pleasant and harmless, and you only need a mouthful."

"Doesn't that make you crave blood?" Emery asked.

"In such a small quantity, it won't be an issue."

"That's good, because you won't be getting blood from me." Penny gripped Emery's hands harder, her core pounding in time with the pulsing magic. It slid over her, incredibly erotic, stealing her breath. "I want to go home."

"It's going to be fine, Penny Bristol," Emery whispered, his sweet breath dusting her face. "You are perfectly safe here. I won't let anything happen to you."

"This type of demon is completely safe, I assure you." Darius stepped up, almost at the dais now. A crowd waited around and behind them, but no one pushed. The entire situation was orderly. "They might ask for your time, but they will not demand it, and they will not attempt to take it by force. It is forbidden. To do so would mean death."

"Who distributes that punishment?" Emery asked, stepping up again, ever closer.

Taste. Lick. Enjoy.

"I assume you or Penny would, should it come to that. It is certainly within your power."

Emery nodded. He'd obviously been asking if they could take matters into their own hands. Green light.

Suck. Fondle. Enjoy.

"Bugger balls," Penny whispered, shutting her eyes and trying to block out that pounding need. She craved the kind of satisfaction only Emery could supply. The deep, hard—"It's getting to me. Their magic is getting to me."

Darius glanced over, a small smile playing across his lips. "*Mon coeur* will be incredibly angry she missed this."

"It would be a running joke until the end of time." Emery chuckled darkly.

Penny elbowed him. "Don't join in with him. You're supposed to be on my side."

"Sorry," Emery murmured.

They stepped up to the front of the line now. The demon distributing the drink on their side of the cauldron was wearing chaps. It turned around, and part of it swung down around its knees.

"Nope." Penny tried to back up. She bumped into the creature behind her. "This is crazy. We're not here for this."

Darius drank out of the offered cup. "This is the best place for us right now. You need to regain your energy and strength. I do not think anyone will look for us here until they've exhausted more obvious ideas. After tonight, you'll be left to your own devices. As R—my dearest would say, suck it up. Pun intended."

"You just sound lame when you say it," Penny groused. "Not to mention we are spreading germs…" She paused as the leader climbed up onto the dais near her, a smile on its leathery face.

"Little *flenchlin*." It took a cup and looked down at her. "I am excited to see you transform."

"I don't like the sound of that," she mumbled as the demon turned and dipped the cup into the cauldron.

Eyes on Penny again, it gave the cup to Emery. "Your partner will go first, just this once."

"Great gravy without a boat," she said as Emery sniffed the contents.

"If you didn't need us so badly," he told Darius,

shaking his head a little, "there is no way in hell I would trust you this much."

"Understood, Mr. Westbrook. You will be able to resist the temptations of the drink, if you choose. It is more potent than the blood you had earlier, but not horribly so, I shouldn't think."

"Resist the temptation?" The leader shook its head and chuckled. "Why ever would you want to resist something so natural? *Enjoy* it. Soak it up. *Revel* in it." Its light eyes flashed.

Emery drained the cup, then handed it back. He licked his lips. "Tastes…*good*." He pulled his hand free of Penny's grasp and ran it down her back. "Amazing, actually. It tastes like…" He licked his lips again.

"It tastes like carnal sin." The demon laughed deeply as it refilled the cup.

She took the cup from it, scowling for all she was worth. The contents swished in the glass—deep purple, not more than a mouthful, as Darius had said.

"It won't hurt you, Miss Bristol," Darius said. "I know very well that I would be skinned alive and eternally slaughtered if I were to ever harm you. That drink is safe."

She growled, steeled her courage, knowing that if Reagan were here, she'd be taunting Penny something awful, and then downed the liquid.

The explosion in her mouth matched the magic in

the air, still pounding through her body. The complex grouping of flavors spiraled through her senses. She couldn't even describe it—rich chocolate, subtle spices, that wine Darius served on his island, home-baked apple pie…

It was as if all the flavors she loved best had been contained in one cup, each in its best possible formation. The best pie, the best PB&J sandwich, the best s'mores. They didn't contradict each other, though they should've.

"Very good, little *flenchlin.*" The leader winked and took the cup before scooping up some of the drink for itself and gulping it down. "If you decide to…mingle, find me first."

"She won't be mingling." Emery slipped his hand down to the swell of Penny's hip and pulled her in possessively.

A moan escaped her as she soaked him in. The feel of that hand, hard and masculine. The rich timbre of his voice and his smell, comforting and arousing.

"The offer is out there." The leader laughed and lifted its hand high, all six fingers of it. "Commence the music!"

A cheer went up, and Darius urged Emery and Penny out of the throng of creatures. "Here, back here. You'll want to get settled in a hurry."

Drums reverberated through the space, almost tribal in nature, a deep, rhythmic sound crashing through her blood. Excitement twisted her gut and tightness took over her core. Emery's hand tightened around her hip, and she knew the rest of his body was reacting, too. Music from a strange sort of string instrument rose above the din, hitting a high note before dipping and then coiling and spiraling through her ears. The sound was sweet and full of longing, but spicy and naughty, too.

"Here." Darius stopped them in front of a little alcove, the lighting so dim she could only see the wall at the back. "It's small, which means it is only for a small group—two or three. No one will duck in here to join, unlike in the larger rooms. The resting area is around the side. This should allow you to…hide from sight. Or, if you prefer, we can look for a different—"

"This is perfect," Emery said, ushering Penny in front of him. "We'll lock ourselves in with magic."

"Fantastic. I will be in the area, in case you need something. Otherwise…" Darius took a step back. "Enjoy yourselves."

Emery smirked, of all things, and guided Penny farther into the alcove. A new instrument joined the others, a base that worked with the rhythmic drumbeat, pulling at her body, pushing, yanking, trying to get her to take her pants off.

"Darius basically just shoved us into a demon sex

club in the Underworld, do you know that?" She helped Emery erect a wall and then nearly buckled and dropped to the ground at the thought of *erect*. "Oh boy, I might be in trouble."

Emery tied off the spell and turned to her, the soft light in the alcove just bright enough for her to see his gorgeous blue and gold eyes, hungry with desire. "That drink is...something else." His eyes roamed her body, stopping on her breasts before dipping to what Reagan would call her fun zone. "Do you want to resist? Would that make you more comfortable?"

Yes was on the tip of her tongue. But that look in Emery's eyes stoked the fire within her to blazing, burning through her blood. She backed up slowly, deeper into the alcove. He stalked her, his big body thick with muscle, his movements graceful and light in spite of it. The light cut across his high cheekbones and accentuated his strong jaw and ruggedly handsome features.

Her core ached for him. Her knees didn't want to keep working. She bumped against the elevated, flat surface covered in pillows. The fact that others had used it for this—that demons had—should gross her out. Those pillows alone should gross her out. But she couldn't tear her thoughts away from Emery. From what was under that shirt. What was in those pants.

He pushed up close to her, his heat dosing her. "I

want to fuck you, Penny," he said, and she swallowed hard. Passion swelled. Lust pulled her under. She couldn't focus on anything but his heat. His words. His unchecked hunger to get inside of her. She wanted him inside of her.

Reading her easily, he slipped his tough palm against her smooth skin. His fingers pointed upward as his hand moved, sliding over the swell of her breast, his thumb finding the sensitive peak.

She groaned, fluttering her eyes shut. His hot mouth was on hers in an instant, swallowing her sounds. His tongue swept through, his taste more divine even than that drink. Better than anything.

His kiss rose in urgency, and suddenly his hands were on the buttons of her pants. They were pushing her pants down and slipping between her thighs.

Her knees finally gave out. She fell onto the springy surface behind her, lifting her legs so he could rip her pants off. She pushed up quickly, undoing his button and yanking his pants down as well. His hard length bobbed up, and she bent forward to capture it with her mouth, his hands on her head and then sliding down to caress her bare butt.

He yanked, pulling her head away before bending down and laying a bruising kiss on her lips. He stripped both of them of their shirts, then lowered.

"I can't wait," he said, crazed, out of control, desperate for her.

Desire pumped through her. A consuming need.

She pulled him on top of her, everything else forgotten, feeling the music pound through her, the drums adding to the ache in her body. The ache *he* could cure.

She lifted, and then he plunged deeply, filling her in a rush of incredible ecstasy.

"Fly, fly, little *flenchlin*," she heard, echoing around their alcove. "Fly to your freedom."

"That's going to embarrass me tomorrow," she said through pants, not able to get Emery close enough. Deep enough. Moving fast enough. "Harder, baby," she said, in the moment again, able to feel nothing but his smooth length sliding in and out of her, in and out. Her back rubbing against the soft surface under her. His kisses dominating her world. "Harder!"

He groaned, lifting a little so that he could bear down. His hips crashed against her. The sound of their lovemaking danced with the steady beat of that drum. Of the music. Of the increasing pleasure that filled up every inch of her world.

An orgasm stole her breath and dragged her down into weightless bliss. She cried out, clutching his back, shaking around him. He swore, shuddering, emptying inside of her.

His lips were on hers again as they moaned with the aftershock. Still inside her, he rose just enough so that he could look into her eyes.

"This is the weirdest and hottest thing we'll probably ever do. We're in a demon sex club in the Underworld in a private…cave or something, on the demon equivalent of ecstasy. Like…is this real life?"

She laughed, all the stresses of the situation melting away. The moans and groans from the creatures outside of their alcove didn't bother her. Nor did the music still beating through her veins. The desire still pooled hot.

"It is weird, yes." She slid her hands across his shoulders and let the crazy scene envelop her, let some of her naivety drip away. "And it is hot. And this is real life when you're friends with Reagan," she whispered. "She'd probably be having a ball, banging Darius on the main floor."

Emery kissed her. "Probably. I'm still hard. I have a feeling that drink is going to keep me that way for…a while." He started to move again. "Whenever you want to go, we'll leave, okay? You are in control of our fate right now. I'm just going to keep giving you orgasms until you say enough."

The fire stole her breath again, and she arched back, rubbing her hard and sensitive nipples against his chest. "When in a demon sex club, you just gotta do like the demons do, I guess."

His laugh was dark and dripping with sin. "Agreed. There could be worse places to hide."

CHAPTER 12

LUCIFER CHECKED THE screens hanging over the large window, looking for anything out of the ordinary within his kingdom. He viewed short snippets of action before moving along to the next sect.

He paid the most attention to the sects he knew to be political, the ones that would stand to gain favor if they used the trespassers as leverage. A few had more activity than normal, but that was likely because Lucifer's people were churning through them, asking questions and searching.

"It has been two weeks. How could those vampires continue to elude us?" he demanded, turning to a small collection of his most trusted advisors.

It was Victoria who answered, easily the most courageous of all his minions, a trait that had kept her as his first assistant and confidante.

"They have proven…incredibly elusive. The vampire Darius didn't travel in a straight line, and his trail largely seems to have vanished. There are no smells for our trackers. No signs of passage. The castle is presumably his ultimate destination, because of the heir, but his initial path didn't seem to indicate any sort of destination at all. It seemed like he was winging it."

"Winging it? *Winging it*?" Lucifer ground his teeth. "That vampire has set up a network of highly aggressive and intelligent traders throughout this kingdom. The more we look into it, the deeper the hole seems to go. He's done this in a matter of Brink *months.* That is not a creature who *wings it.* There is a reason to his madness. We need to find it."

"Yes, sire. You are entirely correct. And we wondered…" Victoria rolled her shoulders. "We wondered if maybe the heir could be prodded for information?"

Lucifer took a deep breath. "I've been working on her. Trying to sever the connection she has to the vampire and her friends. It's proven…difficult."

That was putting it mildly. She'd seemed more pliable since he showed her the garden dedicated to her mother, just like he'd hoped. But that only went so far. The woman was viciously stubborn, and she seemed to completely shrug off his manipulation tactics. Grand dinners and drunken nights and training—she often seemed like putty in his hands, to mold and shape how he would. But the second he tried to implant thoughts or coax information out of her, she shrugged it off, or made a flippant comment, or laughed at him. She disarmed him like he was used to disarming others. If the situation weren't so dire, he would've felt a surge of pride.

That wasn't true. He felt a gush of pride every time his anger rose at one of her comments. Every time he lost his cool and then realized she was waiting for his explosion. Waiting, and ready. Not scared.

If he did explode, he knew she'd thwart it as best she could, and it would be enough to save her life. He knew it, and she knew it. She'd grown in her magic incredibly fast. Faster than anyone he'd ever trained. Faster than he had thought possible. They now shared the same power level, but her magic was more complex. More diverse. She had the gift of those blasted angels, and it made her stronger. Harder to beat.

Those stupid creatures would laugh at him if they knew. Or maybe this was their grand joke. Just another parting gift.

But she could never feel completely at home here if she held on to her mortal attachments. And she *had* to feel at home here—she was born to rule. The mantle was hers; she had but to claim it.

That cursed druid wasn't helping. He was whispering in her ear just like he had with the last heir, and if he wasn't watched—carefully—he'd drive her to madness, too. Lucifer wouldn't be able to watch that. Not with her.

"She is used to subtle maneuvering from that vampire Darius," Lucifer said, watching his screens. "She knows when I'm trying to coax information out of her. And when I am trying to implant ideas."

"She is yielding, I have heard," Victoria said. "Her attendants see the change. She relies on the druid less, for example. She looks forward to her time with you more."

Lucifer nodded. He had heard that, and it gave him hope that she was coming around. If she weren't so stubborn, he'd think it was in the bag. As it was, he had to constantly keep his wits.

"What of Vlad?" he said. "He's never been past the Edges. He can't know how to maneuver in this kingdom."

Victoria shifted her position, noticeably agitated. "It is a great mystery, your highness."

He tightened his fist, fire running over his skin. "What is so mysterious about it?"

"The sect he usually does business with in the Edges said they did not see him. We turned their living quarters upside down. Nothing. We did find a trail leading from the river, though." Her eyes narrowed. "It didn't smell like him. Our trackers are sure. But they don't know who it might be."

"Not Vlad?"

"He could've disguised his smell," said Durgess, another trusted advisor. Standing nine feet tall, he had large, muscled arms covered in chartreuse skin. "Both vampires seem to have access to magic."

"Yes," Lucifer said, realizing the hole in his own arsenal. It was currently thought that a team of highly powerful mages had created the disturbance last week. The very same mages that had been supplying the vampire Darius with their magic.

Lucifer had ordered his people not to kill the mages until he could speak to them in person. If they could be harnessed for their power, he might find a place to store them. Otherwise, as the saying went, if he couldn't have them, no one could…

"Continue to look. I'll be taking my daugh—" Lucifer cleared his throat with the slip. None of his advisors reacted. "I'll be taking the heir to see the dragons today."

Now, they did react.

"Are you sure that is wise, sire?" Victoria asked. "A few of them have neonates. They are extremely vicious when protecting their young."

"She can handle it." Lucifer puffed up in pride. "I'll have her bring that wet blanket of a druid, too."

"Maybe we'll get lucky and the druid won't survive," Durgess rumbled.

"That's the hope." Lucifer strutted away, angry still about the vampires, adrenaline fueling his blood at the thought of what was to come.

Reagan was ready. She had to be. She had the magic and the courage. The only other thing required to tame a dragon was the refusal to give in to pain. She'd shown she was capable of that after the elves' treatment. More than capable.

He couldn't wait to see what she did to those elves when she was able to claim her vengeance.

First, though, she had much to learn. If she survived the dragons, he would step her up into advanced work. She was ready. By then, he hoped she'd finally be ready to get rid of the druid and, with him, her ties to the outside world.

CHAPTER 13

I WAITED WITH bated breath for Lucifer to show up. Today was the day. I'd get to meet the dragons and maybe even bond with one, though I had no idea how. They were fearsome beasts, which was cool, and they flew, which was cooler, and they allowed their person to fly on top of them, which was a life goal.

A huge life goal.

I could barely stop from peeing, I was so excited. Something Cahal had mentioned was TMI when I told him.

"I fear you are starting to slide," Cahal said as he waited near the window, looking out.

"When we got here, you said I was supposed to feel like this place was a part of me."

"Correct. It should feel that way. But not the only part of you."

I dropped my hands. "We're going to see *dragons*, Cahal! You yourself said you were excited for the dragons."

"You haven't mentioned missing Darius or Penny

in a few days."

I ran my fingers through my hair, knowing he was right. I'd been distracted. Lucifer had been training with me every day, complex magic that bolstered me to the point that I felt like I was flying. And then he'd brought up an actual date for the dragons, which promised literal flight. It had kept all my attention.

"He subtly asked about Durant's operations yesterday at dinner, did you notice?" Cahal pushed.

I waved it away, annoyed, before strapping on my boot. "Yes, I know. And I informed him that I didn't know much about Darius's operations because he never included me in anything."

"And then he pointed out the secrets Durant keeps from you."

I threw him an exasperated look. "I caught that, yes. He was correct—Darius has always kept secrets from me. He promised to be totally open when we got together, and obviously that was a big lie."

A *big lie* was putting it mildly, since I'd had no idea about Darius's efforts in the Underworld. Yes, I'd known he was selling or trading magic in the Edges, but his elaborate schemes within the kingdom itself? No. I didn't even know when he'd had time to do all of that.

"Durant keeping things from you rankles," Cahal said, trying to work under my skin, much like Lucifer had been doing. It felt like I had two incredibly strong ropes tethered to my wrists, pulling me in opposite directions.

"You already knew that," I replied.

"But I've never tried to use it against you."

"Because you've never wanted anything from me. Until now."

Cahal turned back as I strapped on my other boot. "I don't want anything you shouldn't also want."

"And what is that? What, in your opinion, should I want?"

"Freedom."

I shook my head and stood. Freedom. What exactly was freedom anymore? Either I had a vampire trying to control me, or a biological father trying to control me, or the elves trying to torture me, or the fae trying to use me...

Freedom was a pipe dream.

What I needed to do was pick a lane.

But first, I needed to see the dragons.

"Are you coming or not?" I asked tersely. He was really dampening my joy about today's festivities. Of all the days to knock me off balance...

Could he not have done all this tomorrow?

"Of course I am coming. I will try to help you until you inevitably kill me."

Rage stole through me, but I forced it back down. "You're trying to manipulate me, Cahal. You know that

I would never kill you. Give me a break."

"I may have been interested in the dragons on a conceptual level, but they could very well kill me. They do not take kindly to trespassers. That's the only reason Lucifer is allowing me to join you."

"Those dragons aren't going to kill you, you insufferable bastard. You know for a fact I won't let you come to harm. Stop with all this melodrama and just chill for a while, would you? As soon as I am done learning, we'll find a way out of here. That hasn't changed. Penny and the gang haven't surfaced since the disturbance. They are obviously lying low, which is fine, because it gives me more time to learn. Just let me enjoy today—*let me enjoy the dragons.*"

"But will you want to leave? Will you allow them to save you, or will you turn them away?"

My level of annoyance with him was reaching an all-time high. I knew where I stood in the grand scheme of things. I knew he cared about me, and that he was trying to pull me back from the edge because he worried I was starting to break. But today of all days…

Honestly, yes. I had to own that a big part of me didn't want to leave this place. I loved training with Lucifer, a guy that I eminently understood. It had taken some work, but I'd learned how to mercilessly push his buttons. And I delighted in both his rage and his good humor. I saw the balance in him. He hadn't exactly shown me the darkness within him, but I had a dark side too. I took comfort in that.

Other than that, I just liked the guy. He was fun to be around. His jokes and easy confidence let me relax. Let me be myself. If I felt a sudden urge to destroy something, he barely noticed. That, or he helped make the destruction into a work of art. If I wanted to design a weird new flower for a garden, he worked with me to realize my vision. If I just wanted to hover in the sky and take in the beauty of a sunset, he hovered with me quietly, enjoying it by my side.

But I knew it couldn't last forever. I knew it. And tomorrow I would gladly hash it all out, and get a bitch slap or get waterboarded or whatever Cahal felt was necessary. *Tomorrow.* Today was dragon day. I could not let him ruin my high on dragon day!

"Come on. Let's go wander the grounds while we wait." I pulled my hair up and fastened it into a ponytail.

"I do not wish to go." Cahal clasped his hands behind his back, still looking out the window. "I'll stay here."

I narrowed my eyes at him. "You're up to something."

"If I see your delight over the dragons, I will more thoroughly understand your reaction to this place. That will blind me. I have an obligation to you, and it requires me to see your slide objectively, without understanding the reasons for it."

Frustration overwhelmed me. Annoyance stoked the fire in my middle, and I knew one moment of blind rage in which I wanted to just hurl him out of the window and be done with him.

"You are coming, Cahal," I said between clenched teeth. "I will not let you miss out on dragons because you think I am emotionally unstable. I'm not. You're coming."

"No. I do not wish to go."

I balled my fists. "This is a test, isn't it." It wasn't a question, and he didn't answer. "I know you want to see their nest, or whatever it is. The last heir didn't command you to stay home because he was looking out for you—he did it to deny you something you wanted. And I know you let that little nugget slip the other day on purpose. If a vampire can't manipulate me, you sure as shit can't either."

He still didn't respond.

Knock, knock…

I turned, stalked for the door, grabbed the handle, and yanked it open. My magic kicked in without any prompting, and I ripped the whole thing off the hinges and tossed it behind me. It was the fourth door in the last week. They never seemed to be put out about repairing them. It was like a fairytale.

My father—Damn it. That *was* a mental slip.

Lucifer's eyes widened, and he stepped back with a cheeky grin. "Was it something I said?"

This was probably one reason the last heir had gone batty. Unbridled violence was entirely normal in this place. Welcomed, even. Someone who didn't express rage wouldn't do well here, especially if they didn't release any of their pent-up rage through love or lust. They'd lose themselves to it.

I, however, considered destruction great fun. It was why I'd always chased shifters around or picked fights with bigger dudes. Cahal might think it was me slipping, but that's because he'd never seen me have free rein.

My constant self-justifications were starting to be exhausting.

"Not you, no," I barked. "The freaking druid is messing with my chi."

"Ah." Lucifer clasped his hands behind his back, the same pose as Cahal, and took an air of patience. He planned to let me handle it.

"Come on," I yelled back at Cahal. "You're going."

"No, I do not wish to go."

"Notice he didn't say he *wouldn't* go," I murmured. "You're trying to force me to *make* you go, is that it? Establishing me as a tyrant?"

"You know what you want, and you know what I

want. What you do with that information is up to you," Cahal called back, resigned yet stubborn. This was indeed a test.

I was so tired of being tested. Speaking of wanting freedom.

I connected eyes with Lucifer. "What would you do?"

He turned down his mouth for a moment and then shrugged. "If I was as annoyed as you seem to be, I'd make him, probably. It's a power play. He used to have power over your actions. He is probably realizing he's losing the upper hand in your friendship."

His words turned to thoughts. *I've seen him do it before. But please know, I lost my last heir to his manipulations. I will not lose you. I will step in if I think you are in danger.*

I read the truth in his eyes. Felt the certainty in my blood. Felt a level of exhaustion I hadn't experienced before, with the different forces pushing and pulling at me, each wanting a different thing, me wanting both. But I couldn't have both, could I? I had to make a choice.

"You're coming," I said to Cahal before pushing forward, through the door. I clicked my fingers for Saint Tits by the door. "If he doesn't come on his own, drag him."

"Yes, your heinous," the demon said dutifully.

"Is it time we learn to make some fish?" Lucifer said, walking beside me down the hall.

"I'm frustrated with him. I'm not going to kill him."

"Noted."

It wasn't until we made it down the steps at the front of the castle that I paid attention to my surroundings. A golden buggy waited out front, an empty harness hanging in the air where a horse would usually go. It didn't have wheels but hovered off the ground as though it did. The door stood open, and a demon attendant in a horsey chauffeur outfit, possibly stolen from a Cinderella retelling, waited beside it.

I stared at it for a long moment, taking in the demon's little jacket with large buttons over its decaying and disgusting flesh crawling with bugs. Crisp white riding pants, adorned with a jaunty golden stripe down the sides, hung off what had to be sticky legs. A white top hat adorned its hairless and flaking head, a gold hat band matching the stripes on the pants.

"Is this some sort of joke?" I asked.

"Yes." Lucifer laughed and stepped forward. "Horrifying, right? Truly a nightmare." He laughed again, and I cracked a grin because the fact that it tickled him so was comedy in itself.

He handed me up into the buggy and took the cushy seat beside me. "How about your druid friend? I'd planned for him to ride in here with us, but I can always summon another buggy for him and his annoying attitude."

I huffed out a laugh. "Another buggy would be best." It would keep me from feeling the guilt that was worming into my chest.

Once we were on our way, I watched out the window as we passed the vibrant green landscape, stippled with pops of color. I didn't look back to make sure Cahal was in tow. He'd apparently be happier not to be.

"Why were you so eager to make the druid come?" Lucifer asked as we made our way.

I continued staring out the window. "He wants to come. Or he did." I ran my hand over my face. "I'm just… It's getting difficult to manage everyone's expectations."

"Yes, I can see that."

"You're part of the problem."

"I realize. What can I do? Do you need a break from training? Should we put off the dragons? We have all the time you need. The elves are stirring, building their army, but so far my spies say they are meeting with resistance. The warrior fae have left the Flush—which you knew—but now they have left the Realm, the shifters with them. They are all congregating in the Brink. The elves are trying to accrue enough people who can pass as human to go after them and drag them back. When that skirmish is underway, we will have an opening to confront the elves for what they've done. We do not need to rush your training, especially at the pace you learn."

A rush of anger stole my breath. Yes, I did want to confront the elves. I wanted to show them what true pain felt like. Unending, merciless pain that crawled into every part of a person until they wanted to beg for death. My stubbornness was the only reason I hadn't broken. That, and knowing Darius would come for me.

I shook my head, forcing myself to remember the big picture. It wasn't just me and the Underworld that had a problem with the elves. I needed to remember that.

Maybe Cahal was right. Maybe I was starting to slip a little. Roger would likely need all the help he could get, and the natural dual-mages were almost certainly down here with me. Darius, too, and maybe some of his vampires. I had the pyramid of power down with me in the Underworld.

But wasn't my training incredibly important? I needed to be down here. Why not just enjoy myself while I was?

I nodded, watching as we passed a sect with a large gothic mansion that sprawled within twisted thorns. I grinned at the sight.

"Yeah," I said, not really sure what that was in answer to.

I sat up straight and looked ahead, my mind churning.

I'd train for a week or two more. That was the plan anyway, wasn't it? I'd enjoy myself, take *me* time, and get to know my biological father. After that, I would leave as planned. Darius and the others were obviously taking their sweet time. There was no reason I shouldn't do the same.

But one thing was for certain.

"I want to send Cahal away. I don't want to kill him, but I need a little space."

"How about we put him in a different wing?"

"I don't want him to be a prisoner. I probably still want to see him. I just need a little space," I repeated.

"Of course. Easily done. I can give you a viewer screen so you can keep track of him, to ensure I am not torturing him."

"Like your last heir did?"

"Ah, you know about that, do you? Yes, my last heir grew tired of him. Grew tired of the same push and pull you are experiencing. It…worked out badly, in the end. I clued in quite late."

"Or did your last heir try to recruit him, and it didn't work?" That was what Cahal had told me.

Lucifer frowned at me. "Recruit him for what?"

I frowned back and then narrowed my eyes. It was a really good question, actually. What was there for Cahal to do here, really? With all of my power, and all of the forces at my disposal through my father, I wouldn't need Cahal as an assistant or for protection. He didn't have the sort of power the top beings here could boast. Nor did he have the know-how to thoroughly navigate this place. He didn't really fit in here, just as my father was implying. So why would the previous heir have needed him for anything but companionship?

Had Cahal just told me a story to pull at my heartstrings?

CHAPTER 14

THE BUGGY RIDE was mostly quiet as we traveled past the neighboring sects and into the wilds behind the castle. The landscape changed from various Brink scenes—rolling hills, rocky mountains, or serene meadows—into ones that would be more fitting for the Realm, like puffy trees and manufactured flowers and golden cobblestones. At one point I'd looked down and asked, "Is that real gold?"

"Why do you want to know, so you can steal some bricks?" Lucifer had laughed. "It is real, and most of it has already been stolen once. I took them from the elves many years ago. I wanted to prove how easy it was to take their things. They weren't pleased."

It was like talking to myself. I could not believe I could be so like this man, whom I had not known growing up. The lesson in genetics was pretty intense.

The various landscapes were apparently his trials. He tested out designs back here, where most people didn't travel on foot or even in buggies. Only the more powerful demons dealt with dragons, and they could alter their shape. Basically, they could fly.

"What do I have to look forward to?" I asked as the landscape subtly morphed into rolling fields of purple and blue. Above, a great winged beast soared through the sky, its aqua scales glittering in the faux-sun. I watched it pump its mighty wings before it dove, zooming down toward the ground and then turning over and climbing back up, enjoying the day.

My heart pumped harder. Excitement curled through me. Forcing Cahal to go was the right decision. I knew he'd want to see these things. He'd just been messing with me earlier, and in the end, he'd be thankful for this.

"Dragons do not like strangers," Lucifer said. "They do not like people interrupting their territory, and they can become quite violent about it. I'll be with you, and if we stay on the path, it negates much of the risk. But the second you approach a dragon, it won't care about me. It will only care about you, and it'll want you to prove your worth in battle."

No problem. I'd been proving my worth in battle my whole adult life.

"How do you coax one to bond you?" I asked.

"After you prove your worth, it will connect with your mind and let you ride. From there, your friendship will begin. The bond is like any bond—you learn about each other, begin to feel mutual trust, and that trust develops into a partnership."

"But...what if, when you're learning about each other, you realize that one of you is an asshole?"

"Their magic gives them a sort of...emotional *Sight*, is the only way to describe it. They can feel your magic, and you through it. If they cannot handle an asshole, they will not engage with you."

"Ah. So if I try to battle a dragon that doesn't want to battle..."

"It'll fly away. Or it will resist, and the other dragons nearby will join with it to kill you to stop unwanted advances."

"Gotcha."

"Dragons are loyal like no other creatures in the world. Once they find someone worthy, they will stick with that creature until the end of time, to their own detriment, if need be."

"Can they only bond demons? Are demons the only ones they find worthy?"

"Not at all. It's just the only option they have. They are loyal to the Underworld, and given I had to cut us off from the Realm, they remain here with us."

"Like the unicorns remain in the Realm?"

"Yes. Unicorns are very similar to dragons, though they tend to be a herd animal. They will work with another creature, but they aren't as fiercely loyal. Great in battle, though."

"And Vlad will help you use them to your benefit?"

He didn't comment, but his ghost of a grin gave him away.

I took a deep breath, and everything within me wobbled again. What Cahal had said hit me. Not having Darius here to chat about strategy was gnawing away at my heart. I wanted to see Penny meet the dragons, because her magical thievery would give them a run for their money, I just knew it. And Emery would fall all over himself to ride one of those great beasts. It was a fitting battle companion for a rogue natural.

I shook my head sadly, staring out the window.

"You're in a black place," Lucifer said quietly. "Can I help?"

"No."

Out of the corner of my eye, I saw him nod. He looked away. And that made it just a little harder.

A TRUCKLOAD OF minutes later, the buggy turned and slowed. I blinked, having been staring at nothing for some time, my thoughts churning. Huge black gates, currently opened, rose into the sky, topped with sharp spikes. Thorny bushes crowded the space at the bottom of the gates and ivy trailed along the top. A thunderous rumble shook my bones but settled down quickly. What sounded like, and probably were, enormous wings beat at the air.

"Your dragon is huge, right?" I asked, my teeth just about to chatter. I wasn't cold—the temperature here was as perfect as the Realm—but I was suddenly nervous. I remembered fighting that rainbow dragon at the circus. That thing had been crazy.

Then again, I'd been trying to conceal my magic at the time. I wouldn't have to worry about that here.

"Very. One of the largest," he said, and I heard a little smugness in his voice.

"And it chose you?"

"Yes. As did several others. But hers was the battle offer I accepted."

"Oh." I climbed from the buggy, seeing the second buggy behind us, black instead of gold, probably matching Cahal's mood. He made no move to get out. "More than one can pick you?"

"Not usually. But…" He pushed his hand against his chest. "I'm the king of the Underworld. There is status in being bonded to me. Many of them wanted to reap the rewards of carrying me on their back. It happens every time I need to bond a new dragon. They are not immortal."

"What rewards?"

"She is the queen of the dragons—she has the choicest nest, gets carcasses brought to her—"

"Carcasses of…?"

"Of various Underworld animals. Once you are

thoroughly trained, we can travel the wilds. Many areas are incredibly dangerous. I know you'd be fine, but some of the creatures are important to the ecosystem, and I can't risk you killing the wrong thing."

It took me a moment to unpack all of that. It was entirely clear there was a good deal of the Underworld I had yet to learn. It was like scratching the surface and then falling down a huge well.

"Anyway, when she is heavily pregnant or with new life, I hunt out the choicest hides and bring them to her. It is something any dragon rider would do, but…"

"You're the most powerful, and therefore can wrangle the best…hide. Hides."

"Exactly, yes. Plus treats and baths and…"

I shook my head, not even able to imagine what it took to bathe such an enormous beast. I let it go for now.

"And why don't the other dragons get those things? Money?"

"No." He shrugged and walked to the center of the gate. "I take care of what is mine. She is my responsibility, and so she will have whatever she needs. She repays me by marching into battle if I need, or taking me for a pleasure cruise."

"Or hunting down the latest disturbance in your kingdom."

He smiled. "Not going to let that go, are you?"

"Not likely, no. She killed innocents."

"No one in the Edges is innocent, and you let her do it so as not to reveal your magic."

A grin wrestled with my lips, and I had to stop from laughing. "You have me there."

"Yes. Trying to act high and mighty when you are no better than me…" He *tsked.*

I did laugh this time. "I should be better than you. Everyone agrees."

"Everyone? Who, the druid? Your vampire? They turn you against me when they don't know me?"

He had me there, too. "So the other dragon owners don't do as much for their dragons?"

"It depends, but largely no. I am overbearing in the extreme when it comes to taking care of what's mine. If only your mother were here—she would back me up on that."

My gut twisted and longing stole over me. I knew she would. I'd heard stories. More stories than I cared to, even. The sexier ones on her deathbed had made me want to pour bleach in my ears.

"And yet I am trapped down here," I murmured, because I had to. I was torn—so torn—and I needed some sign that he was terrible. That I was trapped, which would make him the bad guy. Which would make the choice to leave easier.

Lucifer waved his hand, and Cahal came floating

out of the buggy, arms firmly crossed over his chest.

"You are learning right now, and hopefully shedding some of the untrue stories you've been fed. After I am sure you know me—really *know* me—and are leaving for the right reasons, I will let you go. It will break my heart, but I will let you go, hoping you will come back."

I stared into his eyes, looking for the lie. Looking for the flat expression that would indicate he was holding something back. I only saw earnestness, and a shadow of worry.

I blew out a breath, apparently the way I dealt with things beyond my control, which was this whole endeavor. I turned toward the gate. "What happens now?"

"We enter the dragons' territory and see what comes."

Something flowered in my middle. "See what comes" was exactly the way I liked doing things. No planning, no strategizing, just walking in and rolling with the punches.

"No sweat." I sliced through Lucifer's magic on Cahal, dropping the druid to the ground. He staggered but caught himself before falling on his face. Lucifer's expression flattened. "He's *my* pet. I should hold the leash."

Lucifer didn't comment, and I didn't wait for him

to. I was a little surprised myself, actually, though I wouldn't allow myself to dwell. I'd just chopped through his magic like I usually chopped through that of mages. Without thinking, I'd learned to counteract him. Was it the godly magic infusing me? Or could he do the same with me and hadn't mentioned it?

"Stop sulking. You want this," I told Cahal as I marched toward the open gate.

He followed me like a shadow. "It is not up to you to determine what I do and do not want."

"No, it isn't. Which is why I relied on what you said about dragons. Remember when you were whining about wanting to see them? I remember. Which is why you are here. You're welcome."

"This is extremely dangerous."

"Yes. All of this is extremely dangerous, and you must be up for it because you followed my unconscious ass down into the Underworld. Seriously, stop sulking. I don't want to have to fight on your behalf."

"You're going to have to. I don't have a sword."

I hesitated as I crested the territory and glanced back. Dang. He was right—I'd forgotten about his sword.

"It's fine." I started walking again. "You'll improvise."

"You sound just like *your father.*"

That was supposed to be a dig. Given I liked my old

man—what I knew of him, anyway—I ignored it. So did Lucifer, who was trailing us.

I'd always figured dragons would live in caves under buildings, the way they did in Brink stories, and sleep on piles of gold or hoarded treasure. And I supposed that was partially true here, since this place *was* an enormous cave. But Lucifer had done up the illusion to make it seem like there was nothing but limitless sky.

The fence stretched into the distance on both sides, and I couldn't see the back of it. Vast tracks of green lands spread out in front of me with rolling hills, tended bushes, and various tufts of brightly colored flowers. A soft orange sky held a few puffy white clouds, the faux-sun shedding warm lighting.

To my distant right, a shedlike structure held a sleeping beast, curled up in the soft grasses, its nose sending up tendrils of smoke. Nearer to us, on the left, a dragon lay in a ramshackle barn. Regardless of their shantylike dwellings, these dragons were magnificent, their scales glittering, their wings tucked in, and their great heads nestled against their bodies.

"These have the weaker…handlers, then?" I asked, continuing on.

"You don't *handle* a dragon," Cahal whispered. "You are a team with them. You are their ally."

"These have the weaker allies, then?"

"Yes," Lucifer said, not stepping to my side as he

would usually do. He wanted me to meet this head-on, by myself. It was almost certainly a rite of passage. "Usually bonded dragons nest in the sects of their riders. But some of the weaker riders aren't given enough space in their sect, or they simply don't have permission because larger, more powerful dragons are occupying the available space. Because of that, their dragons stay here with what provisions they are given. Dragons can hunt for themselves, and the weather is always perfect, so it isn't a hardship for them by any means."

"So the dragons that live here are mostly riderless dragons or weaker ones?"

"Basically, yes, though bonded dragons do come to stay in their old nests from time to time. They visit each other, like demons or humans do."

"And the stronger dragons…"

"Typically reside to the rear right of the territory," Lucifer supplied.

I headed back that way. There was something new in his eyes now. A soft light had taken over the cunning gleam. An openness had diluted the analytical intelligence, giving the illusion that one could look down into his soul. Love glistened in his gaze. Adoration.

He noticed my assessing stare, my slowing gait, and glanced off in the direction I assumed his dragon resided. "I enjoy seeing her. She's been with me a long time. No one else in the worlds knows me better."

"You have a soft spot for your dragon." I continued on, my heart warming. "That is a vulnerability, no?"

"Vulnerabilities aren't something to be afraid of. They make us stronger in the end. You cannot really hate unless you know how to love. And you cannot revel in rage if you don't know great passion. You cannot claim true vengeance unless you've felt the rush of fear that something you love has been hurt or lost. You will never know your true strength unless you give in to your greatest weaknesses. I enjoy vulnerabilities. I enjoy feeling the edge of my comfortability. I enjoy the rage that comes from fear. A rage I will unleash on the elves when the time is right."

I pondered that as we traveled a path laid with small white-yellow stones. The area had ample space but little magic, most of the beasts sleeping right now, curled up tightly and not bothering with me at all. I'd expected a little more alarm at the stranger in their midst. I said as much.

"Dragons hunt in the night or early morning, when the wilds are most active. The larger, more powerful dragons usually make the first and largest kills. The smaller, weaker dragons go out after they do. As such, the weaker dragons make it to their nests later. The more powerful ones should be rousing now, at their height of energy."

"You didn't plan to make it easy on me, huh?"

"What would be the fun in that?"

The dragons were getting larger now, some glittering with multiple colors and others more monochrome. A few lifted their heads now, peering at us as we passed. Their acute stares, intelligence behind those slitted eyes, made my stomach churn with equal parts fear and excitement.

"They sense your magic," Lucifer said quietly. "They wouldn't bother looking up at me, knowing I have already bonded. But you are just as powerful in a different way, I am sure of it. It is rousing their interest. You will have your pick of the best today, mark my words. You will make a good match. A noble match."

I preened. He'd said "noble."

"We are coming up on the larger dragons now," he murmured. "Most of these have not been bonded, to my knowledge."

Pushed off from the path, none of these had shelter, unless they'd created a sort of burrow between the trees. They lifted their mighty heads to watch us as we made our way past, their wings fluttering at their sides. One's tail lifted, the end spiked like a dinosaur. That would put a few holes in my middle.

"They are regal creatures, and they don't settle," Lucifer said. "They are pure of heart and intent. If they choose you, it means they believe in you. They will never let you down, not if they can help it. They will fight with you to the death. Once they choose someone, that's it for them, for life. It's a decision they do not make lightly."

A strange sort of tension wormed through me as one of the dragons pushed to its feet, the motion shaking the tall grouping of trees next to its bed. It didn't move forward, though, and it wasn't looking at me. Its focus was on Cahal behind me, who was watching it with wary eyes tinged with excitement. We were clearly entering the territory of dragons of the level that would take notice of him.

Great trees rose into the sky, much denser the farther in we got. Bushes grew in size, too, covering more of the land. Shapes moved within the shadows, looking out at us through the cover of foliage. Some dragons stepped out now, watching us pass.

"Those have riders," Lucifer said, noticing them. "They are taking an interest, though. I have never escorted someone through here, not even my staff. I always come alone. These dragons are wondering why the change. Soon everyone will know of my heir."

"Because they'll sense my magic?" I asked, my voice unnaturally subdued. Anxiety ran through me as I witnessed the raw power of these creatures pushing up to their feet, moving toward and around us.

"Yes." He left it at that.

A pastel-pink dragon roared, the sound infused with magic, and a wave of darkness swept over me. Depression rose and tried to pull me under, dragging tears from my eyes, until the last echoes faded away. The beast stomped out through the trees. Wood cracked and branches swayed, leaves raining down. Into the clearing it went, its great wings snapping out to either side, the ends sporting wicked claws. It huffed, and smoke billowed out of its nostrils.

"That's yours, obviously," I said to Cahal.

"Dragons don't belong—"

"Yes, yes, I know." I fashioned a sword out of air and stepped in front of him, blocking the way. "It's your favorite color, though. Match made in heaven."

His large, strong hand covered my shoulder, and he gently pushed me to the side. "I would rather die by the efforts of this mighty creature than watch you slowly lose your mind and eventually give in to madness and kill me. I will take what comes, sword or no."

"Its roar especially suits you, Mr. Downer."

The dragon lumbered closer, at least twelve feet high, its broad chest filling before it blew out a blast of blistering fire, spraying the area in front of us. I threw up an ice shield immediately, keeping the heat from washing over Cahal and rendering him crispy.

I sent a blast of icy air to push the beast back until we sorted this out. It trumpeted, surprised, before crashing through the trees behind it and lowering its head, focused on me now. It crouched there, waiting.

"I didn't bring you here to see you get killed," I said. "What's the plan? You wanted to see them, but you didn't say anything about choosing one. You don't have your sword, remember?"

"What would a sword do against a dragon? Let me by." His hand was on my shoulder again. His gaze was on the dragon watching us. "You've scared her. Let me by."

"Well, I'll be damned," Lucifer said softly behind us. "And I was."

I glanced back at him.

"By the angels, those bastards," he supplied, winking. He jerked his head at Cahal, who was walking forward slowly, his arms out. The dragon shook itself, still crouching, and ruffled its wings. "He's hearing the call. The dragon has offered to spar with him—to see if he is worthy of a bond."

"I mean." I held out my hand. "It's his favorite color."

"Yes, it's a hideous color for a hideous man. I hate pastel. There's no life in it."

I had to agree with him there, except for the bit about Cahal.

"Just so we're clear." I put up my hands and walked forward a little, speaking to the dragon. "I will not let you kill him. Beat the ever-loving shit out of him if you must, but do not kill him. Do you understand?"

The dragon rose slowly to its full height, the leaves sliding off its scaled back.

"Leave me. It'll be fine." Cahal waved me away before stepping toward it, his boots lost to sight amidst the dense greenery off the path.

I gritted my teeth but moved back slowly, stopping when I felt Lucifer's hand on my other shoulder.

"I regret bringing him now," I mumbled as the dragon lunged forward, its fangs reaching down from its open mouth.

Cahal dodged to the side easily before punching it in the side of the face. His whole body went taut, and he gracefully darted backward. He shook out his hand. Dragon scales were like armor. Now he knew.

"He should have his sword," I mumbled, hands on my hips, adrenaline running through me.

"You really care for that druid," Lucifer said.

"He's a pain in my ass, but he's my responsibility. I don't want him killed."

Cahal grunted as the dragon turned and whipped its tail around, lashing out. But he was already rolling to the side, still so graceful even while taking on a dragon single-handedly, with no weapons. He did have magic, though.

Shadows pooled and coalesced around him, blurring his form and making him all but invisible. The dragon roared, and the depression pushed on me like a weight, hard to carry.

On my first trip through the Underworld, a dragon's roar had spread fear. Panic. Clearly they each had a different magic, and this one was just as effective. On me, anyway.

Cahal ran under the dragon, bending to do so, before punching upward and hitting it in the stomach.

The dragon belched out fire and hopped, trying to look under it, missing him running out to one side. His magic clearly worked on these creatures.

The dragon roared again, frustrated, I could tell, before stomping all around. Cahal started back in, launching onto the lowered head and scaling its neck to its shoulders.

"He should've tried for a larger dragon," Lucifer said, a little bit of awe in his voice.

"It isn't about the size; it's about the motion in the ocean," I said without thinking.

"I am thankful I've never had to give that excuse to a woman."

"Ew."

"You brought it up."

The dragon trumpeted, surprised again, and its wings beat the air. Its body lifted into the air, and it was off and away, Cahal hanging on for dear life.

"Dang it," I said, wanting to jog forward, to trap it in the air and lift Cahal to safety. But in a moment it was beyond my reach, soaring into the orange sky.

"And there you go." Lucifer started forward. "The druid is powerful enough to attract a dragon."

I jogged after him, watching the dragon continue to climb. "Are they going to keep battling in the air? We should stay here to make sure he doesn't get bucked off."

"The dragon would've thrown him immediately if she didn't want him on her back. They will get to know each other now."

"So that's it?" I held on to his arm while I watched the dragon soar through the sky, my adrenaline still firing, my excitement growing, and a little jealousy soaking through the other emotions. I hoped I got to soar like that. That a dragon would choose me.

With my luck, the one I tried to bond with would stomp on me and then get its dragon buddies to help kick me out of their territory. I doubted my father would be very proud if that came to pass.

"That's it for him, yes. For you? I doubt it. The higher-level dragons are this way, and I have a feeling you won't be satisfied until you pick the most fearsome one you come across."

CHAPTER 15

HE HAD ME all wrong. I didn't want the most fearsome dragon; I just wanted any old dragon. I didn't care if it was the scrawniest dragon in this whole place.

They were more spread out now, the beasts we passed larger and more robust. They stared us down, many taking a few paces forward. Strange presences touched me, like fingers jabbing my chest, but they all felt wrong. Annoying, as any finger jabbing your chest would be.

That was when I realized I'd been fooling myself—not just any dragon would do.

"I'll fall back now," Lucifer said, and he did, leaving me to walk alone. No druid by my side this time. No safety blanket.

I didn't need it. Didn't want it.

I picked up my pace, because that was my jam. I'd prefer to run at danger than from it, more often than not. And this was dangerous, I could feel it. The dragons' exploratory touches were harder now, packing more force and power.

At the end, way at the back, I saw the big black dragon that I knew was Lucifer's. I remembered that thing chasing me out of the Underworld, burning everything in its path.

It trumpeted out in pleasure, feeling its—her—rider. A big pile of bones sat to her side, and trees and foliage covered her area, Lucifer obviously taking great pains to make her as comfortable as possible. He hadn't been lying.

She was taken, though.

To my left I spied a few others of equal size, all standing now, looking my way. Annoyance flared through them. Surprise too, though. Could they feel my magic or power scale even from this distance?

They waited near their nests, the nearest a good fifty yards out.

I eyed them all, not sure what I was looking for.

The closest to Lucifer's dragon held its wings tightly to its body, the faux-sun glistening off its forest-green hide. Two white horns rose from its otherwise smooth head, and its wide chest was currently filling with air. It was readying for battle.

Magic shoved my middle, like an opened hand slapping my chest.

I rubbed it away and looked at the next dragon, a stunning metallic gray-blue with a metallic purple chest and underbelly. Its wings rested loosely against its sides, shimmering like gems, with curved claws at the ends. It also had horns rising from a spiked head, these in onyx. Its burst of magic dug into my chest, rooted around, and squeezed my freaking heart. I sucked in a startled breath.

It didn't let go when I tried to mentally brush it away. It didn't give me a chance to look at the sparkly dragon next to it. Instead, it held on, daring me to act. To push back. To tear its hold from my body.

I did, ripping through its hold with my magic, slicing like I had with Lucifer's. Its hold fell away, and I felt its shock. It didn't trumpet, though. It didn't give any outward sign that I'd surprised it.

The last dragon waited, somewhat tense. I had no idea why I knew that, but I could sense it as plain as day. Its white scales glistened, each outlined in dusty gray. No horns crowned its head, and its touch felt like a beautiful day at the park, welcoming and lovely. It ruffled its wings, and I took that as a gentle come-hither. The thing was incredibly beautiful, and I knew it would be sweet and kind and made for Penny. It probably liked rocks and killing things over its shoulder while it ran away.

I refocused on that steel-blue-gray dickhead who'd tried to push me around. It needed a lesson in politeness, and I was going to give it.

Lucifer's laughter followed me through the grass as I charged at the blue-gray dragon. An air sword filled my hand, and suddenly fire was spurting down on me. I brushed it away as the magical hold filled my chest again, pounding now, trying to distract me with its intense gust of power.

"Two can play at that game, you bastard." I sent my own shock of power, punching for its middle.

It fly-lumbered at me, its wings barely skimming the air just to make running a little less awkward for it. These creatures weren't meant for ground combat, their true prowess soaring through the sky. This dragon, though, had figured out how to reduce the handicap.

Male.

The thought reverberated through my mind. Its shape loomed over me, at least twenty feet at the shoulder.

"Yeah. That's what I said—dickhead. Same thing."

He spun at the last minute, his tail whipping around. I'd seen this trick. I jumped over before cleaving one of his legs with my air sword. Power reverberating off him, he hastened to turn back. I copied Cahal and ran under him, but it didn't work out quite like I'd planned.

I was about to slash my sword upward at its belly…and suddenly the ceiling was falling.

"Holy—" Sword forgotten, I pushed air up with all

my might, stopping the dragon from squishing me beneath him. "Good call, bud," I ground out as he thrashed, trying to break my hold. "Smart thinking."

I gave a big shove and rolled out from under him, jumping to my feet and lighting the grass all around him on fire.

He lit an even larger area of grass on fire.

"Fine." I punched him with air and, for good measure, sent an air spear under him before shifting its trajectory so it cut upward. I didn't have to deliver the pain in person. I kept forgetting about that.

The dragon howled, and blood poured down from his belly in a steady gush.

"Oh shit—" I grabbed him in a vise of air and ran under him, the strain from holding him in place covering my forehead with a sheen of sweat. He roared, and I felt his anger, pain, and surprise. "Let's remember who started this."

The blood was only dripping now, the cut already healing. Good—dragons healed like vampires. I closed the gash with air before running back out, releasing my hold on him but leaving my air bandage. It probably didn't help all that much, but it was all I could think to do.

His head, half the size of my body, dipped until his eyes were even with mine, fifteen feet away. Too close, but I didn't want to look like a coward and back up.

Deep yellow eyes with black irises surveyed me, his focus beating into me, his magic now warming me from the inside out. He huffed, and steam washed through the air between us. His head dipped a little more.

Your magic is unknown to me, he thought, and I nearly peed myself.

A dragon was speaking to me!

Dragons could speak, and one was speaking to me!

I grinned like a lunatic and nodded like a fool. "I'm different."

The dragon had washed away every ounce of cool I possessed. Now I knew what Penny always felt like.

He didn't move, and it seemed like he was waiting for something. I remembered what Lucifer had told me about the bonding, something I'd witnessed with Cahal and his dragon, and hoped I hadn't hurt the dragon too badly for what came next.

Barely able to contain my excitement, I ran and jumped, using my hovering abilities to keep me airborne for longer. I landed on his shoulders and quickly turned, slinging my legs to the sides of his neck and hoping he didn't call out *psych!* and kill me on the spot.

The great wings pumped, lifting us up immediately, leaving the ground.

"Oh my God, is this really happening?" I giggled like a little girl as we climbed up and up, zooming into the air faster than I would have thought possible.

I am Archion. I have been waiting for a creature worthy of my flight.

The air whipped around me, and I was so glad I'd fixed that glitch. This wouldn't be the same without wind making my eyes water. I fashioned air glasses.

I'm Reagan. Reagan Somerset. Of the Brink. If I didn't get a hold of myself, I was going to punch myself in the face. Unicorns were cool, but unicorns didn't want to give people rides and they didn't talk. Or fly.

This was blowing my mind. Cahal missing this? He was so going to say, *You told me so*. Maybe I was still going mad, but that didn't change how right I was about the dragons.

What are you, Reagan Somerset? Archion asked. *I know your magic, and I also do not. It is incredibly powerful. I think I have gotten lucky with your choice in me.*

I might've preened a little at that.

I'm only half from the Underworld, on my father's side.

Lucifer.

Yeah, good guess.

Not a guess. Part of your magic is just like his. It is the other part, the one that makes you more, that I do not know. Is it Brink magic?

He banked hard left, and I caught sight of a sparkly pink spot up ahead.

Oh. I leaned forward and pointed even though my finger was still mostly behind his great head and he wouldn't be able to see it. *Can you catch up to that one? My friend is riding it. Her. The pink dragon. With my friend.*

That was it. Punch in the face warranted. How did Penny get through life?

Her name is Coppelia. And it would be my pleasure.

He straightened out like an arrow, and if we'd been in a movie, he would have shouted, *Hold on!* as he darted forward. His wings beat fast and hard, incredibly powerful. My grin was so wide that it stretched my face.

It's godly magic, on my mother's side, I thought as we blasted through the air. Another dragon, yellows and oranges, almost lost to the sky, glittered way off to the right.

Godly magic. I am not familiar with that. It is jarring, the feel of it. I like it.

Yeah, I liked the warmth seeping into my middle from his magic, too. Comforting and energizing and so freaking cool. I was riding a dragon!

We came at Cahal from behind. Directly behind, so the pink dragon—Coppelia—wouldn't be able to see us. Archion slowed to her pace, still creeping up on her, then darted forward once more and bent to nip the underside of her tail.

My kind of dragon.

Coppelia yanked in her tail and dipped. I barely heard Cahal's "Whoa!" He hadn't been expecting that.

We dove down with them, Archion larger, stronger, and much faster, gaining on her and then pulling to the side. She hit the brakes, Cahal holding on for dear life, and Archion continued on, banking softly in a big circle before heading back around. That must've been the sign of *just messing with you!*

Coppelia slowed the harried beating of her wings, waiting for us to catch up.

"Good, right?" I gave Cahal a thumbs-up when we soared alongside them, Archion needing half as many pumps of his wings to stay in flight.

Cahal's smile matched my own. *I thank you for this.*

"Ha!" I pointed at him. "I told you."

Incoming, Archion thought, giving no notice before diving.

My smile turned into a grimace as I scrabbled with my hands to find purchase. My legs slid. I definitely shouldn't dare looking down…

Oh crap, that was a long way to go splat if my hovering skills went on the fritz.

What's happening? I thought desperately, finding the edges of his wings with my feet and bracing myself.

Your father would like to test you, which means testing me. Grip me tightly. Trust in my ability to keep you on my back.

The smile dripped off my face. I chanced a look back this time.

The large black dragon was coming up fast on our heels, Lucifer braced on its back, a grin on his face.

Let's do this. I found a ridge along Archion's shoulders and squeezed my knees in close, which was as good as it was going to get. This might be like riding a bike, but the first time doing that wasn't fun either. Not without training wheels.

Archion banked hard, then dove, gaining speed. The force flattened my cheeks, but I pushed up like a jockey on a racehorse. We curved right, and then Archion was pumping those incredible wings, not gaining height but going faster, so fast the ground was a blur, much too close now, the treetops skimming his belly. I didn't know if I'd have the presence of mind to hover if I fell off. I'd probably freeze up and go splat. Lucifer was still on our heels—or tail, in this case.

How do we win this? I thought as Archion left the dragon territory and sailed out over the green landscape.

I do not know. I can evade Tatsu on my own, but you are a new rider, and I fear you might fall off if I—

Go for it, I thought, bracing myself. *Don't evade, though. Attack. Just get higher so I have more room to catch myself. It wouldn't be the first time I fell off a dragon.*

I felt the surprise in that, and up we went. Higher and higher, Lucifer still on our tail, his smile somewhat less satisfied. He had to know the lengths I would go to in order to win. It was a problem. I was not working on it.

Give him hell, I thought as Archion kept climbing. And climbing.

I was almost having second thoughts. In a moment, I knew I would be.

Archion straightened out, curled up his wings, and curved back over himself. The force of the turn nearly yanked my right hand and legs from their hold, but I tightened my muscles and held firm, moving across his back and lowering until my front nearly touched his back.

Lucifer's eyes widened as we bore down, and I bet no one had ever dared attack him before. I added a little injury to the insult, smacking him with air as we hurtled by, Archion just barely clipping his dragon's tail with sharp teeth.

I looked up as we dove, but the little push of air didn't seem to have displaced Lucifer. I gripped on tightly again, swearing as Archion rolled.

Well done, he thought as he pulled out of it, and then my stomach dropped out. He was diving, the other dragon rushing to clash with us.

Holy…balls! I dodged a very aggressive swing of a

spiked tail before a blast of fire rolled over us, Lucifer probably afraid to knock me off the dragon. I wouldn't begrudge him that fact.

Archion was hurtling downward one minute, then soaring up the next, and the force of it ripped me loose.

"Ooohh shiii—"

I fell through the air, back pointed at the ground, watching as Archion raked the underside of the black dragon's belly with his claws, opening up deep red scores that immediately started dripping crimson.

"That is some dirty fighting right there," I mused, still falling through the air, amazingly not worried about it.

It was probably panic. Panic had made me numb.

I awkwardly spun and pulled my magic around me, putting on the brakes slowly at first, and then more quickly, seeing the ground rushing toward me. A couple of football fields to go. I had time.

Almost there, I heard. Archion was trying to be everywhere at once, clearly battling the handicap of a new rider all on his own.

Sparkly pink caught my eye, coming closer on the right, Cahal rushing to save me. It was then I noticed the sky around us, glittering color everywhere. What must've been every dragon in the area was currently flying, probably watching the mock-battle between Lucifer and me. That, or they'd taken to the air to impress the boss.

Slow yourself a little more, I heard. Cahal's dragon banked, leaving the air clear for Archion to rush in.

I did as he said, my energy draining rapidly, although I had plenty left to get down if I needed to. But I didn't.

Metallic blue-gray slipped right below me before putting on the brakes for a brief moment. I released my magic and fell the rest of the five feet, hitting his back and latching on tightly.

Sorry about that, I said as he immediately climbed, no time lost. *Beginner's foibles.*

Do not be sorry. He straightened out, heading for Lucifer. *That was masterful. Not many would allow that move, knowing they would need to fall.*

I didn't realize what you were doing, or that I would fall, actually. But it's not like I can't catch myself. I'd do it again, no problem. I shrugged.

You are courageous. Your father must be very proud.

I didn't mention that I was just an heir to Lucifer, or that I felt like preening again because a dragon, *a dragon*, was complimenting me. Instead, I leaned forward, gearing up for another attack.

Lucifer pushed up until he was basically standing on his dragon's back. He held his palms together in front of him and then pulled them apart, his gesture of peace.

Archion slowed, and Lucifer glided past us once,

and then again, a smile on his lips. Cahal trailed us.

Fantastic, Lucifer said, and gave me a thumbs-up. *Excellent! You are a natural. You were born for your post.*

Pride welled up in me and I shrugged, still not accustomed to praise.

Let's go for a ride, shall we? he said. *Let's grace the skies with our presence. It's time we officially show you off as the rightful heir and princess of the Underworld.*

I tried to ignore the thought: *You're entering the point of no return.*

Instead, I focused on my dragon, and how completely at home I felt on him. This was a good day, regardless of what tomorrow would bring.

CHAPTER 16

"WE GOT DRAGONS." Penny pointed at the sky from within her bush, just at the edges of a large weeping willow in one of the rest spots. She didn't necessarily need to be in a bush, but just in case her invisibility spell wasn't working, she wanted to take extra precautions. That spell worked for almost every type of demon, except for the crazy-powerful ones, and neither she nor Emery could figure out why. It would take Reagan to patch the hole.

They'd left the demon sex club, thankfully, after staying for nearly a week and having way too much dirty sex in too many positions. They'd even done it in public a few times! She'd given herself to Emery, over and over, completely sober. Drunk on ecstasy. On his body. On the forwardness of the place and the beings in it. It had been sexy and dirty and taboo and fun and oh my God what would her mother say…

The number of times they'd gone at it with Darius in the room…

She shuddered, feeling her face redden. Darius

hadn't seemed to notice, and obviously vampires did that kind of stuff around each other all the time, but still…she was mortified if she thought about it for too long.

The drink must've had lasting effects. That was what she was blaming it on, anyway. Certainly not the allure of getting the green light to let it all hang out…

"There's three…" Penny squinted into the azure sky, the colors changing depending on the area. It was like always living in a painting. "And two are bigger than I've seen yet. They must be important."

Emery scooted to the edges of the tree line and looked up.

Darius didn't move, crouched near the base of the tree, thinking. He was going over every possible route to the next sect, a violence one. Back when the whole place wasn't looking for them, they'd planned on taking a fairly straightforward route. That option was no longer afforded to them. Darius's demon guide had met them at the lust sect and point-blank told them there was nothing it could do. Their cover had thoroughly been blown with the stunt at the entrance, and Lucifer's minions were turning every sect inside out, starting with the more political ones, trying to find them. It had given Darius's spells back and walked away.

Darius wasn't giving up, though. He'd chosen to target a sect that wanted more magical leverage in the

Underworld. Right now they weren't political, so they would be among the last searched (Penny still didn't understand that bit), but they *could* be politically incentivized, or so Darius claimed. He had a plan laid out to get them refuge for a few days while he worked out how to get into the inner kingdom, and then what to do once they got in.

They just had to get to the violence sect he'd chosen. At present, he was thinking it would be two or three days.

The good—or weird—news was that they weren't the only ones that Lucifer was tearing the Underworld apart looking for. A group of vampires had apparently snuck in while the fog was down. Vlad, almost certainly, and surprise, surprise, he hadn't been caught either. Two masters at strategy, but what was Vlad's game?

Undermining Lucifer, probably. Laying the groundwork for when the elves were defeated.

"That's not the same patrol," Emery whispered, pulling back. His shoulders tensed as he retreated a bit more. His voice dropped and took on a hard edge. "You'll want to have a look, Darius."

Goosebumps spread across Penny's skin, and she shrank down farther into her bush. It was highly uncomfortable, but better that than to suffer whatever horrors Lucifer had in store for them. Darius's contact had said that the Great Master intended to make a public spectacle of them.

Three dragons rode overhead. The two big ones were much bigger than the typical patrol dragons, so large they nearly blotted out the sky. One had glittering black scales and the other was a metallic blue-gray, both regal in their carriage, as if they knew their riders were important people. Behind them soared a smaller pastel-pink dragon, like a little duckling. The way they lazily soared, the big ones hardly flapping their great, veined wings and the smaller one keeping pace a respectable distance back, it didn't look like they were in any sort of hurry. Actually, it looked more like a joy ride.

Her throat lodged in her chest and magic coalesced around her.

"Penny," Emery said in warning.

A human face came over the shoulder of the majestic blue-gray dragon, and Penny thought she might be sick. A familiar face, flying low enough that Penny was positive it was Reagan. It had to be. They hadn't seen anyone even remotely matching her description the entire time they'd been down here. Even the ones who tried to look human often failed in some way.

All the breath left her lungs. Tears of relief filled her eyes. Reagan was okay. She was safe, as long as she held on to that great beast. She was riding a dragon!

"I can't figure out if I am incredibly jealous or incredibly relieved." She wiped her face, shaking the bush.

Reagan's face disappeared, and then the underside of the dragon passed over them, metallic purple and really super pretty. The pink one came next, but no one looked over the side. Penny hoped it was Cahal, looking out for Reagan, being her support system and making sure she kept her head.

As the dragons continued on, Penny could just make out the back of the black-haired man atop the black dragon. Her gaze lingered on him for just a moment before returning to Reagan. Her pose was easy and effortless, her hands braced on her legs or hips as she checked out the landscape below. For all the world, she looked just as regal as the dragons. As the man beside her. Like she was checking out her kingdom.

The wide shoulders of the human-looking man behind her had to belong to Cahal, sure as rain. His pose was somewhat awkward, as though he wasn't quite comfortable. As though he wasn't having the time of his life even though he was riding on a mother-dunking dragon.

Was Penny projecting all of this? This seemed crazy. Reagan out for a joy ride, calm and pliant, even though she was basically a prisoner down here? Cahal troubled and tense, even though he was with her? That guy was never troubled. He just minded his business and waited for any unpleasantness to go away.

She had to be projecting.

Darius was at the edge of the trees now, watching them go. Penny turned to him with the question on her lips, asking what he saw with his superior vision.

She felt the blood drain from her face.

Pain flared in the vampire's eyes as his expression melted into one of obvious fear.

Her heart beat faster. "What is it?" she asked.

"We gotta go." Emery quickly stuffed his things into his backpack. They'd intended to stay here awhile, since rest stops had rules. *Mind your business. No fighting. No canoodling.* Demons went out of their way not to notice other demons. With the various types of sects, it was a necessary rule to keep the peace.

"Why?" Penny asked, needing an explanation for the sudden lead weighing down her gut. Her temperamental third eye throbbed with danger. "What's the matter?"

"That was Lucifer, right?" Emery asked Darius.

"Yes," Darius replied, staring after them. He pulled back, his eyes downcast, worry etched in every line on his face. "He is showing her the empire, and he trusts her enough to allow her and her…helper to ride dragons, without any kind of additional escort. He trusts that she is not a flight risk. Cahal's body language suggested that he disapproves of the situation. He's lost ground. His opinion no longer matters to her, or Lucifer wouldn't let him be there at all."

Penny crawled out of the bush and into the canopy beneath the tree, a little too exposed for her taste, but they were leaving anyway. She packed up her backpack.

"Okay," she said, uncomfortable pressure on her chest, "but Reagan is just pretending. Of course she is. She knows the timeline. Never bullshit a bullshitter." Tears clouded her vision. She swallowed down the lump in her throat. "She always says that. Remember, Emery? In the Flush? She'd know how to get one over on anyone. Even Lucifer. She's a survivor. She respects Cahal. She would never hurt him."

"No, but she would push him away, maybe tell him to get us to safety." Darius's face transformed back to its usual granite, empty of emotion. He was locking all the fear inside. "She isn't lost yet. He is still with her. As long as he is still with her, there's hope. We have precious little time."

Penny stood, ready to go, feeling the urgency even as her brain recoiled. "I can't believe it." Anger flash-boiled her blood. "I won't believe it. She would *never* give up her freedom to stay down here. She only did it on the island because she loves Darius, and that we all knew that wasn't going to last forever."

"It doesn't look like she *is* giving up her freedom," Emery said softly, directing Penny after Darius.

"No. Lucifer is allowing her a nice, long leash." Darius started out of the rest area at a quick pace. "So long that it probably doesn't feel like a leash at all. He'll have spies everywhere, posed as assistants. As friends. He is winning. We must hurry if we want even the slimmest of chance to…take her back."

The question rose in Penny's mind even though she would have preferred to keep it trapped in her subconscious.

What if Reagan didn't want to be taken away? What if she was truly happy down here, with her remaining parent and a royal family line? She was a princess. She probably had a huge house and unimaginable riches. She wouldn't need Darius's money. Darius's people. She'd have her own. Should they really ask her to trade all of that if she didn't want to? Could they?

CHAPTER 17

I COULDN'T BELIEVE I'd known Archion for only three days. It was insane. I felt connected to him in a way I hadn't felt connected to many others. And he wasn't even human! Although…neither was Lucifer. And neither was Darius. And Cahal…and, well, me.

Okay, being human meant nothing.

I threw my leg over his neck and hopped down to the ground. Before heading toward the castle, where Mr. Boobs waited at the bottom of the steps, I glanced back at Cahal, who was getting down off Coppelia. Both of them were mad at me—Cahal for putting him in his own apartment, and Coppelia because she was a united front with her rider. Very prickly, those two.

"At least you got to go for a ride, though," I told Cahal as he ran his hand over Coppelia's shoulder in goodbye. He was allowed to ride as long as I was with him—Lucifer's rules. He needed to be picked up at the castle steps and dropped off at the same location.

I, on the other hand, could ride whenever and however far I wanted. My restrictions were slowly being peeled away. If I wasn't followed by skittering demon assistants all the time, it would be perfection.

"Your royal heinous," Tits McGee said, hands behind its back. I lifted my eyebrows, waiting patiently and not giving in to my sudden desire to give it a little shove and see if the enormous boobs finally sent it toppling. "Your father awaits you in the eatery."

"Dining room, remember? It's a dining room," I reminded it.

"Yes. That. Your father would like to dine with you this evening."

I glanced up at the decreasing light, faux-day giving way into the eternal darkness of the cave we were in. A huge cave, much larger than made logical sense, but it was a cave all the same. The Brink would be really weird after this, with its grounding in physics and its smaller color palette, changing depending on the day or season.

"Sure, yeah." I turned to Archion, placing my hand on his leg. *Until tomorrow, friend.*

Until tomorrow. Dream sweetly.

I patted his glittering scales and turned. "Do I need to dress for dinner?"

"It is…as you…what you want."

I frowned at the demon for a moment. "Did you short out? What's the matter?"

It looked at the ground. "Nothing, your heinous. Brain chasm."

Brain fart, it meant. It was trying to learn my sayings to make me feel at home, apparently. It was so delightfully weird that I went for it.

"And the druid?" I hooked a thumb at Cahal, slinking up the castle steps behind me. He wasn't happy, I could see. Since I'd moved him, his only joy came from riding. He hated seeing me practice, or create practical jokes in the castle. He hated my delight and good humor, basically. He no longer liked that I didn't need a safety blanket. And if he weren't so damn melodramatic about it, I'd probably take him more seriously.

"Not this evening," Mr. Boobs said as we entered the castle. "The Great Master worries he might have to attend to some business for a couple days, and he would like you alone for the evening."

"Sounds good. You can escort Cahal to his apartment."

"You're not even going to walk me to my estranged home?" Cahal asked, arms straight at his sides, back bowed just a little.

"Cahal, I just spent an entire afternoon riding with you. Surely your balls must hurt? Get some ice. Or a pretty demon to rub them better. Then chill out and stare out the window while brooding. It's your favorite pastime, and I want to make sure you have ample time to do it. I'll see you tomorrow."

His gaze lingered on me for a long beat, but then he

ripped it away and started off toward the opposite stairs. I took a deep breath and hovered up to the correct landing before jogging to my rooms to get freshened up. He'd be fine. This way, he got alone time to read without being annoyed by me, my unwanted assistants, or my requests that he drink more. This way, he wouldn't have to spend his evenings telling me I was derailing. It saved us both the hassle.

In a passable dress and leather pants, I made my way back down again. Lucifer didn't seem to mind my odd fashion choices, and I liked to wear pants, just in case. He basically wore the same thing day in and day out.

On the second floor, at the back of the castle, I arrived at the closed double doors of the private dining room, a demon attendant standing to either side. Each wore a type of tux, with long flaps at the back and a bow tie but no actual pants. Instead, they had hairy goat legs ending in duck feet.

"Odd choice for formal wear," I said as they opened the doors for me. "You got the pants wrong."

"Yes, thank you, princess," the one on the right said.

"We thought that we wouldn't need pants, since we have animal parts," the other said, obviously with a better grasp of the nature of my comment.

I'd just learned to go with this place making no sense. "Yup, good logic."

They puffed out their chests and waited for me to enter before shutting the doors again. Lucifer sat at the head of the table, as usual, and stood when I entered the room.

"Reagan." He stepped to the side, dressed in his button-up white shirt and jeans.

I laughed and took the antique-looking chair beside him, the back carved with lion heads and topped with spikes. The large oval table—dark brown, almost black—held three candelabra, each with three candles, all lit. Paintings in gilded gold frames depicted battles or love scenes. Two crystal chandeliers set in the paneled celling dripped down over the table.

"What's funny?" he asked, sitting down as I did. Attendants, previously waiting around the room, stepped up to push in my chair.

"Nothing. Just the fashion of this place. It's very different from the Brink."

"Good or bad?"

"Good, because I never cared much for fashion."

"Yes, it's an arduous waste of time." He leaned back as an attendant filled our wine glasses from a brown jug. The deep burgundy drink was not wine, however. It almost tasted like punch, and it was quite a bit more alcoholic than its grape counterpart. "How are you? I missed our training today. How was your flight?"

"I'm good. The ride was great. Archion did a flip in

the air, and I stayed on."

"Fantastic." He beamed, reaching for his glass. "That's great. You are taking to the air like a squirrel takes to water."

"Not…no. A duck—It doesn't matter. But yeah, it's a good time. It's a rush."

"Yes, it is. I have always enjoyed it."

"Were you busy today? Why'd you have to cancel training?"

His eyes darkened for a moment, and he waved the thought away. "It's nothing. There is a problem with a couple of the sects—a highly political sect, and a more dormant one built on violence. Some of the members are…breaking the rules. Flouting my law, as it were. I'll need to make a public display. It is the dirtier part of running a kingdom. We'll conquer that, in time. You are too new here to be involved in something like this. We must wait until you are more established, with a better grasp on how things work."

"Yeah, no problem. I didn't think you'd want me to come."

He paused in sipping his "wine" and dropped the glass a little. "I want to involve you in all facets of this kingdom. You will have a fresh take on our operations. New ideas. I am eager to hear about them. Archion has spoken at length with Tatsu about his conversations with you. About the things you say as you fly over the lands. They are both intrigued to see what you can dream up. I am, too. It will be nice to finally share the burden of leadership. It's a lonely role, without family. Without visitors."

"If we can beat the elves back a little, maybe we can open things up a bit. Not be so closed off…"

He did take a sip then and set the glass down as the soup arrived. "Yes. We will need to make a plan for the elves. I had hoped to bring in some vampire help, but…it seems we weren't on the same page, he and I. I will rectify that misunderstanding soon. I believe I have found the vampire in question."

"Vlad, you mean? Is he the reason you closed everything down?"

To his credit, Lucifer hardly skipped a beat as he reached for his spoon. If I hadn't been watching for it, I wouldn't have noticed his surprise. Servants talked. All one had to do is hang around the hallways in one of those invisible spots and listen in. All was fair in tomfoolery and shenanigans, after all.

"Yes. He snuck in. We're not sure how. I had expected him to report to the castle, but he has not."

I tried my own soup, reached for the not-quite bread, and dipped it. I filled my mouth and talked around it, much less guarded without Cahal here, watching everything I did. "He's cunning. He'll be your best ally so long as you have what he needs. And you do.

He's probably just…" I shrugged and swallowed.

"Finish your thought." An edge had crept into his voice.

I grabbed my wine and leaned back. "I'm guessing."

"We're all guessing at this point."

"He's probably creating a network for after we handle the elves. Vampires think of the long game, always, and he's more cunning than the others."

"He should know better than to keep me waiting."

"Agreed," I said. "He and I…don't see eye to eye, so much. I've threatened him a few times. Nearly followed through the last time, but I was stopped."

"By?"

"Darius."

"Ah." He spooned soup into his mouth.

"I have been wondering where Darius might be. I thought he'd try to save me."

Lucifer ate a bit more before dabbing his mouth. "He had ample opportunity to get in before I closed everything down. If he was in a hurry, that is."

"I guess he wasn't."

Lucifer watched me for a beat. "Does it pain you, his absence?"

I ticked my eyebrows up. "That's the first time you've asked."

"I've been afraid of the answer."

I pushed my soup away, no longer hungry. Guilt

gnawed at my gut. "I was going to marry him. Maybe try for children."

"Marry a vampire?"

"I brought out his humanity. We're not sure why."

"He is a vampire—maybe he was giving you what you wanted to see…"

"Oops. You must be tired. That little dig wasn't very subtle."

Anger flashed in his eyes, and he blinked, leaning forward for the wine. "Yes. You've caught me. It would be easier for me if he wasn't in the picture. If he wouldn't barge into the picture, I suppose, given he hasn't tried to assert himself thus far. And yes, that's another dig, I suppose. Please, forgive me."

I allowed a smile and waved it away, leaning my head back and downing my drink. "I'm not going to lie. I miss him. I've been trying not to think about him. Eventually, though, I'll need to make some hard decisions."

"Eventually, but not today."

"I don't really want to talk about it, but no, not today. I'm not ready to make decisions. There's too much going on, what with Archion and practicing my magic and getting a handle on the castle and the kingdom…from the air, anyway."

"Would it help to visit a lust sect for a few days—maybe sex him away?"

I widened my eyes and then coughed out laughter. "Dude, you're biologically my dad. You can't say stuff like that. It's weird."

"You are half demon, and within that half is a representation of every facet of this world. Lust, passion, sex—they are meant to be experienced and explored. It's natural, for all creatures. If it weren't, it wouldn't feel good. I don't think it's weird at all to bring up."

I chuckled and shook my head. "It would be if you'd raised me in the Brink, trust me. No, I don't need to bang it out. I just need to think on things for a bit. I need to consider what I want my life to be. What makes me happiest. Where I can compromise. I just..." I waited for the attendant to fill up my glass again. "I need more time, that's all. And I need a clear headspace."

"A clear headspace?"

I looked away, hating myself for what I was about to say. Hating what I was about to do.

"It's Cahal. I think his usefulness has come to an end." I smoothed my hair back. "He's convoluting everything now. I can't seem to think straight when he's around."

"Look." He held out his palm. A goldfish stitched into existence.

"I'm not going to kill him. I might just send him home. Can I do that? You let him leave last time—let him leave this time."

He steepled his fingers, resting them against his lips. "I don't know. He has a bad habit of turning back up. At this point, he'll probably have to be killed. Consider it a mercy kill. He can't find his true mate, and so he is stuck in a life he does not want to lead. Put him out of his misery."

"Jesus, you don't fuck around." I rubbed my eyes.

"No, I do not. And I see the confusion he brings out in you. I saw it eat the last heir from the inside out. I will not allow him to do it to my daughter. I will kill him before he can."

"Right, fine, great, but I'm not going to kill him, and neither are you. I just need some space, that's all. So send him home and lock him out."

Silence drifted between us, and suddenly I was exhausted. Usually I could hold my own at these dinners, accustomed to dealing with manipulative people—and non-people—but this one felt...different. He wasn't his usual self. The business he had to attend to was clearly gnawing on him. If I wanted an example of the darkness residing within him, I had it.

"I will not kill Cahal." I stood. "We can talk about what to do with him when you get back. Until then, he can stay in his room, okay?" I met his gaze. "Just give me that. Give me a few days to sort things out in my head."

"Yes, of course." I turned to go. "But Reagan…" I turned back. "Think about what I said. About the mercy you would bring. Ask him if that is something he might want. He could've tried to escape, knowing I would inevitably try to talk you into killing him. But he has stayed. He confronted dragons without a weapon. He is taking chances because he is tired of this life. He needs someone stronger to grant him salvation. Ask him and see. I'll see you in a few days. Be good. I love you."

I paused by the door, my back rigid with the last thing he'd said. "That's a dirty trick."

"Yes, I know. But I *do* love you. You are my daughter, and it will pain me if something happens to you. I want to protect you. Deal with it."

"I don't love you."

"Yes, you do. You just don't want to admit it. See you in a few days. Don't get into trouble."

Lost to a fog, I barely knew where my feet were carrying me. I'd known his affection for me was growing, that I had wormed into his walls. He'd called me his daughter a couple of times since the dragon thing, and the servants had signaled a change too. I didn't know if I believed him about the love stuff, though. It was too soon. Wasn't it? Or was the situation different between a parent and their offspring than it was the other way around?

I was in front of Cahal's door before I knew it. I

didn't knock, just busted in. Why bother pretending I suddenly had decorum, especially around here?

He sat by the cold fireplace in the two-bedroom apartment, leaning toward a lit candle, book in hand. He straightened up when I entered the room.

"Let's go for a walk," I said, motioning him out.

"Did you learn how to make fish?" He put down his book calmly and followed me, bringing nothing with him.

"Is that what you want from me?" I led him down the stairs, noticing the servants and attendants glancing our way before shuffling past, curiosity in their gazes. They knew something was up. News traveled fast.

He didn't speak as we left the castle and walked down the path to my favorite garden—my mother's. Once inside, we sat down as we had that first time, only this time I didn't take his arm or hand. I didn't sit so close. Over these last couple of weeks, a wedge had been driven between us. This place had done it, but I was ultimately responsible for it.

I rubbed my eyes again. Time to shed the confusion. Time to do what I had to.

"Do you want me to kill you, Cahal?" I asked quietly, looking out at the garden, feasting my eyes on the flowers and the plants. I soaked in the silence for a moment, waiting for him to answer. Or maybe waiting for him to judge my mood and situation. On the island with Darius, he'd grown very good at reading me. Here, he'd gotten outstanding at it.

"Is that what it has come down to?" he finally asked.

"Yes. A mercy killing. Do you want a mercy killing?"

No one would disturb us out here. It was the one place my attendants let me cry in peace, mostly because I threw enormous tantrums afterward and tried to kill them. I'd thrown the fits for fun but also for insurance purposes. Now it would finally pay off.

"Sometimes, yes, I do. I'm the best at what I do. I'm god-touched, which should be something to envy, but I think that's why I'm so incredibly alone. It makes me different from my kind. I believe it has also made me incapable of finding my true mate. That, or she just isn't out there."

"Maybe it's a he?"

"I've left that possibility open. Same result. Those of my kind who don't find their true mate typically die in the line of duty. I don't know that I ever will. Sometimes the solitude is unbearable."

"Christ, I didn't realize I'd get a truth bomb."

"You asked."

"Yeah, but…not really, know what I'm saying? I'm not going to mercy-kill you, Cahal."

"Then why did you bring me here?"

"I have no fucking idea. This place has always been

a mind-fuck. I feel like I'm slipping in and out of sanity."

"No, you don't. You're happy here."

"Under the circumstances, I'm happy, yes. Under the circumstances."

"He didn't read you very well. You are very like him. He should've known you are not a person who could ever get used to a cage. Darius has always understood that."

A pang hit my heart so fiercely that my vision flickered and I swayed, my longing for Darius nearly dragging me under. Cahal's arm was around me immediately, holding me up.

"Sorry," he murmured.

"Yeah, keep that stuff to yourself. I can't let Darius distract me right now. Time has run out. It's time to leave. We need to put the dangerous part of our plan into effect. I think Lucifer has found them. He's leaving for a few days. He said something about a public display. Obviously that means he'll kill them gruesomely. He asked about Darius for the first time tonight. He knows I'm headed for heartache, and while I do think he cares that I'd be in pain, he's still going to go kill my boyfriend, I have zero doubt. Zero doubt. If not now, then when he eventually finds him. I would think I'd fucked up at dinner, maybe revealed my hand, except he was all over the place too. I don't think he caught my attempts at information grabbing. We were both off our game, but I've still got him hook, line, and sinker. He won't realize his slip-up until I'm long gone."

Because I was leaving. I'd been planning to leave all along; I'd just had to disguise my intention so he didn't clue in. I had been playing him from day one. From the moment I knew Penny had gotten through. I'd known he'd be on top of things. That he'd shut this place down and find them before they found me. When he did, he would make sure they didn't jeopardize his plans. All the while, he'd be trying to manipulate me into wanting to remain here. He'd trapped my body in the hopes of trapping my mind. It wasn't a new strategy—kidnappers had been doing it for ages.

I'd started talking to Cahal in whispered tones the very next morning, after my freak-out the night before, careful not to let the watchers overhear. We'd worked out a plan, one we'd never overtly mentioned to each other since, until now. We'd mostly never broken character. There were too many invisible watchers around the castle, and I didn't trust any of them.

My ultimate goal was to get enough wiggle room to slip out. That would require Lucifer to trust me, and *that* meant I had to let him believe this place was winning me over. I already had a playbook from the last heir, complete with a villain who would play on his fears—Cahal. I had all the pieces. I just needed to sell it.

And that was where the personal confusion had come in. Honest, genuine confusion. I *did* really like it here. I liked Lucifer. I didn't want to leave. All of that was true.

The trick was honestly feeling it—getting lost in it—and then letting Lucifer see my reactions to it. He wouldn't buy my confused mental state if I wasn't genuinely feeling it. I had created an illusion with my emotions as surely as he could create one with magic. I'd let it progress naturally, responding to each new situation as it arose. And Cahal had been right there beside me, always playing whatever role the moment called for—the martyr, or the villain, or sometimes the much-needed friend.

He had played his part perfectly, spinning me up when I needed it. Confusing me a little more by mentioning how happy I seemed here, how fulfilled. Careful to only mention Darius and the others when I needed to be pulled back just a bit. He'd kept me on target like a champion, though it had been hard to forgive him the day of the dragons. The day that he'd thought was the most crucial, the butthead.

Ultimately, though, I owed this Academy Award to Darius. I never would've been able to keep everything straight if not for my crystal-clear memory from the bond, and I never would've been able to compete with a master manipulator like Lucifer if I hadn't had a lot of practice with a cunning and intelligent elder vampire. I didn't love the manipulation game, but obviously I could handle it when I had to.

And I'd had to, there was no doubt. My superpower was my drive to survive. I'd brought that to the table all on my own. I'd been surviving all my life—hiding my truth from people. The stage had changed, but the show continued on.

One day, maybe I could just be me. One could hope. But this wasn't the time to get soggy about it.

"Did you reveal any part of the plan?" Cahal asked.

"No. He brought up Archion. Thank God I followed your advice and came clean with Archion. Apparently I picked out a dragon who is as good at lying and pretending as I am. He's eager to finally see the Realm. And maybe the Brink if I can sneak him in. Roger has tons of land in California—he should be fine with me borrowing some… Anyway, we leave tonight."

"Will you be sad to leave?"

I chewed on that question for a long time, needing to disentangle the game from reality.

"Yes. I like it so much, it hurts to think of never coming back. But I would never consent to staying here under these conditions. If I come back, it needs to be my choice, not Lucifer's. I would never sacrifice my friends." I pushed his arm from around me, trying to loosen up a little. It had been a tough few weeks as I purposely pushed away the things that really mattered to focus on the shallower pleasures and joys of my day-to-day existence. “Good thing we trained together, huh? I don’t need to worry about Darius or the king of the Underworld manipulating me, but you can clearly read my cues like a book.”

“I helped you do what you wanted. That’s the only reason my influence worked. If you didn’t want me pushing you around, you wouldn’t have allowed it.”

That was probably true. And it made me feel a bit better about letting him see me run the gamut of emotions.

“Right, okay. We need to get back in character, and then we need to sell the next leg of the journey. We don’t have any time to lose. We have to get to Penny and them before Lucifer does.”

“You’re sure you know where she is?”

“Yes. Her spells are like bright beacons in this place. They almost vibrate with magic. I thought for sure Lucifer would’ve noticed her concealment spell the other day, when we first flew over the kingdom. His magic is definitely different than mine. It must be because my mother was a mage with godly magic, but yeah, finding her trail hasn’t been very hard given how low we’ve been flying these past few days. I’ll need to talk to her about that. She needs to rip those down when she moves from place to place. Regardless, if they haven't moved, I know where they are. And if they have, I can track her—it'll just take longer. Worst case, I have a very foggy idea of Darius's direction. The bond is still muffled, but there's a wisp of direction. That might take too long, though."

I moved to get up, but he didn't follow. Given I had to escort him back in a terrible temper, I did actually need him to join me.

I sat back down.

"What is it?" I asked.

"Lucifer did open himself up to you. He regards you as a daughter, not an heir. He never called the last heir a son, not that I heard. You two have a connection. I can see it. Lucifer can see it. How can you so easily discount it?"

"I barely know the guy. He's cool, and we have a connection, sure, but it is more teacher and student than kid and dad. I can pretend otherwise with some conviction, but that's the honest truth."

"Why is that?" he asked, giving me a searching look.

"Because I barely know the guy, like I said. It bugged me that he pretended to understand my pain, when he so clearly doesn't. He asked me not to destroy this garden, hinting that it was special to him. That we shared the same grief. We very clearly do not."

"I'm not following."

"As if I *could* destroy something that reminded me

of her. As if I could do anything but treasure it for the rest of my life. I miss her so much it feels like the blackness is going swallow me whole, even now, after she's been gone for a few years. If he thought he had to say that, then he doesn't understand me at all. He was trying to manipulate me, and to do that with my mother—with the pain that is locked inside of me at her passing—is all kinds of wrong. It is a forgivable offense in the grand scheme of things, since it was early in our relationship and he has goals, but I won't forgive him until I'm safely out of here. You were absolutely right—her memory has kept me grounded, especially since I couldn't let myself think of Darius and Penny and everyone else. He doesn't have that kind of pull with me yet. We need to work on real trust before I can let him in."

He nodded, and this time he did stand. Apparently I'd passed the test, whatever that was.

"I am sad for you," he murmured before we started walking. "I'm sad you have to be torn like this. That you can't experience the full happiness you deserve."

"We all make sacrifices for those we love. If I can get Penny, Darius, you, and Emery out of here in one piece, I won't regret a single thing. Let's just hope Daddy Dearest doesn't have any tricks up his sleeve."

CHAPTER 18

"GET HIM OUT of my sight." I waved Cahal away when we reached the second-floor landing. "I will not be granting you a fucking mercy killing, Cahal. You and my da—Lucifer can suck it."

He turned and showed me his back, straight and broad, like he was about to march into death without flinching.

He probably was, just not in the way our demon observers thought.

I kept my own back from straightening, my chin from rising.

I sensed battle coming. It was almost time to fight for my life in the best way I knew how—magic, steel, and fists. But not yet. I couldn't show that side of myself without alerting everyone that I'd had a *drastic* change of heart. They knew me as a temperamental teen, basically. The broken heir who spent her days being coddled and training with her father. The moody, hormonal kid who was just getting her bearings. It was a façade that never would've fooled anyone who truly knew me. They would've called bullshit immediately.

I ripped away a wall hiding a little creepy demon and sent it scurrying with a ball of fire. I pulled Darius to the forefront of my mind, letting the longing soak into me. Drag at me. It would take the fire out of my eyes. The determination out of my jaw. It would help mask my desire to kick some ass long enough for me to get to my room and get things in motion.

Mr. Boobs found me on the third floor. I turned and blasted it with a shock of air, knocking it over the stone railing. It would catch itself before it went splat. Not like it mattered—it was a spy for Lucifer. It kept me in my place, happy as could be, and alerted the masses every time I did something big, like ripping down a huge wall that had sectioned off part of the castle or cutting a hole in the ceiling.

They must've thought I was incredibly gullible all these weeks, acting up but largely falling in line. I could just imagine Darius asking why he'd never gotten this Reagan, who could be trapped and cowed, happy with only friendly banter and fun training sessions.

Yes, I did like this place. But I liked being *me* better. This return to decisiveness felt damn good. It was like I was pulling off a smothering sheet. I had a job to do: save my friends, bang my boyfriend, and then knock the elves down a peg so Lucifer could open up the Underworld and I could come and go as I pleased. *That* was the real end game. That was what I wanted. I wanted to be here on my own terms. I wouldn't mind taking a spin in the ruler chair, but I'd need freedom, and to also keep my home in the Brink.

And maybe I'd never get all of that. Fine. Then I'd make the elves and Lucifer both terrified to mess with me. Plus I'd steal a bunch of those gold bars on the walkway to the elves' castle, smuggle it back to the Brink, and live out my days however I wanted. There would be no compromises. There would be no more confusion. Mama wasn't playing anymore.

I made it to my room and slammed air into the doors, throwing them open. I turned and shouted, "Do not bother me unless it is an emergency. And let that druid go hungry. See what he thinks about death when he's starving. I bet it won't be so attractive then."

I slammed my doors behind me, putting the most intricate air lock on them that I could devise. Over that, I created a fire illusion, a way to lock my fire magic into place without actively feeding it. Thanks, Dad, for the training. It would serve me well.

I couldn't wait to ring Penny's bell. Assuming she hadn't learned more than me down here and threw whatever I dished out back in my face. That would hurt. Still, I couldn't wait to see her again. All of them again. I even wanted to hug Roger, of all things. This place had knocked a screw loose.

It took me five full seconds to realize something was dreadfully wrong in my room, and another two to realize I was fucked.

A grisly monster hand grabbed my throat and squeezed. Pasty white and old as sin, the creature shoved me up against the nearest wall, pinning me there. The fecking thing was blindingly fast, and I hadn't been even remotely ready.

This was what happened when you let your guard down for weeks at a time. Death by old-ass vampire.

Its black eyes stared into mine as it hissed, saliva dripping down long canines. Three other vampires were stationed around the room, ready to attack should I fight back.

"My, my, Grandmother, what big teeth you have," I said, walling the other vampires off. The one that had me didn't squeeze any harder. If she'd meant to kill me, she would've done it already. "What are you doing here, Ja?"

She pulled back a little, releasing my throat, and then changed into her human form. Small and petite, also now naked, she looked like a stiff breeze would blow her away. Dainty features and large eyes hid the predator within. Vlad had nothing on this vampire, I was sure of it. None of them did.

"Reagan. So nice to see you."

"There, you see?" I winked at her. "When vampires

say it, they don't really mean it. There's something reassuring about that. When Romulus says things like that, he actually means them."

"The fae's kindness makes them facile. They are practically asking to be used by smarter beings."

"Good gracious. Tell us how you really feel."

She put out her hand, indicating the sitting area in the corner of my bedroom, where a bottle of demon whiskey sat, half-full.

"Don't expect this to taste like Irish whiskey," I said, heading over and taking a seat. "It'll disappoint you."

She followed me, but I put up my hand when she bent to sit.

"Cover up your junk. I want to come back to these rooms someday, and I don't want your ass crack all over my furniture."

Her feral gaze made me grin. I had missed vampires. What fun they were. What a rush. Lucifer would get a real kick out of them.

She didn't comment, but she did wait for me to allow one of her minions through my air wall so it could hand over a sparkly red dress. I waited for her to slink it over her person before taking a seat and reaching for the glasses.

I held up my hand again. "None for me, thanks. I've got places to be."

"Is that so?" Ja sat back and crossed an ankle over

her knee. I wasn't sure if she was intentionally flashing me or what, but it wasn't the choicest of views. "You do not plan to stay holed up in this fine castle like a little pet?"

"Oops. Your judgment is showing." I let seriousness take over. Time was ticking. Cahal and I had to get to the dragons before midnight so we could be well ahead of Lucifer, whom I assumed would be leaving in the morning. I hoped he would, at any rate, or the battle was going to kick off a lot sooner than I had expected. "What are you doing here, Ja? And how the hell did you get in?" It dawned on me. "It wasn't Vlad who snuck in at all—it was you and your people."

"You would've realized that long before now had you been paying even an iota of attention."

"I had my own demons to see to." I waggled my eyebrows. "Get it?" Her flat expression said she didn't care. "How'd you get Lucifer to think it was Vlad?"

"I've known about Vlad's efforts in the Underworld for quite some time. I've watched, quietly. He doesn't understand it like Durant does. Or like Durant will. He certainly doesn't understand it like I do. If he'd made it through, he would've been captured and brought to the castle immediately. Maybe he would've sought it out himself. And then he would've woken you out of your comfortable sleep, told Lucifer things he had no business knowing, and everything would've gotten incredibly messy. But thanks to the distraction created by Ms. Bristol and Lucifer's haste to close everything down, I didn't have to hunt Vlad down within the Underworld and kill him to ensure his silence."

Holy crap. Usually vampires didn't gun down other vampires. Not elders, anyway. This lady was like a cowboy in the Wild West of vampires, and suddenly I really wished Darius was here to handle her. Or even Cahal. Anyone but me.

"Still, how did you fool Lucifer?"

"I went to Vlad's chief contact, killed everyone loyal to him, bribed those I could to create false truths—"

"Those are called lies…"

"—and disappeared into the Underworld. Lucifer has been chasing a phantom. A loose end. Now he realizes foul play, of course, and will likely wipe out the sect loyal to Vlad. It's better that way. They weren't well organized. Vlad has been playing them for fools."

I couldn't do much more than stare. She was terrifying.

She studied me within the silence. "I am here because Darius assured me that you would be on the winning side."

"The winning side of what?"

"Playing dumb just eats time." She had me there. "I agree with him. I used to think Penny Bristol was at the center of this. Or maybe I just really like her, I can't tell.

I would like to taste her."

"Good luck with that."

"Thank you. But she is not the leading point in the pyramid of power. You are. You are more than just the heir of the Underworld. You're much more, aren't you?"

She paused, looking me over, and I checked the imaginary watch on my wrist and then tapped the skin to make sure she got the point. I could just walk out and go about my business, I supposed, but she'd likely get annoyed and sound an alarm. Or do some other crazy thing I would never expect. I certainly hadn't expected her to be in here. Or in the Underworld.

"You know a bit about me," she continued.

"A bit, though I had no idea it typically took you so long to get to the point…"

"You know something of my history with your kind. The demon kind, I mean."

"I just know that it is mostly gross, what you get up to—banging and bonding the ickier versions of demons…"

"We all have our tastes." Penny wouldn't like to hear that she was valued on the same level as gross demon sex. Or maybe she would, that dirty little birdie. "I have many allies in the Underworld. I have extensive networks from all my dealings here. I was able to hide easily. Much more easily than Darius Durant, who has been found out."

She paused once again, this time to get my reaction. She was about to get nothing for her efforts.

Her flat smile said she'd just clued into that. "You knew."

"I suspected."

"And that is why you are suddenly shifting into action after frittering away weeks?"

"You have spies in the castle, then?"

"I have spies *every*where."

"I needed training."

It was my turn to study her. What the hell was her game? If my battle of wits down here had been against her, I was pretty sure I'd have lost.

"Your training has raised quite a few eyes." I didn't bother telling her that she'd gotten the saying wrong. She uncrossed her leg and entwined her fingers in her lap. "Your ideas have made people nervous, especially because they have excited Lucifer. Many don't want change, even though he has always welcomed new information. New knowledge. He is one of the few good rulers, in my opinion. It is a shame he was locked down here, mostly cut off from magical society. He'd do well to move in the elite circles again. It would make the Underworld stronger."

"Ja, honestly, you need to chat with Darius about all this stuff. I can get myself out of a pinch, but I can't plan…whatever it is you are talking about. I'm not that smart. Or bored."

"Simply put, the vampires belong in the Underworld. We should never have been left in the control of the elves. I want what Durant wants. What you now want. I want the treaty with the elves broken. The current regime must be toppled. I am fine with those silly little fae running around with their swords, promising…rules or order or whatever it is they howl about. If that is your cause, and you will be on the winning side, then we all will win."

"That was a threat, right? If that isn't my side, you'll try to kill me?"

"Not at all. We both know I couldn't. Though…if caught by surprise when your mind is numb from pampering…maybe…"

I scowled at her. That was a good dig. I didn't have a comeback for it because it was true.

"Well, lucky us, that *is* what I want," I said, sitting forward. I was running out of sand in the hourglass. "I don't want to bother with the fixing-up side of things, in any of the worlds, but I do want to demolish everything so that it can be made better. In order to do that, though, I need to leave. So, again, what do you want, Ja? Other than to ascertain my plan?"

She spread her arms. "I want to help, obviously."

"Oh yes, obviously."

"I have a misdirection ready to go. One of Vlad's people has always been loyal to me. He is deep within Vlad's faction."

I nodded knowingly, remembering back to when I'd first helped get Charity into the Realm. Vlad's people had stood in our way, but they hadn't been controlled by Vlad. He'd learned of it, and I'd thought he rooted out all the bad apples. Clearly he'd missed a few.

"Soon he will be sacrificed to the cause. Lucifer will be told he is one of Vlad's people, and Lucifer will then try to torture information out of him. A futile effort, of course." She smiled, and butterflies filled my belly at the gruesome mischievousness sparkling in her eyes. "I've acquired one of Penny and Emery's spells. The *sacrifice* will not be able to say anything of use."

"But it'll take a while to kill him, I assume?"

She winked. That was a yes.

I took a deep breath to still my suddenly rampaging heart. "You are doing that for your own benefit. You need me, and I need Darius. So if you hoped to get an extra trade out of it, you're pissing in the wind."

"I will sort out the terms of all of this with Darius. There is one more thing."

"Maybe. Keep it within reason."

"I will help you with Darius. You will need to fight him out of there. They are holding him for Lucifer. They think that'll give them some sort of boon. And they are probably correct, though what favor they would've gotten from Darius would've been far more lucrative. Simple-minded fools."

"And they'll die for their sins."

"Of course."

"What's the catch?"

"You will then need to help me get out of the Underworld. I can get you to the safest exit point, but you or Penny Bristol will need to tear down the walls that Lucifer has newly erected."

My smile spread, and it was my turn to pause.

She was trapped here, just like everyone else, and it was only a matter of time before someone turned her in. Without help from Penny or me, she was up shit creek.

"Darius will certainly be sorting out the 'implications' of all this," I said, because she would owe us, big time. When it all shook out, she needed us to save her skin, and that was worth more than what she was offering us: a boost we maybe didn't need.

"Quite," she said tersely.

"The only problem is, we haven't accounted for you in our plans. We have dragons. What's your mode of transportation?"

"Very fast speeds and the absolute fastest route already cleared." Ja stood and shrugged out of the dress. She tossed it to the vampire behind her. It hit my air wall, which I then ripped down. "It'll take time for you to collect the druid and get to the dragons. By the time you get to the sect in question, we won't be far behind. Clear the perimeter and we should be on hand to head into the fray."

She'd clearly thought this through.

"Fine." I stood and looked her squarely in the eye. "If you fuck me or jeopardize my people, I will either trap you here for my father to deal with or find you on the outside and kill you and every vampire close to you. Do you understand me? You might be cunning and incredible at sabotage, but I am a nightmare from which you will not escape."

Fire lit in her eyes before her eyelashes fluttered. "Oh yes, you will win. Darius Durant found a diamond in the rough. I am absolutely green with envy. Here. This will help."

A blur was all the warning I had before she was directly in front of me, so close my breath dusted her face. Her hand stopped right before it touched my skin, and a grimace creased her lovely face when I squeezed her with air.

"I'm not sure if you've caught up with the times," I said, holding her there. "But these days, you must get consent before you touch a person's chest."

I am glad to see that you are back to operating at optimal capacity, she thought, probably because I had her locked down so tight that not even her jaw could move.

I meant to circumvent the binding on your bond with Darius when I was in the elves' castle, but Lucifer showed up too quickly. I didn't want to get caught with my hands on the prize and end up down here like Cahal did.

What was this now? She had been in the castle?

I've had a bond muffled by them in the past, she continued, *so I did a lot of research on the subject. To break their magical suppression, you will need to take each other's blood, like bonding again. It will be much quicker and less intense, of course. In the meantime, there is a workaround. You simply need a vampire more powerful than the bond holder to flower the effects of the bond so that you can feel it. Given Darius is the bond holder, your only option at present is me. Shall I?*

"I mean…it goes without saying that I need to live through this, right?"

Don't be an idiot.

That was apparently a yes.

I released the air hold and allowed her hand to continue until it rested just over my heart.

"Boy will I feel stupid if this was all an elaborate scheme to rip my heart out," I said.

"In that case, we'd both feel stupid. Being elaborate just wastes time."

"You're not real moody, are you? Just super sweet all the time, huh?"

Claws elongated from her fingers and dug into my

skin.

"I'm having second thoughts," I said, and then held my breath as the pain spiraled outward from my chest. I would've pushed her off if I hadn't felt a strange stirring in my chest, like the haze on my bond with Darius was lifting slightly, letting the feeling of him seep out and into my person.

My body tensed, the world stilled, my entire being focused on him re-entering my world.

The pain in my chest increased, her claws digging in, her power amplifying.

"He has grown mighty while under your care," she whispered, her voice strained.

Anxiety and worry bled through the bond, followed by confusion, and then a gush of love so powerful my knees weakened. He felt me as I was feeling him. Relief washed in next, and suddenly I knew exactly where to find him. I could sense his direction in relation to mine.

"Interesting. I never took you for a crier." Ja pulled her bloody hand away from my red-stained chest. I barely felt the pounding of pain, focused as I was on the feeling of Darius within me again. Coursing through me. Filling me up. It wasn't just the bond, which was still half muffled. I could finally let myself miss him again. Ache for him. Want him near me.

How could Lucifer ever think I could sex him away? That was a person who didn't understand deep, soul-crushing love. He might've really liked my mom, but he hadn't loved her. Not like this. Not even close.

"It's been a rough few weeks," I said, wiping my cheeks and not even feeling remotely embarrassed about the show of vulnerability. Something Lucifer had said popped into my mind.

Vulnerabilities aren't something to be afraid of. They make us stronger, in the end. You cannot really hate unless you know how to love. You will never know your true strength unless you give in to your greatest weaknesses.

Ja was watching me with a tilted head.

"Come on. Stop wasting time." I brushed past her so I could grab a different top. This one now had holes in it.

"Don't fail," she told me, and then she and her cronies went running across the living space and leapt out of a window that would dump them out onto a very steep incline. I didn't have time to see if they'd tumble off.

Dress off and tank on, I tied my hair tighter and grabbed the demon whiskey and one glass from the table. I emptied most of the whiskey to look like I'd drunk it and then put the bottle on the table in the main room and the glass on the table near the window. If someone got into the main room before they should, hopefully they'd see that and my closed door and wait for my hangover to wear away. Assuming they could get in at all.

I opened the window that looked out over the darkened kingdom and sailed through it, pulling in tightly to the building and dodging windows as I made my way to Cahal's apartment. I'd chosen it deliberately. It was a big production to get there from within the castle—you had to take stairs and go down halls. Go out the window, though, and it was very accessible. I loved it when a plan came together. Especially because I never usually planned at all.

He stood in the window with only dim light at his back. He didn't have his sword, which would be a problem, but there wasn't anything we could do about it. I'd tried to devise a way to get down to the armory to get it back, but I'd never been allowed to go there. I wasn't ready to see the darker parts of the kingdom, I'd been told, as though I didn't know how torture worked. As though I hadn't been tortured right before being brought here.

They just didn't trust me. They thought I would try to steal the sword out from under them. They were right.

He pulled the latch and swung the heavy pane inward. He glanced down the side of the castle to the ground far below. Then back at me.

"Wanna hug?" I put out my arms.

He glanced down again before stepping up onto the ledge and reaching out for me. I cinched my hands around his big body, grabbing him beneath the pits, before wrapping my legs around his middle. While I'd discovered I could hover two entities, he could only wrap himself in shadow. Unless I was glued to him, of course.

What took you? Cahal thought.

"I had a lovely surprise meeting," I whispered, sliding down the side slowly, working around windows great and small. "Ja showed up."

His large slabs of muscle bulged, his arms squeezing my back uncomfortably.

"Yeah. Surprised me, too." I tried to glance around his big arm to the ground, but no go. "How close are we?"

Half a floor. How did… It wasn't Vlad.

"Correct. She scolded me for not having seen that. She had a lot of disparaging things to say, actually. She doesn't think too highly of the way I've spent my time here."

She was in the elves' dungeon when I got there. She cleared the way for Lucifer, though he didn't know it. Or need it. I don't know what else she was doing in there, but she mentioned that you needed training. She wanted you here.

"She was going to release the hold on my bond with

Darius, but she ran out of time, I guess. She just did it there, in my room. Well, halfway. It's enough. I can get Darius's direction. I'll be able to find them easily this way."

We bumped into the ground a little harder than we should've. Whoops.

"Let's go, druid. Let's see if you can keep up."

I took off like a jet, needing to get the hell out of there as fast as possible. Cahal was right beside me, hopefully close enough to impart a little magic. He wouldn't last long at this speed, but we could slow down once we were out in the nothingness.

"I do not…get that…vampire," I said as we went. "She told me…some of her…end game—"

I hit a rock and stumbled. Cahal braced me. The guy was like a dark guardian angel. He was dangerous and rough and deadly, but when he was helping you stay alive, no detail was too small.

Do not trust anything she says. Her mind is dizzying, and her motives are never clear.

I was glad I wasn't the only one that thought so.

Cahal looked back and then slowed, breathing heavily.

Thank you for the air, by the way, he thought. *I may not technically need it, but it is uncomfortable to live without it.*

"Yeah, I was thinking the same thing when I did it.

Also, I was throwing a tantrum."

He continued on at the slower pace, and I took that opportunity to tell him all Ja had said, repeating her plans in slow detail.

She will let them kill the spy she had with Vlad?

"It seems so."

She must have others. She likely brought him in case the worst should happen.

"Which it clearly did if she is now asking for help."

Yes, exactly. She is learning the hard way what it is like to enter into a situation with you and Ms. Bristol. It takes some getting used to.

"You've done well."

Yes.

His delivery was deadpan. Who would've thought that was possible with a thought? I laughed as we reached the dragon territory. We slowed, and Cahal stepped in front of me. He bent, and I climbed onto his back so his magic would mask both of us. Most of the dragons were asleep, but the big ones would be heading out soon for the hunt.

"And here I thought you'd carry me like a bride," I murmured as he started jogging through the trees. He'd drop me at Archion before he went back for his dragon.

Only a madman would consent to carry you like a bride and mean it.

"I'll tell Darius you said so."

He is not a man.

I rolled my eyes. I'd walked into that one.

Hey, I thought as Cahal put me down next to a sleeping Archion, all curled up like a dog in a comfy, big bed. Trees and bushes closed him in on all sides but one, a setup I'd made for him over the last few days, much of it an illusion. It gave him privacy, which he deserved, but it would also keep Lucifer from noticing his absence.

Hmm? A sleepy dragon lid lifted slowly, the pale orb beneath glowing slightly. Huh.

We gotta go. It's time. I patted him again, hard as a rock. Way prettier, though. *Hurry!*

His eyes snapped open now and his head came up, quickly alert. He snaked his long neck out and twisted through one of the trunks, spying what lay beyond.

Go tell Saphira that we are ready.

Who?

Saphira. The white dragon.

Oh. I turned to hurry away. I turned back. *What?*

She is my best mate. Our eggs hatched close together. I trust her with my life, and I told her about our journey. She wants to come. She will help carry your friends. The bond requirements will be withheld while we are running for our lives. Because if you get caught, we will all be trapped here forever, or killed. We wish to leave. With you.

I didn't have time to argue. Or say thank you. Or ask if this was a good idea. I just listened, running toward Saphira's hangout, using the roundabout back way so none of the other dragons would see me. This close to Tatsu, Lucifer's dragon, we need to take the utmost care, especially since the big dragons would be getting up to hunt pretty soon.

Reaching the dragon with the lovely snow-powder scales, outlined in dusty gray, I patted her shoulder.

No reaction.

Hey!

Still nothing. Oh, right—I could only think thoughts between a dragon that accepted me as a bond mate.

"Hey." I kicked her this time. She was a dragon. She would barely feel it.

Her eyes snapped open, and her head jerked up, smoke pouring out of her nostrils.

"No, no." I held out my hands. "It's me. Archion's rider. Remember? I guess he broke my trust, blabbed to you, and you consented to be a fifth wheel?"

Those luminous eyes, the "whites" a soft blue, blinked slowly. The black slit within enlarged, and she looked in the direction of Archion.

I put my finger to my lips. "Shh. Hopefully he also told you that we can't let Tatsu know we're leaving…"

Her body rocked back and forth until she was

pushed up into a crouch, very graceful for a dragon.

"Get out of here without people—dragons—noticing." I took a few steps away. "Then meet us in the air. We'll be flying high. We have no time to lose."

Back at Archion, I belatedly remembered that I should've probably put up some sort of illusion to show her sleeping in her spot. Then again, if Lucifer noticed the magic, he'd know I'd deliberately set out to hide her. If he noticed she was missing, on the other hand, he might just think she was out for a fly.

Okay, let's go. I hovered up onto his back. *Cahal is probably wondering where we are.*

I thought your friend chose a dragon under his power level. Archion lifted into the air and flew forward a ways, staying low to the tree line. *But his magic is able to cover Coppelia perfectly. With a larger dragon, that would likely not be the case. They will be stronger as a pair with that magic able to hide them.*

I nodded, because I'd wondered too, but his insight made sense. We kept moving, and a little farther out, hopefully past the notice of Tatsu, he zoomed into the sky, meeting Cahal and Coppelia. Saphira joined us a moment later.

I tapped his neck on the side to adjust our direction. I had Darius's bond to guide me now. His location was a glowing spot in my mind, and I could barely keep from pushing Archion to hurry faster.

We'll be going into battle, I told him. *I think it is a violence sect, so they'll be able to defend themselves. We'll need to clear the outside of the sect so a group of untrustworthy vampires can rush in.*

I have not been in battle before.

I know. Trust me, it'll be fun. You can do a sweep and then drop me off so I can fight on foot. I'm better off if I'm participating.

I'd hate to lose you.

Then help out when the time comes. If you feel fear, just—

I am a dragon among peasants. Why should I feel fear?

He wasn't too old in dragon terms—a hundred and fifty or so—and male. He was basically a teen boy. He probably wouldn't feel fear, stupidly so. But in this situation, that would help instead of hurt, so I let it go.

Cahal pulled up alongside us, high above the ground. He looked over, hard to see within the darkness and his swirling shadow.

We'll need to give it all we have, Cahal thought. *This is your only chance at escape. You fooled Lucifer once. It will never happen again.*

CHAPTER 19

"I'VE GOT NOTHING." Penny wiped her face of sweat. Or maybe they were tears.

She sat back on her haunches with her hands braced against her thighs, staring at the iron bars locking them in a windowless ten-by-fifteen-foot cell. Stone blocks surrounded them on all sides but one. Only a sparse glow filtered in from the barred opening, which faced another stone wall. They couldn't see anyone coming and going—hadn't seen anyone since they'd woken up, as a matter of fact.

"I have got literally nothing." She pushed up to standing and started pacing. "How did we get into this mess?"

Emery sat on the ground in the back corner, his arms draped over his knees, sparing his energy. Darius, too, sat calmly, taking up the other corner.

"We were outnumbered, that's what happened," Penny said, not one ounce of calmness in her person. Not one. She didn't know whether she should scream, cry, throw up, or pace. She'd opted for pacing, because she'd already scratched "figure out how to get out of here" and "use every real and made-up curse word known to man" off the list.

They had been put down here while they were asleep. Drugged, more like. She'd been cuddled up in a fluffy bed with Emery one minute, and facedown on a stone floor the next.

"Why would they just flip on us like that?" She rubbed her pounding head. "I mean, we were all good. I thought everything was good. They were hearing Darius out, they were giving us a nice place to sleep, a good meal…and then *wham*. Here we are."

She turned right and stopped at the bars again, wrapping her fingers around the cold metal.

"There has to be a way out. Magic has to help, somehow."

But she'd already tried everything. She could do a lot with magic, but she couldn't bend metal. She couldn't move it. There weren't even enough ingredients in this godforsaken place to make a decent spell. They must've known how little it would take for them to wrangle up some magic to get out of here.

She sighed and leaned her head against the hard surface.

"What happens now?" she asked, at a loss.

"Lucifer shows up," Emery said. "And we hope Reagan is with him."

"She won't be—" Darius cut off.

Penny turned to see if he had some miraculous great idea to get them out of this jam. If anyone could create something out of nothing and form a plan, it was this vampire. The trip into the Underworld had given her a new respect for him. More than respect, even. She might just start worshipping him as a brain god or something—he was *that* good at navigating dangerous situations and coming out on top.

Except for their current predicament, of course. Which was definitely his fault. She didn't really know what had gone wrong, other than the super-violent and terrible demons had refused Darius's trade, it had landed them in the stink, and it was his fault.

No, never mind. She would not worship him. She'd punch him. Just as soon as she wasn't caged up with him and could quickly run away.

"What is it?" Emery asked, sitting forward.

Darius tensed, and then his face and eyes softened. Penny had seen that look before—he'd worn it almost constantly on the island where he kept Reagan hidden away.

Hope surged within her. "Say it. Say what it is." She'd become incredibly pushy from all of this.

He relaxed a little. "Our bond is…partially mended. She's…" He bowed his head a little, clearly plugging whatever was coming through the bond into his big, fat brain. "She is eager and determined. She's making a move. She must be."

"Oh good." Penny let out a relieved sigh before her thoughts caught up. "Wait, does that mean she is coming here with Lucifer after all?"

"No. If I'm not mistaken, she's coming to our rescue."

Penny deflated and looked back at the bars. "Dang it. Why are we always the damsels? She better not ride in on that freaking dragon. That would really push me over the edge."

"Why don't you have a seat, Miss Bristol?" Darius said. Penny knew that tone. It was his "you're losing your mind and need to get a hold of yourself" tone.

Usually she ignored it. But this time, she pulled up some stone beside Emery and worked on deep breathing. If Reagan was coming, that meant she was breaking out of the castle on her own. And *that* meant she'd probably have the enemy hot on her heels.

IN THE FRESH new morning, with soft light illuminating the inner kingdom, Lucifer landed in front of Tatsu's habitat. He changed into his humanoid form and strode toward her. Going into a direct conflict, one that might get out of hand, he usually flew in himself with Tatsu on his heels, the two of them working side by side to quell the feud or uprising. But this conflict wasn't active so much as smoldering. Riding in on the queen of the dragons would lend a little prestige to the affair.

When dealing with vampires, he wanted to convey a little prestige. Especially for the vampire Durant. That vampire needed to see why Lucifer's daughter was so thoroughly out of his league. She was a princess. She was of higher caliber than any of the other heirs, and her unique combination of magic would make even the elves quake. She was the pride of the Underworld, and no vampire was fit to be her companion.

But first, he needed to attend to another vampire matter.

He'd gotten word an hour earlier that they had one of Vlad's people. How that vampire had eluded him for so long, he didn't know, but it ended now. He would pry information out of that creature before he broke him. Vlad had had a good run, but it was the end of the road for him. No one snuck into his territory, hid from him, and then received a pardon. No one.

As he stalked forward, he noticed an unusual emptiness in his peripheral vision. Saphira wasn't in her sleeping area. She should've been back from hunting by now. He turned a little, eyeing Archion's resting place. The dragon was a fierce and fearless fighter with the courage to carry someone like Reagan. He'd been a fine choice.

Expertly crafted trees and canopies blocked his view. Reagan had built up the illusions to give her dragon privacy. She was already taking great care of him. As she should. Soon Lucifer would make room for a habitat for Archion near Reagan's side of the castle. If it weren't for Tatsu's duties overseeing the other dragons, he would've made her a place nearer to him as well.

His heart warmed and he continued on, finding Tatsu standing and ready to go. He'd called down to her from the sky, but he'd decided to take the longer route through the dragons' territory to let her wake up and ready herself. She walked forward, her gaze catching on Saphira's empty resting area before it turned skyward.

He smiled. Like rider, like dragon.

Early for a fly, Tatsu said, her gaze going to Archion's space next. Saphira and Archion were hatchmates, although from different mothers. They were mostly inseparable. *Is Reagan out? I can't see Archion's nest anymore.*

He hadn't checked on Reagan this morning. He'd gotten word that she told the druid she would not be mercy-killing him, but it was only a matter of time before she gave in. It likely put her in a bad mood, however, and Lucifer didn't want to disturb her if she had tucked into the demon whiskey, as she called it, last night and needed the day to shed the hangover.

I don't know, he said as he hovered up to her back.

She blew smoke out of her nostrils, clearly annoyed. She watched over the dragons like Lucifer watched over the sects. She didn't like unexplained behavior or absences. Although rare, it wasn't unheard of for a sect to try to kidnap a dragon and use it for their purposes.

You would've woken if someone had attacked, he reminded her, situating himself.

She didn't comment as she spread out her wings and prepared to fly.

She doesn't typically get up early, especially these last few days, Tatsu thought. *She has been depressed, now that Archion has found a rider. She wishes for one too.*

It's hard for a dragon of her standing and power to find someone worthy. Lucifer kept his patience in check. Neither vampire would go anywhere, and the sect that had harbored Vlad in the past had nowhere to escape to, not with the borders closed. He had time to appease his dragon friend.

She understands that, but it doesn't prevent her jealousy and depression. Tatsu pushed into the sky, but not very far. She pumped her wings, sliding forward, peering over the illusion wall of Archion's nest. Empty.

That was unusual.

Judging by the deep rumble in Tatsu's chest, she thought so too.

Reagan probably went for a ride to calm herself, Lucifer thought. *Maybe they felt bad for Saphira and brought her too.*

Your daughter is worthy of the title of princess. There is no comparison between her and the last heir. She fits in the Underworld. She is strong already, and with more practice and training, she will be incredible.

Yes, I think so too.

Tatsu kept moving forward, looking over the nests, checking who was there and who was not. *She is untrained in the more advanced areas of her magic, but in personality and resourcefulness, in deed and duty, she is your equal. And she is cunning.*

His patience was wearing thin. He didn't comment, nor did he look down at the other dragons. He relied on her to watch them, but it certainly wasn't time for a roll call. The issues with the kingdom right now did not center on dragons.

I saw her truth when she picked Archion over Saphira, she went on. *He is an unruly dragon. Wild. He will never be tamed. And she will never try to tame him. They are perfect for each other.*

I am growing very fond of my daughter, and I enjoy hearing your accolades, but what is your point, Tatsu? We have business.

She is unruly, too. Tatsu stopped her forward progress. *Wild. She will never be tamed. If you try to tame her, she will chew out of her bonds, and you will cry over her loss.*

Yes. She's like her father.

No. Not like her father. The elves trapped you down here, for the most part, and us with you. Like you tried to trap her. You grew used to it, because you love this place. She loves the Underworld too, I can see. I can hear the hum of it from Archion when he speaks of their time together. But she will not be trapped. And she would never kill someone she values as highly as that druid. Look.

She doesn't value that druid…

The thoughts dried up in his mind. The nest of the pink dragon—he couldn't remember its name—was empty.

She vowed to protect him, Tatsu thought. *She gave him the gift of bonding with a dragon. She rode with him every day, side by side. She is loyal to him. Tell me, what lengths would you go to in order to protect someone you are loyal to?*

His rose-colored glasses ripped off, he considered his memories from the last few weeks in a new light. Little things Reagan had said. Little things she had done. Her confusion at how much she liked his kingdom. Her joy in learning, her quick responses as a pupil…

Her flashes of defiance when he chastised her. Her

incredible bursts of anger. Her quick wit, able to cut him to the quick after only a short time of knowing him. The look on her face when he'd mentioned sexing away her vampire lover.

That hadn't been disgust at a father bringing up sex to his daughter. It had been disgust at the suggestion such a thing could be done.

Why did she send the druid away? he wondered. *Why did she form an attachment with a dragon if she planned to leave? How did she so thoroughly trick me?*

Because he *had* been tricked. He still couldn't quite believe her capable of such an elaborate ruse, as a matter of fact. He did not believe she could've snuck out in the middle of the night, with the druid of all creatures, and tried to escape his paradise. Tried to escape *him*.

Rage twisted in his gut.

Go to the castle, he mentally barked.

You won't find her there.

GO TO THE CASTLE!

Still his mind pored over every detail of their interactions. The nuances he had missed in his eagerness to connect with her.

One thing stuck in his mind: the look she'd given him when he told her not to destroy her mother's garden. He hadn't understood that look at the time, but he did now.

Detached abhorrence.

He had leaned into a fond memory, trying to create a deep connection, but she'd seen straight through him. It was then she'd shored up the wall between them—one he couldn't hope to penetrate with friendly banter and declarations of fatherly love.

She didn't want a father. She wanted her mother back. If he hoped to gain her trust and her affection, it couldn't be through calling up his connection to a woman he'd, admittedly, barely known. He'd been entranced by her, incredibly fond of her, but he hadn't loved her.

She had been Reagan's whole world. Her sun, stolen from the sky. And he'd played false with that memory. With her pain.

"Vulnerabilities make us stronger," he said softly, smiling sardonically as they flew.

Reagan's raw grief for her mother was a huge vulnerability, and it had kept her mind focused in this new world. He hated how right he'd been.

This can't go unpunished, he thought, leaning forward, knowing that Tatsu would take that as an indication to go faster. *If she has lied to me all this time, and fled, it cannot go unpunished.*

The question is, who will you punish—her…or yourself? For you were the one who forced this on her. You were the one who tied the chain around her ankle. Can you really blame her for an action you would've taken a couple of centuries ago?

He shook his head as she touched down, blocking out her unassailable logic.

Why hadn't Tatsu raised her doubts before now? Why had she waited?

He asked her.

I have only known her for a few days. It took the end result for me to interpret her actions.

Not helpful.

He ran through the castle. At her quarters, he quickly studied the magical work blocking the door. It was exemplary. She truly had reached power level—his level—although her magic had a unique twist caused by those infernal angels, may they stay trapped in their "haven" forever.

His mind stuttered.

…like he'd been trapped down here…

Frustration rose. Overcame him. Quickly turned to anger.

He hated when Tatsu was right, which was usually always.

He worked at the blockage as her attendant drifted closer.

"Sire, what is the matter?"

He ignored the demon, tearing down the last bit of magic work before finding the fire spell that lay beneath. *Excellent.*

"Damn her," he said, pain eating through him. "Please don't do this to me. Please don't turn on me."

The last bits of magic down, he burst through the doors. A nearly finished bottle of alcohol sat on the table. An empty glass on another surface.

A setup.

If she'd drunk all of that, in the mood she *should* have been in, she would've carved out another hole in the ceiling. She'd missed an important ingredient in her tableau—passion. She carried it about her person like a birthright, and this scene was sorely lacking in it.

He strode to the closed doors of her room and kicked them open. As expected, her bed was made. Not slept in. Her window was open.

He ran at it, looked out, then turned back to run…before pausing.

"No," he said softly, and chuckled a little to himself as his heart broke. He backed up and stepped out of the window, hovering around the corner of the castle, and to the druid's wing. So easy to reach this way. So hard to get there through the castle.

She'd orchestrated even that, and he'd bought it. He'd relished the thought that she was casting the druid out.

Not so. She'd tucked him away somewhere he could be easily reached when the time came to escape. The brilliance of her ruse made him chuckle, even as pain lanced his heart. She'd ordered them to let Cahal starve for a couple of days, ensuring no one would check on him.

The druid's window was unlatched, slightly ajar. Within, utterly empty.

Lucifer stopped in the middle of the sitting room for one solid moment, staring at nothing, feeling the pain of deception. Of trickery. Of regret.

Then, all action again, he leapt out of the window and changed to his other form. She'd left with the druid, obviously. There was only one place she would go.

He didn't drop down to Tatsu. He couldn't stomach her telling him, *I told you so.* He flew past, and she followed, blessedly silent.

How long had Reagan been planning this? Since day one? When had she cultivated such a plan, playing him at every turn?

Fire kindled in his gut.

Cahal fucking Druer.

The druid must've helped her in this, just like he'd hastened the other heir to ruin. That cursed druid, favorite of the angels, had never stopped being her safety blanket. His daughter had only wanted Lucifer to think that.

He didn't know whether to laugh or cry. He didn't know whether the pounding in his chest was love or hate, pride or sorrow. Which was fitting, because she was a blend of everything the Underworld had to offer, even though she hadn't been raised here. She was him when he was younger. She was him as he wished he were now.

Damn it. He'd played this all wrong, content because she'd tricked him into complacency.

Fire followed him as he flew, pushing his limits, aiming for the sect that housed the vampire Darius. He couldn't let his daughter escape. She was his more than any other offspring he'd had in history. Wasn't that ironic, that the one who was most like him, worthiest of the title "heir," was also partly made from those cursed angels? Bastards.

She would not leave this place. He'd make sure of it.

CHAPTER 20

HERE WE GO, Archion. Finally! I pointed down at the violence sect. Darius's light and energy pulsed below, waiting for me.

Light was creeping into the sky. We'd lost precious time helping Ja and her vampires escape the inner kingdom. She hadn't accounted for a patrol, something that wasn't there when she'd come in. It made me wonder just how long Ja had been spying on the castle.

We'd had to kill the border patrol. We couldn't afford them running back to the castle and tattling on us. It had thrown our plans all to hell.

Thankfully, Ja's team was incredibly vicious and effective. It had been a little unnerving to watch, actually. Even Archion had gotten squeamish. Saphira had been altogether useless. Hopefully she'd just been shell-shocked and would redeem herself with future carnage. The vampires were still headed to meet us at the violence sect, but they might be a bit delayed. We'd need to get Darius and the others out while the dragons burned everyone in the perimeter. When Ja finally showed up, she'd join the fray.

What's our plan? Archion asked.

Don't have one. I figure...we just dive down and scorch them all.

What if they don't scorch?

Then I flatten them with air.

Good plan.

My kinda dragon. No plan was a good plan.

Cahal flew right behind us, Saphira behind him.

What about Saphira? I asked, taking stock of the minimal activity going on around the squat stone building. There was an expansive courtyard, but the building itself was only a couple of stories high. Either most of it was built below ground or it simply wasn't that big. Hopefully it was the latter.

This is new to her and she is on the timid side. She'll follow our lead.

I looked back at her, not sure how to get her going. With Penny, it was easy—I just shoved her in front of danger. But how did you do that with a dragon?

My foot slipped and shot off Archion's shoulder. My weight shifted and my body followed.

"Oh crap—" Archion adjusted immediately, but I held out my hand and slowed my fall with a hover.

Why wait? The plan started now.

Burn it all, I thought to Archion. *Work the perimeter. Keep the way as clear as you can for when Ja gets here.*

I righted myself so that my feet were pointed downward and then released my hover, falling fast. Near the ground, I firmed up the air around me, slowing my descent drastically, and dropped down in front of a very confused demon with five horns on his head, no eyes, and his dick swinging so low he should consider knotting the thing to keep it out of the way.

"Horns and a big Johnson don't make you better at violence, idiot," I said.

He startled, his hand slapping toward the sword strapped to a bare, furry hip. I punched him in the face. His head cracked back, and I reached beside him and yanked out his sword before torching him.

His high squeal indicated this sect would not take kindly to fire. Good.

He flailed his arms and ran, a horned torch.

"Stop, drop, and roll, bub." I looked up as Archion flew by. The dragon opened his great jaws and blew fire at the ground, rolling over me and then scorching everything in its path. Demons came away from the walls, just now cluing in that there was danger in their midst. They clearly didn't spend a lot of time getting attacked from the air. Or maybe at all. They didn't seem very good at the violence game, given the way they threw up their hands and just took the fire as it blackened their skin or fur. More good news.

How the hell had Darius, Penny, and Emery gotten taken by a sect this bad at violence? Maybe there was something I was missing.

"Reagan!"

Cahal shot down from the sky, nearly to me. That was the problem with not having a plan: you nearly missed important moments, like when it rained grumpy druids.

I slowed his flight as his dragon bellowed, a thick wave of depression flowing over the area. It dragged me down for a moment before I labored to shake it off. Archion followed with a roar of his own, but that didn't impact me at all, probably because of our growing bond.

Cahal wasn't recovering so easily, though, arms and body stiff from Archion's paralyzing roar, reaching for the sword I held.

"Come on. Push through it." I grabbed Cahal around the wrist, the effect like thawing him out. He blinked and shook his head.

"Effective," he said, and I felt a burst of pride. That was my dragon. I totally got the best one.

"Here. Hurry! If my dad isn't on his way yet, he will be soon." I handed over the sword before I sprinted toward the nearest door.

"You called him your dad," Cahal said, running behind me and scooping me up with one hand. He held me tightly to his uncomfortably hard body, swirling his shadow magic over us.

"Stop. I want to kill people. Also, eat a donut. You could do with a little padding for situations like this."

"You can kill people after we find the others. This will be faster."

Annoyingly, he was right.

"Yeah," I said as he ducked into the door and flattened us against the inner wall. Demons ran by, strapping armor to their bodies, trying to find the fight. What they'd find was fiery death from the sky. "He *is* my dad, after all. And after this, we'll be even. If he wants to make up, great. If not, I'll just call him a deadbeat dad and be done with it."

Usually people like you have daddy issues, Cahal thought as he stayed near the wall and ran down the corridor. My feet dangled down his side, my toes occasionally touching the ground as he moved and dodged people. His shoulder clipped a demon and sent it reeling into the rushing crowd, which was large enough that this place definitely had more than just two stories.

"There is no usual for a person like me."

He cut across the corridor at a gap in the onslaught, and I suddenly wondered how the hell we were going to get out of this place. They had a whole lot of people, it turned out. Without Ja—or even with her—we didn't.

A faint echo of a dragon wail made my bowels watery. Not with fear, but like they would let go and I'd physically soil myself.

"What the hell," I said softly as Cahal put on a burst of speed, cutting through a gap in the crowd heading to the front and to the other side, where a window looked out over the courtyard in the middle of the building. Weapons were strewn about in a way that suggested the demons had been training when the warning bells went off. Clearly, they were practice weapons, though they still seemed metal. Hardcore. The fae better be wary of going up against violence demons.

"Darius is at a diagonal to the right—" I shook my head in confusion. We'd have to snake through the building to find the way to him. "Where are you going?"

He turned a corner and slowed, looking for something. In a moment, I found out what.

My feet hit the ground, and I staggered into the wall to catch my balance. Cahal grabbed a humanoid demon with a wrinkled suit and bare feet and shoved him against the wall. The shadows peeled away.

"Where are the prisoners?" Cahal asked in a low voice born of nightmares. Rough and wicked and dangerous.

The man-demon's eyes widened to the point of comedy. "Wh-wh-whaaaat?"

"The vampire and mages. The prisoners. Where are they being kept?"

"Dungeon. In the dungeon. In the stone cage so they can't magic their way—"

"How do I get there?"

"D-down the rear steps. B-ba-back of the building." He put forward a shaky finger. "That way."

Cahal stuck his sword through the center of the demon, twisted, and ripped it out again.

"Make sure he dies—" Cahal started, but I was already on it. One swipe of an air sword, and the demon's head fell to the ground. I ran in the direction he'd pointed, wiping goo from my hands. Cahal caught up and smashed me to his side again, covering me in the shadow. It was like physically being between a rock and a hard arm.

He hit the end of the corridor as someone shouted behind us. I glanced back over Cahal's shoulder as he turned right. The dead demon had been discovered and the discoverer was currently looking around wildly, either for the culprit or someone to help. It had missed our escape entirely.

I sulked a little, because right now it was the Cahal show, and looped an arm around his shoulders so I could haul myself up just a little. His hip was digging into my side.

He slowed a little as a few demons ran around a corner up ahead, wearing helmets with metal nose guards protecting nothing above wide mouths full of large, sharp teeth. Metal breastplates covered wide chests and thick, hairy arms held spiked weapons or spears.

Better than guarding a prisoner… one thought as they rushed toward us.

I slammed all but one of them against the wall. Blood splattered and bodies crumpled to the ground. Cahal dropped me, immediately launching into a flurry of action—sticking them with the business end of his sword to make sure they didn't get back up.

I caught the last one in a vise grip of power and immediately felt the same sort of power trying to shove me away. It froze. It knew who I was.

"Where's the dungeon? Which way?" I asked, stepping closer, then back again because I didn't want to tilt my head up that much. Given the width of its shoulders and the size of its massive arms and chest, the demon looked shorter than it actually was.

"Princess. I'm sorry… I have to wait for the Great Master. I can't tell—"

I lit his legs on fire. "Tell me or I'll kill you very, *very* slowly." It couldn't possibly know that I didn't have that kind of time. "I won't tell my father how I found out."

It licked its thin lips, its expression one of consternation and agony. It didn't give any other signs its lower half was burning.

"Two rights and a left. Down the stairs to the bottom. The Great Master said to hold—"

Off with his head, I thought, and stepped aside as his body hit the floor.

"I really didn't need—Ugh." I winced as Cahal squeezed me to his side again. "Seriously, how about a piggyback instead? This situation is not amazing. As I was saying—"

He ran around the next right, then veered to play Dodge the Demon as another group of huge, armored creatures jogged through.

I put my lips to the shell of his ear and used very little sound as we took the next right. "I don't think I needed to storm the gates. I probably could have just told them who I am. They won't fight the heir."

Please back off a little, he thought, and I frowned and pulled my head away.

"Why? What's the matter?"

He took a left, the hallway empty now. Midway through was a door labeled with what looked like a picture of stairs drawn by a five-year-old.

I am almost always your platonic friend, but sometimes, in certain situations, I remember that I am a man, and you are a beautiful, fiery woman, and my body responds accordingly. I have a thing for women in battle…and a thing with my ears. You are hitting too many buttons right now. I need you to back off.

I couldn't help an evil grin. Too bad this wasn't the

time to mess with him.

He paused by the stairs and looked up and down the connecting hallway. An elflike demon in a fuchsia dress walked by at the other end, rounding a corner.

Cahal opened the door and stepped into the stairwell, stairs curving up and down. He set me down on the landing, turned his broad back, and flared his arms backward for me.

"Oh yeah," I whispered sarcastically. "This'll be much better. I won't be near your ears at all this way…"

Most notably—he caught me as I jumped up and left it to me to hang on—*you won't be randomly brushing against my cock.*

"Wow. So I was hitting buttons *and* working at a lever…"

Please stop.

"Too bad Penny is taken. You guys could really explore the weird together."

I do not know why she puts up with you.

"Yeah, me neither. I don't push her buttons like I apparently do yours."

I regret mentioning it.

"You certainly will, yes."

Changing the subject for obvious reasons, he added, *They won't fight the heir specifically, no. But they'd try to kill me and surround you with the intent to hold you for your father. Any sect leader will know the situation with you.*

He was taking the steps two at a time, a big guy with a muscular woman strapped to his back, and yet he barely made a sound. He was great at sneaking.

The light dwindled as we got lower and lower, the fairy lights affixed to the stairwell walls not all lit. They'd have no way to fix the problem, since demons weren't allowed in the Realm, and fairies weren't allowed down here. It was an incredibly crazy situation, and I was surprised the guy I'd gotten to know had been willing to put up with it all this time. Sectioning people off like this was crazy.

While I wasn't sure about Lucifer's goal to obliterate the elves and take over their castle and their world, I *would* help him rectify this wrong. Romulus was right—order needed to be reintroduced into the worlds. The coming war was necessary, even if it promised to be a great big hassle.

At the bottom, the light was nothing but a dim glow. I felt Darius's nearness and his calm expectation, waiting for me. Knowing I would show up.

"Put me down," I said, heart in my throat, needing to see him so badly it was a complex.

Cahal didn't waste any time, and as soon as my feet hit the ground, I was running along a stone wall. Three furry guards waited outside of a doorway with no actual door. I lit them on fire and let Cahal stick them with his sword while I ran through the opening. Around a corner, still hugging the stone wall, I made my way down a small hall that dumped me into a torture chamber of some kind, filled with complex contraptions that were apparently meant to cause pain for long periods of time. They looked like they'd kill a human pretty damn quickly.

Penny better still be alive. Emery with her.

At the other end, the smell down here horrifically musty, like the place had been used a few too many times and never aired out, I found another doorless opening with a few glowing fairy lights beyond. Darius waited right in there. Right on the other side of that—

I crashed into a huge form stepping around a corner. Startled, I stuck it full of air swords and knives and added a little splinter on its right pinky, just in case it was one of those people who said a paper cut was *so much worse* than any big wound. I shoved fire in the middle of those holes, expanding it so the heat would boil its insides, and then ripped it out of my path as it gurgled its way to an awful death.

Don't fuck with my friends.

All the cells were open save one in the middle. Fingers came through and wrapped around the bars. Lady fingers, belonging to one very bedraggled mage badly in need of a shower.

"What happened to your hair?" I asked her, stunned

to see a mostly bald head with a tiny bit of stubble and face cleared of hair.

Tears covered Penny's luminous blue eyes as she beheld me, her lip quivering. "I was supposed to save you this time," she said.

I couldn't help but laugh. "Next time, I promise. And it'll be *ah*-mazing!"

"We nearly lost a battle to a fire field," she said.

My gaze zipped to the man uncoiling from the ground, dangerous and deadly, corded with muscle and pent-up aggression. Darius's beautiful hazel eyes took me in, feasting on my face, then my body, then my lips. His relief and pleasure at seeing me flooded the bond.

I flicked my fingers, and the bars bent away from each other, my air power stronger than their steel. I was in with him in a moment, wrapping my arms around his neck and crushing him with my kiss, so grateful to see him again.

"Hello, *mon coeur*. This isn't quite the rescue for you I had in mind."

I laughed and kissed him again. "It was perfect. You gave me a reason to leave. Do you need blood?"

He grabbed the back of my neck and moved his lips down, blindingly fast, his teeth piercing my flesh. Sweet pleasure quickly covered the bite of pain, and I groaned with the feel of him taking from me. He pulled back with an intake of breath, his elongated canines stained crimson.

“Better than memory,” he murmured, and then licked the wound, sending a jolt of pleasure through me.

I pushed away from him, needing space. Especially from the urge to drag him down to the ground on top of me. Now I felt bad for making fun of Cahal.

A glance up revealed that Emery had already hastened Penny, who was still crying, out of the cell.

I nodded at him and stepped through. “Emery.”

He returned my nod. “Reagan. Good to see you.”

“I’ll bet. You all got yourself into quite the pickle, huh?” I patted him on the shoulder. We weren’t at the hugging stage yet. Penny I just let cry, because she seemed very close to shattering, and we needed her to hold it together so we could get out of here.

“Okay, here’s the plan…” I said, leading the way back to the torture chamber room. Cahal didn’t so much as nod hello. It was clear why he had no friends.

“You develop plans now?” Emery asked, following with the others as we headed for the stairs. “You really did learn some things.”

“Yeah. As I said, here’s the plan—we’re going to fight our way out of here, hopefully with the help of Ja and some of her vampires, collect the dragons, and then make a break for the Realm.”

“Ja is down here?” Darius asked.

“She snuck into my rooms in the castle and ambushed me with an offer to trade for help, yeah. She came into the Underworld after Penny tore down the fog—not wise, by the way—and framed Vlad. Lucifer now wants to kill Vlad. Until he finds out what really happened, obviously, which he likely will, and he will want to kill Ja. And you, of course. And probably Penny and Emery."

"Happy to join the club," Emery said.

"How will we rendezvous with Ja?" Darius asked.

"No idea. Hopefully we'll meet her along the way as we try to bust out of here."

"And the dragons? Do we have a meeting point?"

"They're out there flying around. I should be able to catch their attention."

"I take the planning thing back," Emery said.

"So what is the actual *plan* part of the plan?" Penny asked, sniffling.

"Freedom. Here we go." We ran up the stairs to the main floor. "How is your energy? Penny?"

"A little hungry, but we've been running on fumes for…however long we've been in this accursed place," she answered, matching my pace. "We'll make it."

"We don't have much choice," Emery murmured.

"That's why we'll make it, obviously," Penny retorted.

"Ohwee." We slowed as we neared the door leading out to the main floor. "Penny has found her inner Karen."

"Yes, I have, and I'm not even ashamed to admit it."

Cahal paused near the door, his magic wrapping around him and obscuring my vision of him even though I was five feet away. He paused, waiting for everyone to gather on the landing, Darius taking up the rear, before he nodded at me and stepped through.

I let the door close behind him until a soft knock came. I pushed out next.

You and he have developed a strong working relationship, Darius thought as I slipped out the door and took a fast look around. One dead monster-looking dude. Cahal worked fast.

"Yeah," I whispered as the others filed out, Darius stepping to my back. "We've had to. I'll tell you all about it when we get out of here. We only know the main entrance. Do you know of any other?"

"No," Darius murmured, probably to keep everyone on the same page. "That's the way we came in. We didn't get a chance to explore before we were drugged and locked up."

"I was wondering how you'd been taken." I nodded at Cahal, who started jogging along the right side of the hall. I crossed to be right behind him, the rest of them trailing me. "I still think I should just demand to leave. I'm kind of a big deal around here."

"This sect knows we came here to free you. They know that Lucifer closed access to the Underworld to root us out and planned to execute us himself," Darius said softly. "They will not just stand aside as you walk out. They will try to capture you, possibly killing us in the process, to turn you back over to Lucifer and gain his favor. Our only way out is by force."

"Told you so," Cahal said.

Oh good, he finally had someone to gang up on me with.

Penny's and my boots echoed against the walls in the empty hallway. I didn't bother trying to be quiet with her thumping around, obviously tired but trucking on. Light flickered around us, very little sound reaching us from the front. Cahal crossed to the other side of the hall, no longer able to use the shadow trick to hide the rest of us, and slowed near the corner. He edged his head out to look around before pulling back. He flattened against the wall, not saying a word. That meant danger was near.

My turn.

I pulled back a little and drifted to the center of the hallway, pointing first at Penny and then at Emery. I turned the point into two fingers and indicated the space right behind me. Darius and Cahal got the next points, behind them.

It was time to finally, *finally* display the full extent of my magic. And I'd make sure it was a spectacular show.

CHAPTER 21

I STRUTTED FORWARD like I owned these halls and the people in it. Just like Lucifer would've done.

A horde waited for us, three wide and ten or so deep, huge bodies standing in the way. They wore metal armor on their heads and across their wide chests. Thick, hairy, weapon-laden tree-trunk arms draped by their sides, and muscular legs ended in feet or hooves or stumps. The last would be easier to knock over.

Glaciem magic swelled. Air condensed in front of me, blocking the way.

"They don't like fire," I said with a grin, stopping in front of them, my team behind me.

"So let's burn their faces off and get out of here," Penny said.

I lifted my eyebrows and spared a moment to glance back at her. Her face was closed down into hard lines, her eyes determined, her bearing tense but ready. There was an edge to her that I hadn't seen before, like she was on the verge of breaking. Like it was her last straw. This place had clearly gotten to her.

While a part of me delighted in this tough, hardened version of Penny, guilt quickly overrode it. I'd been pampered and treated with kid gloves, flying on dragons and playing games with creepy demons; she'd been scared and hurt and dragged through hell, almost literally. She'd probably endured horrors she'd never dreamed of on this trip—the kind of things that well and truly might show up in her nightmares. And she'd done it all to help me.

"Fuck," I said to myself as anger thrashed within me like a vicious serpent. "Move or die," I said, turning to the host.

"We will not hurt you, princess. Let us get you back to your—"

I sent a blast of hellfire down the center of the hall, punching through the center of their faction. I didn't run forward as I might've once done. I had an image to uphold. If they were going to call me princess, I'd kill them like royalty.

I ran my hand through the air, unraveling their *Glaciem* magic as though it were a containment spell set up by newbies. Their power level didn't compare to mine, and while it had been expertly woven, they didn't have my special secret sauce. Penny's secret sauce, even.

"Light 'em up, Penny." I pushed my way down the hall, using my own *Glaciem* magic to ram them backward.

"With pleasure." Her voice wobbled, and I felt another pang in my chest. I'd pushed Penny at danger a time or two, but always with the awareness that she had a line—one I shouldn't cross. Something told me this trip had finally shoved her over.

I'd have to make amends later, though—more demons were coming around from behind, trying to trap us. I could feel their magic pulsing.

"What's the story, Darius?" I called back.

"Work on the front. We have the back."

Penny blasted fire from beside me, catching my arm in the crossfire. At least it wasn't my eyebrows.

I joined with more hellfire, ripping it through the heads and bodies of the demons on the left. A wicked spell let loose, Emery joining the fray.

"Fuck it," I ground out. I might be royalty, but I still hated walking into battle. There was nothing for it but to charge.

I picked up the pace, running now, closing the distance. I stopped the hellfire as we circled the last corner before the entrance. The breath whooshed out of me.

The place was packed.

The larger creatures blocked the way, but I could see the smaller variety behind them, and another demon in a wrinkled suit. Power pulsed, hard and hot, from their crew. It shoved me, tossing me backward into Penny and Emery, before hardening into a wall.

"How's that rear?" I called, working at that magic, applying fire to rip it apart. It wasn't as intricate as some of my father's creations, but these demons were obviously more powerful than the ones we'd just roasted and toasted, and their block was robust, since they were all working together, constantly rebuilding the wall as I tried to tear it down.

"All dead," Cahal called up.

It isn't a continuous stream of enemy from back here, Darius thought. *We've dispatched them. There is likely nowhere to escape to in that direction. We must leave this way, or not at all.*

"Oh, we're leaving." I rolled my neck and took a second, studying what was in front of me, like I might any spell. "It's really not so different," I mused, tracing the magic with my eyes, feeling it, noticing the complexities of the construction. "I have to break it down all at once, like tearing off a Band-Aid, and then attack before they can get their bearings."

"What can we do?" Emery asked. His arm brushed mine, and a zing of magic worked through me. It reminded me of taking down that massive spell at the Mages' Guild when we somehow merged our power and were able to tag-team a robust spell to bring it down.

The pyramid of power…

I put out my hands. Emery's rough fingers wrapped

around my right wrist. Penny's hand filled my other hand. Usually I would shrug it off and tell her to grab me in a not-so-friend-friend place, but, well, if she wanted to hold hands, I owed her that.

Plus of a lot of dead things.

Electricity rolled across me, and our magic swelled, filling the space and beyond.

"Wow, you boosted your power," Emery said as he pushed up to analyze the spell.

I punched holes through weak parts of the construction, spurting fire through them, while Penny and Emery worked on a spell. She bent to look at a section, and Emery let go of my wrist to hook his arm through mine and waggle his fingers. In a moment, I felt their magic join together, and then it joined mine as I continued to poke holes in all the weak areas.

"Thank you, you vile little creature, for bequeathing me your magic…" Penny muttered, and I knew she was talking about the Red Cap that she'd stolen the godly magic from. The demons' air wall blackened from the middle, the damage working outward like spiderwebbing glass. A hole developed and started growing.

I pushed the fire through faster, my own secret sauce aiding the dual-mages' combined efforts—the three of us tearing the wall down.

Emery flinched beside me.

"What?" I asked.

"Something's...coming. My..." He paused again.

"His premonition." Penny's breathing came faster.

"A large demon with black wings, followed by a black dragon..." Emery said. "I keep getting it, over and over. It isn't immediate death, but—"

"My father. Shit. He's coming." I glanced back for Cahal. His eyes were flat and hard.

Go, he thought. *You cannot get caught.*

"How's your pain tolerance?" I asked through gritted teeth, working faster, feeling the enemy trying to rebuild. They were building a new wall of air down the way, too, knowing they only had to delay us, not stop us.

"I look like a cue ball, how do you think?" Penny asked. "We have something that helps."

"Great." I shook them off and pushed forward, the edges of the fraying wall catching me but not hurting. It was my magic; of course it wouldn't hurt.

Penny grunted. No one else made a sound.

I reached the first line of demons like a falling star, anger exploding out of me in bursts of complex, incredibly powerful magic. I slashed and struck, summoning fire from the ground and reaching into ten of the weaker demons and grabbing control.

Kill... I commanded them, turning them on one another, their swords swinging, arms and chunks of flesh flying. Blood spattered me and a demon crashed to the ground on the right, Penny's spell taking half its face off. Large bodies fell on the left, Emery's fighting having always been wicked.

Darius pushed up beside me as I used air to shove the demons in front of us into a funnel, letting us fight a dozen at a time instead of the whole host. His swampy, whitish vampire form hissed, and he burst into action, ripping and tearing with his claws and magic. He lunged forward and tore into a demon's neck, drinking while he was there, and then picked it up and threw it ahead of us.

Penny exploded it in midair.

"Good grief, Penny, he was already dying," I said, working my hellfire in bursts, needing to keep firm control over my energy. I couldn't fade like I had at the elves' castle. This time, I had to make it through to the end. We all did.

"And now he is decorating our enemy, isn't he?" she said.

"I think I just got lady wood," I said with a grin as I activated my air sword and skewered a demon. I blasted fire down the way and held the air funnel, fighting against those trying to tear it down.

Ten more demons turned against their peers, aiding Darius's rip-and-tear-fest to my right. Spells were lobbed over us, vicious and deadly, leaving ribbons of flesh by the time we got closer.

There are still too many, Cahal said.

"I got another premonition," Emery yelled. "Whatever is going to happen is going down soon."

"Dang it," I spat out, pushing harder, faster.

Another pulse of air shoved against mine, this one the strongest I'd felt. Had to be the sect leader—the *conspector*. They'd pack the most punch.

"Take the others," I said, veering that way. I'd need to take the head honcho out to give us a fighting chance.

A wave of inhuman shouts and yelling filled the hall, followed by a chorus of hissing. A demon body flew high. Then another, blood gushing out and raining down on those below.

"More vampires," Penny said. "Ja…" The name was spoken on a sigh of relief. She clearly thought Ja wouldn't betray us. She was almost certainly correct. Hopefully.

I kept my focus, pushing to the right, toward that pulse of power I'd felt. I released my hold on the remaining demons around Darius, stunned now and easy pickin's for him. I grabbed a few other demons, keeping the effort small to save strength, and directed them at that pulse. I caught sight of it, a female form in a man's wrinkled suit, on a little dais, overlooking the shifting, seething crowd.

"What is the deal with the wrinkled suits?" I asked as I closed the distance, shoving demons out of my way with a swell of magic, then lighting them on fire and letting them burn.

The leader's beady eyes flicked and shifted until they landed on me. It didn't make any sign that it knew me. Or show any emotion at all, actually. It stared, blank-faced, with a pug nose much too close to its eyes and a hairline starting where its eyebrows should be.

"You didn't get that quite right," I said, pointing as I approached, creating a channel of fire around me.

"Your highness." It bent slightly.

I clucked my tongue. "It's your *heinous*, actually, and that wasn't much of a bow."

I paused as the demons I controlled battled around me, through the flame, dying as they killed to create a little bubble around the leader. I motioned to the demon, knowing I needed to hurry, but stopping in front of it all the same. There would be survivors, and I wanted them to know who they were dealing with here. If I ever came back to the Underworld, it was important for them to know that I wasn't just some human off the street—I *belonged* here. I had the power to prove it.

"Bow," I demanded, and let the demons go around me. They staggered through the flame, faltering and falling.

It tensed, I could see. Its power pulsed higher as it prepared to act.

I squinted a little, tilted my head, grinned, and

thought to myself, *Are you sure?* I wanted to see if he'd read the cues.

Nothing in its demeanor changed. Its expression didn't shift. Its body didn't move. All the same, I knew it suddenly doubted whether it could stand against me.

"Bow," I said like I was chomping on glass, speaking its language, something that came naturally when down here. I didn't add the ending to that command, but we both knew it all the same. "Or die."

Slowly, as though an old granny was winding its crank, it bent toward me, spine curling. Fire raged around us. A pasty-white vampire ran by, splattered in black blood, crimson dripping from its fangs.

"Good," I said when the leader's head was closer to the floor than the ceiling. "Do not trouble yourself about your efforts here. I know you think you are acting in my father's best interest. I will let you make it up to me at another time. Kill one of my friends, however, and I will pull your insides out through your mouth."

I gripped its middle in a tight fist of magic, knowing it would be much too strong for me to fully control but wanting to give it a jolt all the same. I let fire shimmy the air around it. Then I knocked it off its dais and turned. It would know my strength, it'd know I had both types of magic, and any question of my lineage would be put to rest. Why this mattered, when I might never come back here, I did not know, but Lucifer had taught me more than magic. He'd taught me to hold my own with underlings, or die when I turned my back. For better or worse, I was the heir, and I felt the need to own my place in this savage sect.

I shoved a wall of demons back, starting to feel fatigue. A spell ballooned to my right, and I knew the natural dual-mages were also fading. It wasn't as strong or vicious as what they would normally put together under dire circumstances.

"Hurry, let's get out of here," I yelled as I ran toward the door, covering my people in magic and raising fire all around them.

Emery grabbed Penny and yanked her after me. Darius ran a moment later, in his monster form and covered in goo. More vampires joined us, Cahal amongst them. He'd traded up for a larger sword, and he swung it like it was an extension of his body.

Another pasty-white vampire—Ja—filed in at my side, sparing a moment to rip the middle out of a smaller demon. Without missing a step, her monster feet turned into human feet and she changed into a petite woman form…with vicious claws.

"Will your whole party take to the dragons?" she asked on the run.

I magically shoved demons out of the way as Penny and Emery fired off spells, toppling bodies. Fire rose behind us, as hot as I could make it given my dwindling energy. We made it outside as a dragon roar tried to freeze me up before the effect slid off—Archion, soaring overhead. Emery staggered, Darius bumping into him, but Penny shoved them both.

"Fight it—it's just magic. Here, look." She conjured a spell before the roar subsided and threw it wide, blanketing the throng of demons in front of us, trying to hurl spears up at the dragons like idiots. The spell hit them hard, their already slowed bodies turning to lead and stopping completely.

Sparkling white scales caught my eye as Saphira dove and unleashed a white-hot lick of fire. It rolled over a group of demons, as near to hellfire as non-hellfire could get. It seared those in its path, sending everyone running out of the way. She beat her large wings to lift higher into the sky before she trumpeted, her bowel-shaking roar filling the air.

"Wow," Penny said on a release of breath, staring up at the dragon with wide, adoring eyes.

"I so called it," I murmured, not quite sure how I was going to get everyone loaded up. To Ja I said, "Yes, we'll double up on the dragons. We'll go out the way we came in. You should take another exit, though, straight to the Edges. Lucifer is coming. We'll tear down the containment spell, but he might be hot on our heels."

"Noted. We'll work out the particulars on the other side." She meant about who owed whom. She put a hand to my shoulder, her eyes serious. "Get out of here alive, heir. Get to the Brink. There is no other option."

She morphed into her other form and sped away, her people with her.

I shepherded the others to the side of the building, away from the panicked crowd trying to fight three dragons. No one else came out of the building after us. The *conspector* had clearly thought better about killing one of my people and going up against three powerful dragons. Wise.

Archion, I thought with everything I had. But he was across what had turned into a battlefield, cleaning up the perimeter with bursts of flame.

"Stay here," I told Darius, sweeping my gaze to Cahal.

"No." Penny reached forward to grab me, her eyes wild. "No! Not this time. If we go anywhere, we go together. I'm not leaving you alone in danger."

I didn't have time to argue, and it would be funny to give her what she wanted. I'd say I'd be going to hell but…it seemed I was already there.

"Suit yourself." I yanked her toward me, and up we went, hovering over the battlefield to my dragon.

"Not what I meant," she yelled, looking down as we lifted farther and farther off the ground. "Why aren't the other demons hovering?"

"Did you just call me a demon?"

"If the shoe fits, you know what I mean?"

I laughed, thinking Archion's name again. "They don't have enough power, I imagine. Or don't want to actually get eaten by the dragons. I'm not sure why they're even fighting."

Coppelia dove to my right before snapping out her wings and watching us. She was off a moment later, toward Archion. He gained altitude after a burst of fire before he got the message.

A spot of black on the horizon caught my attention. I squinted into the growing light of the day, trying to make it out. A black blob against the bluish sky. Was it a trick of my eyes, or had Daddy Dearest finally caught on?

"We need to make shapes," I said softly as Archion sped toward me. A spear flew past him.

"Why? What is it?" Penny asked, following my gaze. She didn't squint, which meant her strictly human eyes couldn't make out what I was looking at. That was good news, at least. We had some time. Not much, but some.

Archion swooped down below us, and I let go of the hover.

"Holy fart bags," Penny shouted before landing behind me on Archion's back.

"Really? After all this, you still can't swear?" I asked, thinking, *We need to drop Penny on Saphira's back. Then we have to grab the others and go. Lucifer is coming.*

Archion wasted no time, his wings beating mightily.

"I have sworn—oh, have I sworn. But I have to regain some sort of decorum and hope Darius doesn't tell you what else I have done."

My smile was wicked, and then laughter boomed out of me as I shoved her off the dragon. Saphira was there in an instant, sliding under Penny, who grabbed on and repositioned herself as though they'd practiced that move a million times. I felt Archion's surprise.

Yeah, right? I thought as he turned toward the guys, waiting for us with weapons out. *I mean, I knew she would be a good dragon for Penny, but that was almost a smoother move than with us.*

Beginner's luck, he thought.

I laughed again as he reached the others and turned, blasting out billowing flames at a group of less-than-smart demon holdouts. Saphira and Coppelia joined, clearing a big space to give us time. Cahal leapt up onto Coppelia immediately, and Emery and Darius stared up at us for a moment.

"Emery with Penny and Darius with me, obviously. Let's go!" I waved them on.

Emery paused, his eyes going distant. Crap, he was having another vision.

"Go, go, go!" I hollered.

Emery started running, looking at the sky. Darius

was beside Archion in a moment as Cahal and Coppelia lifted into the air.

I have no clothes, he said, looking at Archion's scales. He was worried about skidding his bells and tackle against rough scales. It was a fair assessment.

I had a sort of sports bra on, a strip around my breasts and upper back, as close as the demons could get to what I'd wanted, so I ripped off my shirt and laid it behind me before I lifted him up. Not like my chest being nude would have stopped me. Glancing back, seeing Emery had already climbed up behind Penny, I told Archion, *We're ready.*

Darius's arms came around me, his skin sliding against my bare sides and stomach. A delicious shiver coursed through me, but Archion lifted into the sky with brawn and power, regaining my focus.

Like we planned? Archion asked.

Yes. Same path out as we practiced, but continue on this time.

We led the way, overtaking Coppelia, as I looked behind us. My heart stopped in my throat.

It was absolutely a black blob in the sky. A big black blob in the hazy shape of a dragon heading our way. Near it, flying on its own, was another winged creature. Lucifer.

Just like in Emery's vision.

Not to pressure you, but hurry*!* I thought.

Darius turned, looking behind us, and then back. *We have time.*

If the barrier Lucifer had laid blocking off the entrance/exit to the Edges wasn't a doozy, then sure, we had time. If Lucifer stopped at the violence sect to see what was what, sure, we had time.

I doubted we had time.

Give it all you have, bud. I patted Archion's side.

Saphira kept up with us, Penny leaning forward like she was racing a horse. Coppelia wasn't keeping up as well, though. Smaller and not as strong, she didn't have the power of the other two. Instead of trying, though, she veered a little to the right and dipped lower. Cahal's magic enveloped them both, and it was hard to see them against the ground far below.

I nodded, turning straight, leaning forward like Penny was doing, hoping to hell we'd have enough time to break that spell.

And, if we managed, that Lucifer didn't follow us out.

CHAPTER 22

"THERE IT IS," I said, squinting through the air at the river passing below us.

It wasn't a fog bank this time. On the other side of the river, beyond the boats but before the Edges, stood a solid black wall. Power pounded from it, even from this distance. I knew the magic would be complex and dangerous, making it so no mages or demons could break it. Lucifer was the master of this world for a reason, and I knew he'd poured his everything into that wall.

"Damn it, damn it, damn it…" I leaned back on Archion, and he slowed as we glided forward.

Climb to the top of that thing where it connects with the ceiling, I thought, *and give me a look from there to the ground. I want to take its measure.*

Archion did so, and I motioned for Saphira to follow. Penny and Emery needed to see this.

It stretched on for miles. Miles and miles. But that was just an illusion, of course. All of this was an illusion, and this wall was bedrocked into it.

I looked back the way we'd come. That spot of black had slowed at the sect, perhaps touching down, perhaps not, but it didn't matter. Lucifer was on our tail again.

Thankfully, we only had one dragon to contend with. He hadn't called in any backup. Not yet, anyway.

Land, I thought, having seen my fill. I needed to talk with Penny and Emery.

"That dragon is amazing," Penny said, her hair windswept. She blinked at me, starstruck, then pointed at her head. "She was speaking to me. *In my head!*"

"Yes, yes, good, good. Come on." I pointed at the huge wall. "We need to get through this, or you will die and that dragon will be riderless again."

Emery pushed toward the wall, looking up to the top and then out to the sides. He leaned in, scanning the magic in front of him. "It's a stroke of genius."

"No, it's the work of a master," I said, running magic over it to see if I felt anything more.

Penny released the spell that usually unraveled my magic—the same one that had likely taken down the fog. The crisp layer over the wall shone and then fizzled, burning away, exposing another finely wrought layer underneath.

"He knows our magic," I whispered. "He clearly built this to withstand it. His yin to your yang. He obviously knows best how to thwart me." My eyes scanned, my magic washing across it, pulling and tweaking and digging, trying to find access. Every time I did, though, I was met with another layer of intricately woven air and fire magic, in a different style. Holy crap.

I started laughing. I couldn't help it.

"He taught me a lot, but he certainly didn't teach me how to do this. That bastard. Those illusions in the castle were nothing. Child's play. Training wheels."

Cahal strode over, his dragon standing with the others.

"What's the story? We don't have a lot of time," he said, stopping beside me.

I explained the issue.

His brow furrowed, and he looked over his shoulder at those black dots, growing bigger as the moments twisted by. "I don't think he meant them as training wheels. His last heir had trouble with tearing down his illusions. It took the last heir a long time to learn how to put them up. But I agree, this is...highly advanced. I can actually feel the power thrumming from it."

"We can do this," Emery said, nodding as he looked it over. "We can do this. Between Reagan and Penny and me, we're powerful enough, and we have all of the necessary elements. We can get through this."

"It was never a question of *if*, it is a question of whether we have enough time." I ran my fingers through my hair.

"We can get through this in enough time." Penny

pushed at the tattered sleeves of her shirt. "I am getting out of this place, do you hear me? I am getting out and"—she jabbed Emery's chest, making him flinch—"you are getting out and"—she stepped forward and jabbed her finger into my arm—"you are getting out and"—she jabbed the air at Darius and Cahal—"you two are getting out. We're *all* getting out, and I am taking my dragon with me. She can't leave without magical aid. I have magical aid, apparently, though I don't know what that means. So she's coming. Try to argue with me. Go ahead."

We all stared at her—her wider-than-normal eyes, her tense shoulders, her balled fists.

She nodded. "That's what I thought. C'mon, pyramid, let's get to work."

Penny has been on the edge of breaking since she was forced to leave you behind, Darius thought.

"Yes, I can see that," I murmured.

"That rat is talking about me, isn't he?" Penny snorted. "I don't even care."

She pushed Emery at me and then stepped up to my other side, facing the wall.

I took a deep breath and focused. Yes, we could do this. He'd obviously put a lot of time and effort into this wall. He'd correctly interpreted what Penny had done with the fog and put up this blockade to prevent it from happening again. I was sure he'd put some safeguards for me in there, too. He was incredibly intelligent and clever.

The magic was too layered and thick, too intricate a combination of *Glaciem* and *Incendium* for me to simply rip it down the way I had with the castle illusions. I'd have to weasel through it and create weaknesses throughout, and then Penny and Emery could apply their magic and break it off in pieces. Only *then*, once it was as full of holes as Swiss cheese, could I tear it down in one magical *rip*. It was the fastest strategy for getting through it. It had to be.

After I'd explained my strategy, Penny and Emery both nodded, determination on their faces. Their magic rose, and with it, electricity ran through us, tingling the ends of my hair and shocking down my back.

"We have the godly magic in common," Penny murmured as we worked, sweat quickly prickling my brow. "That's why it feels like this when we connect, don't you think?"

A large, familiar hand closed around my shoulder. Cahal, his magic zipping through us.

"Yes, that has to be it," Penny said, answering herself.

My mind wandered, considering everything I'd learned here, trying to find a lesson that could be applied. A key that would loosen this spell and make it as easy to pull down as the fog must've been. As easy to pull down as the castle illusions. What had made them different…

"The dragon shape is clear now," Cahal said, apparently our timekeeper.

"Lucifer is flying beside it, a separate entity," Darius murmured.

"Super," I said, squeezing my eyes shut, working and thinking, poring over everything. Plunging holes in the spell, working on its weaknesses, pointing the way for Penny and Emery to exploit any flaws, of which there were virtually none.

"Lucifer looks like he is rejoining the dragon," Darius murmured.

I glanced back, heart speeding up. Lucifer changed shape mid-flight, turned, and lowered onto the dragon, the shift as seamless as a magnet clicking onto metal.

Beginner's luck, my left foot. We've got work to do, Archion, I thought, not sure whether I was close enough to be heard. He didn't answer.

"Shall I get on Coppelia and get in their way?" Cahal asked.

You are not enough, Archion said. Clearly he'd heard me just fine. I relayed what he'd said. *I will go.*

"Wait. Just wait a minute," I said, working faster, pouring everything into it. "Wait, let's see if we can—"

"Saphira wants to go with Archion to stall Lucifer and Tatsu," Penny reported.

"We're not making much headway." Emery laid more spell. It barely ate away at the barrier. "We can't work fast enough. We need more time. A *lot* more time."

Let them go, Darius thought to me, clearly not wanting to usurp my authority here by saying it out loud. *If you don't, we have no chance.*

"There must be a way," I said, biting my lip, racing through every memory stored in my head. "There must be. How did he make it so strong and those other spells so…" I rolled over a thought, then backed up and analyzed it. The flower, hovering over my palm. The walls I'd created in the castle. The ice and fire magical blockades I'd put up at the doors of my chambers. I hadn't anchored any of them. I'd done some pretty good, delicate weaves, but I hadn't anchored a single one.

Mages' spells, when not properly anchored, were weaker. They were much easier to tear down.

The illusions in the Realm were anchored to the ground, even in places that didn't require it.

Anchoring gave strength.

I looked down at the base of the wall, way down into the very foundation of this place. Up at the top, it had been the same thing. He'd rooted this thing down into the floor and nailed it all around.

I spun, looking at the endless miles of desolate,

sandy beach. Of the piers, only one in sight. The sky, covering the cave ceiling. None of those illusions were as finely wrought. They'd been slapped up, almost, just like many of the castle walls. They'd been good enough for the moment. He'd probably intended to repair everything once he came back to take down this wall.

"Tear it down." I pulled at our surroundings—the bank, the docks—picking through the illusions easily, eroding them with holes and cracks and crevices. Destroying the base for the roots. "Take away the foundation, weaken the spell."

Penny's eyebrows pinched together, but Emery wasted no time. Magic flew from his hands immediately, helping me with the beach. Finally, Penny joined in with gusto, understanding what we were doing.

"Go get the ceiling," Emery said, and he jerked his head at Archion.

I took a running leap onto Archion, my hovering ability kicking in, and up we went, climbing quickly. At the top, I yanked and tore at the spell, pulling it down. Roots hung down through the rock and dirt on the ceiling, little spiderwebs of life. Water pooled in areas. I watched a drop wobble on the end of a glistening rock and let go, falling to the ground far below.

I'd ponder how all of this was possible later.

Black wings beat at the sky, Tatsu so close. Lucifer on her back, looking straight at me.

"Oh crap, get to the ground, hurry!" I said, Archion diving immediately. I held on, willing him to go faster—willing *myself* to go faster. "Oh crap, oh crap."

I landed in a rush and stumbled to the others, continuing to break through Lucifer's magic work. The desolate ground pulled back to reveal weeds and dirt and sand, with clumps of clay holding moisture. The dying illusion raced toward the docks, and several emerged from the haze, and then all of them, the boats tied to their docks, the Boatmen looking our way. The turbulent sea was slowly exposed, rolling and racing past.

"Good, good. Hurry, guys, we have to hurry." I cleared the rest of the illusion away and then refocused on the thick wall in front of us. "All you've got. The dragons can do the work after this. Fast as you can."

We went after it like a starving man jumps on a steak. I punched holes and created nails of swirling fire and ice, breaking apart his design so Penny and Emery could exploit the damage.

"He's right on us," Cahal said.

"What do we do?" Darius asked urgently.

What could we do? Keep going and hope for the best.

CHAPTER 23

T*HEY ARE ALL there,* Tatsu thought as they closed the distance to his daughter.

Not all. There are no vampires beyond Durant.

They'd stopped briefly at the Haedus sect, knowing full well that Reagan had escaped with her friends. The place was in chaos. Sure enough, they'd left not long before, having severely rattled and cowed the powerful *conspector.*

Lucifer hadn't allowed himself to feel the pulsing of pride that she had donned her mantle even while running from it. He'd grabbed the briefest bit of info from the leader—none of the vampires helping her sounded like Vlad—and had taken off after her.

They are working on the wall, Tatsu said, as though he didn't also have eyes.

Urgency pumped a solid beat within his chest. He could not let her get away. She would make a fool of him. She would show his weakness as a ruler.

She has showcased the strength of your bloodline, Tatsu said. He must've let his thoughts slip. *She will show the powerful pedigree of her friends. Of her dragons. Of her person. She is your heir, through and through. She is worthy of the Underworld. Of the title of princess.*

She is trying to escape all of those things, or don't you know what fleeing in the middle of the night generally means?

She is trying to escape one she sees as a tyrant.

You're on her side, are you?

I am on your side. You *need to be on her side.*

She won't get through that wall. I used all my best conspectors *to help form it. Maybe if she had a few hours, but not in mere minutes. I'll have her. I'll apologize and we'll start again. This can be amended.*

What is… He let the thought linger.

The illusion of the beach unraveled before his eyes. Magic ate through it like acid, ripping it into tatters and revealing what lay beneath.

His daughter stood with her friends, grouped around the wall and working on one spot.

If she wanted to break it more quickly, they should spread out, work at different parts of it. But then, there was only one with the magic to do that, he supposed. The other two, the mages, weren't as strong. They could erode old constructs, but they seemed to need Reagan's help on his latest work.

Faster, he said, leaning forward, his heart speeding up. *We can reach them before they go. Faster.*

They will attack.

The mages are nothing. I've confronted angelic magic before. Or how do you think I survived?

Reagan will attack, and Archion with her. He is a handful. If Saphira joins...

He shook his head. She might attack, that was true. But she lacked experience. She had brute power, but no finesse. No advanced knowledge. She would not stand a chance. He'd have her, and they could put all this behind them.

Fire flared in front of Reagan, followed by a swirl of what looked like frost. More, in patches, one location and then another. He could not see what else was happening, not from such a distance, but they were working fast, urgently. Another burst of fire, bigger than the last. A white crack wormed up his onyx wall.

"No," he said, half standing, looking harder. It grew, the crack, before another one started. And another. "No! Go, Tatsu, go!"

She put on a burst of speed. She might not think this was the best course of action, but she was loyal—she'd help him now, just like he always helped her when she asked for something.

The wall began to erode. Cracks ran through the structure, racing for the sides.

How? He squinted, trying to see into the distance. He'd made that wall incredibly complex. It was some of his best work. "How…"

The hole kept getting larger, growing and growing. They now raced for their dragons, Reagan helping them mount with bursts of air, faltering slightly when it was her turn to lift. She was exhausted, panting from the effort; he was close enough to see that. Right on them now. They still had to get up to speed and fly over the Edges. They still had to exit, one dragon at a time—the exit too small for them all to leave together. He could grab at least one of her friends. She'd sacrifice herself for them.

Is this what you want? Tatsu asked as they closed the gap.

All three dragons had made it through the crumbling wall.

"Go," he growled, willing her to go faster, half wanting to fly himself. He couldn't compete against a dragon, though. He needed her.

Is this what you want? she repeated as they barreled through the hole, the edges continuing to recede. With time, it would dissipate to nothing, the same way the fog had.

He ignored her. Because yes, this was what he wanted. He wanted his daughter to live down here with him. He wanted an equal to talk to. To rule by his side. He had never wanted to elevate someone to that post by marriage or something so unpoetic as a promotion.

He'd wanted his bloodline to dictate the right candidate—the person literally born for the role. All these long years, and he'd never found anyone. He'd never given up hope, though. He'd never bent, always believing it would happen.

And here she was, the woman born to rule. She must want the title that went with her talents. How could she resist? How could she turn away from the beauty down here, the ability to create her dreams and laugh at her nightmares?

"She is confused," he said through gritted teeth. "Her friends are making her confused."

They soared over the pits, everyone scattering. He wanted to burn them all where they stood. Clear this place out. It was a cesspool, had been for…countless quantities of time.

In a way, he'd created this mess, this eyesore on the entrance to his kingdom, by putting up the fog. They'd gathered here, the ones who could no longer travel freely inside.

No, he wasn't the one who'd done it. The elves had pushed this on him. They had forced his hand. He should've pushed back before now. He shouldn't have been so willing to follow their terms.

Reagan neared the exit. Tatsu was right on them. If she got through, then they would get the druid, easy.

No, the druid was pushing up to go first. Reagan

was holding back.

You shall have your dragons back, he thought to Tatsu, his focus acute. *Most of them, at least.*

I do not want them back. Let them go. They've been suffocating down here for too long. Let them see clear skies and bask in real sun.

The druid disappeared through the exit. Reagan motioned Saphira on wildly, her movements erratic, desperate to get everyone out. It must've been like this when the elves took her. She'd stayed behind and sent the others to safety.

The vampire rose from the back of Archion. He must not have expected it, because he made a wild grab for Reagan, not wanting to leave. The girl on Saphira leaned toward Reagan, her face desperate, as the vampire touched down in a wobbly landing. Her friends did not want to leave her. She was forcing them out, sacrificing herself for them again. Dooming herself.

She thought of him in no better terms than she did the elves.

What Tatsu had said filtered through his mind.

Saphira pushed forward, eagerly, and disappeared from his kingdom. Only Reagan was left, and they were on her now. She had no hope. One push and they would have her.

"Stop."

His heart broke to hear the word fall from his lips.

"Stop," he said louder as Reagan turned to him on the back of Archion, not even trying to push through. She must be worried he would follow her. She wanted her friends to get to safety.

Her expression was defiant and resolute.

These last few weeks, he'd gotten the pliant Reagan. The student. The trickster.

Now he could see the steel that infused her backbone. She would never back down, not like this. She could not be forced, Tatsu was right. Just as he could not be, in his younger years. She had been born for the role of heir, and stubborn defiance was part of that.

"Let her go," he said, needing to hear himself say the words, refusing to sag as his daughter beheld him. Refusing to let her see him breaking. He held up his hand, wishing her well.

Confusion stole over her expression, followed by understanding. She placed a hand on her heart and bowed. Respect given, respect returned.

Turn and go. He tore his eyes away. *She won't trust me to stick to my word. Turn, and let her see us leave.*

Tatsu did as he'd instructed, blowing a trumpet to Archion. They got it back, and then they were away.

Shall we go after the vampires? Tatsu thought as they flew over the Edges.

No. Let her deal with them. But if any vampire should come into my kingdom without her, they will see me directly. If they do not, I will make an example out of them.

So you aren't going to repair the fog?

No. We are going to prepare for war.

They flew, and he let Tatsu handle the details, thinking of his daughter leaving the kingdom. His kingdom. He wondered if she'd ever think of it as hers.

He wanted to ask her.

This time, he would do it on her home turf.

And we will prepare a visit to the princess of the Dark Kingdom. For that will be her title whether or not she accepts it. After this, she has earned it.

CHAPTER 24

"IT'S FINE. NO one will notice, honest."

Roger stared at me like I'd grown two heads. Three dragons crouched on his lawn beside his very private, very secluded, and not-so-secret house. You could keep a great many things from a great many supernatural creatures, but you could not keep much from Darius. When Darius wanted to know about an enemy turned acquaintance, he learned everything. Including Roger's previously secret hideaway in the Sierra foothills that only a few other people in the world knew about.

Well, a few other people…and the government. Shifters largely followed the rules. Vampires did not. Being a good guy came with its drawbacks. And now Roger knew.

He continued to stare at me. He was clearly at a loss for words.

"Look." I gestured around us, to the sprawling house that could fit a wife and a whole litter of children, the gorgeous grounds that would thrill even the fae, and the woods stretching for four hundred acres. The guy might dress like he was just another kid on the block, but he was clearly loaded. Being an alpha paid well. Somehow. Or maybe he'd just stolen some golden bricks from the elves. "Who is going to see them? They won't bother you. They'll just hang out here until the battle, and then they can hopefully head back to the Realm and fly around there. It'll be great. You'll love them."

Penny sat off to the side, basically draped over a patio chair, her arms hanging limp and her legs sprawled out in front of her. A plastic bottle of bubbles sat beside her, which had been her pastime for the last hour, until she'd just given up and opted to stare at nothing for a while. We were taking it slow. She needed some time to back away from the edge.

It had been two days since we'd returned from the Underworld, and I still couldn't shake the image of my dad lifting his hand in salute and letting me go. It hadn't been an acknowledgment of defeat. He would've had me—if not there, at the gate, then he could have followed me into the Realm. I'd known it when I sent Darius with Penny. I'd known it when I stopped Penny from desperately trying to leap from her dragon to mine.

The jig had been up. My escape plan hadn't gone smoothly enough, and he'd caught me.

But instead of actually capturing me…he'd let me go. He'd respectfully said goodbye.

That fact made me want to go straight back to him. To my wing. To the castle and its weird gardens. It made me want to continue training and then maybe tour the kingdom and scare more *conspectors*. That had been a great time. Better than freaking out shifters, because demons were crafty and would give me some real trouble if they fought back.

But that was probably a pipe dream. Lucifer might have let me go this time, but it was hard to say what plot that worked into. What game he might be playing. I needed to just count my lucky stars and look on his kingdom fondly.

In the meantime, at least I'd gotten Archion out. Apparently, dragons couldn't leave the Underworld unless escorted by a card-carrying member of the magical society. They had to have someone on their back who wanted the dragon out.

Given none of the demons were allowed in the Realm, and they wouldn't want their dragons heading to a place they couldn't go, the dragons were mostly stuck with everyone else. Some of them hadn't liked that fact, obviously.

But we couldn't just leave our dragons in the Realm. The elves wouldn't allow them to wander freely, so the only option had been to take them with us. Which led to the conundrum of where to keep them.

It was Darius who had suggested this place. There were a few options, including his island, but this was the closest to a gate to the Realm.

Roger hadn't been home when we got here. He hadn't come home because of us, either. Apparently he'd needed a break from all the tireless organizing he'd been doing, of his people and of the fae, now hiding in the Brink from the elves' minions. He'd left them in capable hands on some of his shifter lands, and showed up here for a few days of quiet reflection.

Surprise!

"Reagan…" He shifted his weight to his other foot, his heavy slabs of muscle straining his white T-shirt. "They are dragons. It's against…"

He let the thought drift away. It was a different world than when he'd started this job, and we all knew it.

"It's against the rules?" I finished for him. "It's against the rules…of the creatures who are currently hunting any shifters and fae left in the Realm?"

Before he'd found the dragons, he just gaped at us for a solid thirty seconds in shock (and dare I say relief?) that I was A) not dead and B) in his secret hideaway. Then he'd just opened his mouth and spilled the whole complex situation of the elves vs. everyone else.

Well, complex to them. To me, it seemed pretty simple. You were with the elves, Lucifer, or us. If you were with us, you were a friend. If not, you were an enemy—and any enemies who showed their faces in the Brink would get dead. Easy.

But the goody-goody shifters and fae? Oh no, they had a thing for questioning intruders. Giving stalkers the benefit of the doubt. Letting minions hang around so long as they didn't attack. He'd apparently ignored a few enemy since we'd been gone. Not cool.

Before I helped him see the error in his ways, we needed a little downtime. *Some* of us, and I wouldn't name names—cough, *Penny*—needed to fix our brains.

"Seriously…" I waved my hand through the air, indicating the dragons as Cahal stepped out of the sliding glass door and onto the patio. He had a snifter with brown liquid swaying within his grasp. It was hard to rattle that druid, but our stint in the Underworld and our very close call at the border had done a good job of it. "Aren't they amazing?" I held up a finger. "Before you answer that, remember that we will gladly kill you if you insult them."

Roger shook his head, not fazed. He knew I wouldn't kill him; I'd had lots of opportunities and never pulled the trigger. It used to be because we needed him, but now it was because I kinda liked him. He was a good, solid guy, even if he was something of a goody two-shoes.

Extraordinary, he thought, and for a moment, I wasn't sure if he'd let the thought slip or had meant to communicate with me. *They are truly magnificent,* he continued. *I find myself incredibly jealous.* His dual-eyed gaze hit mine, one blue eye, one as green as a faded dollar bill. *I want to hear about the Underworld. About the elves. I want to know what you've been through.*

"You don't need to add that to your list of burdens, Roger," I said, softening my tone.

Darius exited the house with a snifter like Cahal's. I half wondered if he'd proposed this place to show Roger that he had one of Roger's secrets, much like Roger knew of Darius's secret island.

Roger studied me for a moment. *It's important to know...*

He didn't finish the thought, but I knew what was troubling him. Leaving me behind had probably been almost as hard for him as it had been for Penny. It wasn't his fault, but to him, it felt like it had been. He wanted to hear my woes so he could shoulder the burden himself. I didn't understand how he could live life like that, but I knew him well enough to understand his motives.

"I'm not fragile. And I will get my vengeance." I said it as blasé as I felt it. I wasn't, and I would.

Oh how I would claim my vengeance.

"Don't trouble yourself about it, Roger. If anyone is to blame, it's the *Seers*. They're the ones who told us we needed to go there. How are they, anyway? Feeling guilty, I hope. God I hate that craft."

He silently studied me for a moment longer. "They have been doing readings constantly… On where we should be settling…what we should be doing…" He paused for a beat again. "Trying to get information on *you*. You have been a black hole in their readings. They never got a single thing about you. Not about the dragons, showing up on my property…nothing. They do not know why."

"Good. Hopefully it's the cosmos telling them to butt out."

He took a deep breath and turned back toward the dragons. It was clearly an easier topic to bear. I had no doubt he'd been sitting in on a bunch of those readings, hoping for a sign that I would make it out. That Penny and Emery would, too. All while worrying about his people, and the fae, and whatever other burden he probably thought was his to bear.

"You're a good man, Roger," I said, and meant it. "A good leader."

He huffed out a laugh. "Now I *know* I'm dreaming."

"Yeah. Everything has gone totally tits up. I know, it's ridiculous."

"What are they going to eat?" he asked. "Where are

they going to…fly?"

"Um…" I frowned at him. "They hunt. You should understand that, right? As a shifter? And, oh, I don't know…over the trees on your massive property, which is flanked by a bunch of other massive properties of rich people who probably dress a whole lot better than you… Why do you always dress like a hobo, anyway? Are you skimming off the top or something? Do you not want the other shifters to know you're corrupt and making a bunch of money off them?" I quirked an eyebrow.

He stared at the dragons for a moment longer, his gaze moving from one to the next, skimming over their wings, their mighty heads, their glistening scales in the bright moonlight.

Incredibly jealous, he thought, and chuckled. Something he didn't do with his pack. Apparently shifters thought tough guys—and gals—didn't laugh. Which was ridiculous, since elder vampires smirked and laughed all the time. It usually meant they were planning something terrible for you.

"Fine, whatever." He turned away, toward an open seat on the patio, next to Penny. "Keep them out of sight of humans."

"Breaking the rules, I like it." I gave a thumbs-up to Archion. "You heard that, right? Go hunt if you want. If you don't have enough, let me know and we can buy a bunch of cows or something."

Where do we sleep? Archion asked as Coppelia took off into the sky.

Wherever you want. Choose a place in the trees. Just don't break too many, or Roger will get mad. He spread his wings before I thought to add, *Oh, and I forgot to tell you, don't eat predators. Like a gray wolf. Roger turns into a wolf. Don't eat him.*

We have a very acute sense of smell, you realize. His thought sounded very haughty. Hello, mood swing. *We can sense magical beings and identify their magic. We will know it is him. As for predators…* We *are the top of the food chain. We are the predators of predators.*

I used to think that was vampires. I stood corrected.

Hey, whoa. I put up my hands. *What's with the attitude? Eat something. Take a nap.*

He huffed out smoke and took to the skies. He was hangry, clearly.

Saphira waited a moment, and Penny swayed toward her, nodded, and slouched back.

She's worried about me, Penny thought, and I wasn't sure if she even realized she was thinking rather than speaking. *She thinks I shouldn't be left alone.*

"Is she right?" I asked seriously. The dragon waited.

"No. Emery has apparently been in my state of mind before, soon after he went on the run. He says I just need to wallow in it for a while until the unicorn blood wears off, eat and sleep for a long time, and it'll eventually pass. He doesn't think I'll turn into him."

Penny and Emery had been given two doses of unicorn blood each, one after crossing the fire field, and another just after we hit the Realm and needed to stall until the sun went down. They hadn't felt the cravings, but lusty urges were another story. And *moods.* At least for Penny.

"Turn into him, hmm… And what is he again…good at survival?" I asked, wandering closer. "Great in a bind? Fast thinking and acting? Is he just trying to keep you down, then…since, you know, those are actually good traits? Who needs independence—let the man do all the work…" It was hard not to smile.

"Keep it up, rat butt. Just keep it up." She picked up her stress reliever, the bottle of bubbles, and pulled the lollipop-yellow plastic wand from the purple container.

The man of the hour, Emery, was the last through the door, falling into a chair opposite Penny, the heavy cast iron squealing against the concrete. "What?"

"Nothing. She just sucks," Penny muttered, then blew through the plastic wand. Bubbles jetted out before lazily hovering in the tranquil breeze, fresh and sweet. I needed to create something like this in the Underworld.

I needed to stop thinking about the Underworld.

"So…" Roger put his elbows on the table.

Penny stopped blowing her bubbles for a moment,

glanced at him, and then swiveled her upper body toward him. She dipped the wick twice and then blew again. The bubbles cascaded around Roger, settling into his hair or popping with a soundless splat on his meaty shoulders. He fluttered his eyes closed as they brushed across his face.

"What are you doing?" Emery asked her.

"Seeing if he'll give in to his baser instincts and try to catch all the bubbles. My dogs growing up freaking loved bubbles. They'd go wild for them. It's got to be in the genetics, right?"

A shocked silence filled the area as Penny blew another stream.

"This is what my life has become," Roger finally said, and the rest of us barked out laughter, letting the stresses of the last few weeks uncoil.

It had been a hard journey, even when I was being pampered. It had been painful, both physically with the elves, and mentally in terms of dealing with my grief for my mom and keeping up a dangerous game with my dad. Penny had been through the wringer, Emery had relived his nightmare time on the run, Darius had navigated the treacherous underbelly of the Underworld while wondering if he'd ever see his love again, and Roger had shouldered the burden of all his people. Cahal…well, Cahal had been my rock in the storm even as he waded through dark waters of his own. If it killed me, I'd help him find his mate. I'd go to the gods or angels or dickheads to do it. And those might all be the same person, according to my father.

I knew there would be more stories to digest when I met up with the others, Callie, Dizzy, Charity, and everyone. Fears, concerns, and apprehension for what was to come.

But for now, I just took Darius's hand and led him away from our friends. We closed the door to the spare room on the second floor, not bothering to lock it in case Penny wanted to bust in and get a peek.

"I was so glad to see your face," I told him as I stripped off the button-up shirt he'd borrowed from Roger and worked at the belt holding up the baggy trousers. Darius was taller, his muscles considerable but less bulky than Roger's, and it showed in the clothes. I could tell Darius wasn't overly enthused about wearing garments that didn't fit perfectly. Especially ones made for "peasants." Roger needed to work on his fashion. Not that he would. He was probably able to buy this place *because* of his simple fashion…

Darius leaned down and brushed a kiss across my nose. "When you uncovered the bond, even halfway, I can't tell you how relieved I was to feel your love. I'd worried that Lucifer had gotten to you. That he had turned your mind to his plans. You seemed so natural riding alongside him on your dragon. I worried you might've forgotten what we had."

"What we *have*." I pushed down his pants and took his hard shaft in my hand. "I had to ignore you, or I wouldn't be able to focus on what I needed to do. I love you too much. It would've unraveled everything. Cahal was a godsend. Whenever I started liking it there too much, he merely had to mention your name. Or Penny's. And I'd start unraveling. It was brutal but necessary. I'm so happy to be back."

"You're so happy to be with us," he said softly, and pulled the baby T from over my head. Two of the guest rooms had had some women's clothes, each a different size. Both adult women. Both with some slinky Underoos. Roger had brought some special ladies to his private pad. I wondered why they'd left without taking their things. I fully intended to ask eventually. "You are not happy to be gone."

"It's complicated."

"Yes. But rest assured, I am fully aware of your struggle, and I will find a way to merge your two worlds together. Unless you don't want me to…"

A rush of love and gratitude poured through me.

"If anyone could, you could. My father let me go…" I blinked back tears and thought, *Ew.*

Darius's smile was sweet. *Don't run from emotion. It's what saved you. It's what will bring you back. His decision means there is a future there. We will find the way back.*

"And I will marry you."

"Are you sure?" He tilted his head at me. "I don't recall asking you..."

"And I don't recall asking if you wanted a punch in the face, but..."

His smile boosted his handsome features, a heart-throb by anyone's standards. "This is true."

Butterflies fluttered in my stomach. He was old school, and I was lazy. I'd wait. And it would be epic, I was sure.

"We need to fix the bond," he said, and slid his tongue across my nipple. I leaned my head back and closed my eyes as he moved to the other breast and fastened his hot mouth around its center. "Will we break the bed, do you think?"

I smiled as he pushed down my khakis and reached between my thighs. "I doubt Roger would care at this point. Between the dragons and us, he's just as broken as Penny."

"I hardly think so." His lips slid across my neck and he bit. Pleasure coursed through me as his fingers moved within me. He drew deeply, his thumb making circles on my clit.

I groaned, running my hands over his cut shoulders and hooking a knee around his hip. He quickly upped the pace of his plunging fingers, his circling thumb, and kept sucking, taking me to the point of danger. It was necessary for the bond—he would take me near death, then I would deplete him.

I'd been scared the first time. I'd reacted in fight mode, pushing him away. I clearly hadn't trusted him then in the way I did now. With my life. With my happiness. With my future. Lucifer had wanted to kill him for his attachment to me. He might still want to. But I knew Darius wouldn't go anywhere. This affirmed that fact.

"I want you inside me," I breathed, soaking in the pleasure.

He pulled off my neck and backed me to the bed before lowering me and settling over me. He wasted no time before pushing into me, taking my breath. His mouth was hot on mine, his tongue swirling through.

"I love you," he murmured against my lips.

"I love you too," I replied, arching as he filled me, over and over.

His mouth returned to my neck, sucking, his body thrusting, claiming me again. I gripped his back as he took me to the edge and then beyond it, again and again, the pleasure scaling impossible heights as my head got light. I'd always maintained that death by a vampire would be a lovely way to go. This was why.

I moaned, gyrating up to him, crashing against him. His body hitting harder, going deeper. Pleasure pulsed until I exploded in ecstasy, crying out his name.

He kept going, starting me up again already, his mouth on my neck, taking my life's blood. Taking all of me. I smiled with the feeling, with bonding him again. Black spots swam in my vision. We were getting close now. Pleasure built. Pounded into me. Consumed me.

I cried his name and he shuddered, groaning against my skin. He finally pulled his mouth back, sucking in a breath as he did so.

He breathed deeply, looking down on me, adoration in his eyes.

"Your turn, *mon coeur.* Take what is yours. What will always be yours, forever."

I would ensure that forever would be a very long time.

The End.

About the Author

K.F. Breene is a Wall Street Journal, USA Today, Washington Post, Amazon Most Sold Charts and #1 Kindle Store bestselling author of paranormal romance, urban fantasy and fantasy novels. With over four million books sold, when she's not penning stories about magic and what goes bump in the night, she's sipping wine and planning shenanigans. She lives in Northern California with her husband, two children, and out of work treadmill.

Sign up for her newsletter to hear about the latest news and receive free bonus content.

www.kfbreene.com

Printed in the USA
CPSIA information can be obtained
at www.ICGtesting.com
LVHW090540190524
780734LV00001B/102